ARIA

Rob Thubron

For Betty Graham. Long may you continue.

CHAPTER ONE

SPAIN

August 5, 1988

This is the day everything changes. Today, aged nine years old, I die.

Dad dragged Mum and me to Spain five years ago, his dream of early retirement from a career as an entertainment agent finally realised – no more booking third-rate acts into dodgy northern clubs.

The Costa Del Sol in the late eighties warranted its 'Costa Del Crime' nickname: drugs, clubs, and ex-pat criminals on the run, all set against a backdrop of Brit-owned bars offering full English breakfasts and happy hours lasting from noon to midnight. Most evenings consist of San Miguel beer, cheap cigarettes, and stories of the good old days back home. It's a summer holiday that never ends for many who live here. In my dad's eyes, this is heaven.

My birth had been a surprise, arriving just when my then forty-year-old mother had given up all hope of having kids. Four years later, she reluctantly left friends and family behind to move abroad.

My parents send me to an English-speaking private school under the assumption that it's easier to make friends. I'm a happy, confident, outgoing boy who performs well academically and is popular among my cosmopolitan class-mates. Dad runs unofficial tours to Gibraltar in his minibus, while Mum has a second-hand bric-a-brac shop. Worry, fear, and pain are still unknown concepts.

My father likes to drink, often heavily, and thinks nothing of driving while intoxicated. He grew up in north-east England during a time when drink-driving was the norm. Virtually every night of the week involves ferrying us to local Spanish bars, where he knocks them back. Dad never gets blind drunk, though, and has avoided being pulled over by the police thanks to the era's more relaxed views on being behind the wheel in an unfit state.

Tonight, however, things are different. Whereas it's the norm for him to have one drink in each of the five or so bars we visit, he's already finished off three beers before we arrive at the second stop; a pace that doesn't slow. By the time we leave the last establishment, it's up to my mum, who never learned to drive, to help him into the car. As we veer about the road, clipping curbs and narrowly missing parked vehicles, the concern I feel isn't for myself. He's been a great father up until now. What's prompted this be-haviour?

We finally reach home around 11, surviving the trip without my sozzled parent killing us or anyone else, despite ploughing into an innocent bush in our estate's car park. After helping him out of the driver's seat, Dad collapses into a heap. He makes a sound so alien while lying face-down on the ground that I wonder if I imagined it. He's crying.

Bob Graham's five-foot-six height means he isn't the most imposing. Nevertheless, Dad's always been a tough, stoic man who believes tears are reserved for women, kids, and 'fairies.' Watching him wailing on the floor like a baby, face buried in the crook of his arm as moonlight shines off a balding head, I feel the burn of my own tears.

Mum tries to act like everything is okay, presumably for my sake, but I can see her wet eyes hiding under that curly blonde hair.

'Come on, Dean,' she says in a shaky voice. 'Your dad's just not very well.'

Picking him up as best we can, the three of us stagger into our villa. Dad slumps on a living room armchair, still sobbing when Mum tells me to go to bed. Wishing this awful night to be over and to wake tomorrow with everything back to normal, I do as she asks.

Our home is a typical, single-level Spanish building with a large, open-plan central area. The top of my bed faces an open door that looks out onto the living room, granting me an unobstructed view of proceeding. My parents are about 15 feet away, though their strangely hushed voices ensure the words are inaudible. Suddenly, Dad pulls himself up from the chair with such force that it slides backwards. I'm relieved, assuming he must feel better.

There seems to be something wrong with his expression. It's twisted up and deformed as if he's wearing someone else's face. That's when everything changes. The volume of his voice increases so fast it makes me jump, but the screams are too slurred and angry to understand. All I can focus on is the white spit flying out of his mouth.

Then he hits her.

Some moments shape the entirety of our lives. I often think about that night thirty-odd years ago and wonder about the person I could have become if it never happened. How different would everything be? Would I have ended up normal? Happy? I'll never know. What I do know is in that instant, the moment his clenched fist split open her lip and sent Mum staggering, I ceased to exist. That child died, leaving something forever hollow and broken in his place.

The violence continues for hours. Years later, a counsellor suggests I blocked out the worst parts of the night. But there's one thing I'll never forget: it's the first time *she* appeared.

Dad pauses the attack and enters my bedroom after noticing me watching from beneath my Star Wars blankets. I've been too afraid to move or scream as this waking nightmare plays out before my eyes, the man I love beating my mother half to death. He sits on the edge of the bed. I can see his lips moving but can't comprehend anything. What is this monster hiding inside his body? I keep the covers held up to my nose. Mum lies slumped, possibly unconscious, across the sofa. Face bloodied and battered, soft gurgling noises coming from her throat.

My head pounds. Tears silently stream. I feel close to passing out when I notice a dim light in the corner. Still paralysed with fear, my gaze doesn't move from the warm glow. I glance back at Dad, who's now stumbling over his words while telling a metaphorical tale about a bear everyone fears but is ultimately a good guy. Even if I wanted to point out the light, my vocal cords aren't working.

An orange radiance floods the room. Dad's lack of acknowledgement is as confusing as its source. My eyes grow wider upon seeing the figure that starts to materialise; a woman, tall and wrapped in white robes with buoyant yellow contrasting her flawless pale skin. She looks too beautiful to be of this world – a perfectly symmetrical face and dark blue eyes that remind me of the ocean on a cold day.

The stranger stretches upwards to stand tall, sinewy limbs reaching skyward. I gasp at the massive pair of wings that unfurl from her back and struggle to find space. Her beauty and presence fill my body, dragging me from this first experience of absolute despair. I hear her say one thing before the remainder of the night wipes from my mind like a dream I can't quite remember.

'Don't lose hope.'

December 4, 1988

Most children love their birthdays, yet my absence of joy is evident upon turning ten.

It's been four months since that night. Despite attempts at acting normal, people have noticed changes in my behaviour: Teachers keep asking why I suddenly can't concentrate on schoolwork; my friends wonder what's made me so cheerless.

A few days after the incident, Mum told me it was the death of his mother, the grandparent I could barely remember from England, that ignited Dad's rage.

There have been plenty of similar moments since then, numerous meals thrown across the room, punches, slaps, screams, cries. I float along in a state of numbness, trying not to show tears or anger as it only feeds his rage. 'LOOK AT WHAT YOU'VE DONE. LOOK AT WHAT YOU'RE PUTTING OUR BOY THROUGH!' Words that cut into me worse than the violence. I lock my emotions deep within, letting them eat away at my mind and soul. I'm a ghost, neither dead nor alive.

Even at this young age, I begin to suspect the angelic woman was imagined – a trick of the mind caused by enormous stress. Maybe I half-dreamed her, a one-off vision that briefly slipped from my subconscious and into the real world. But during another night of alcohol-fuelled attacks a few weeks later, she made a second appearance.

Dad closed my bedroom door before starting his assault on that occasion, not that it stopped me from hearing the yells. I remember lying there, once again wondering when it would end. There was no light; she just appeared at the foot of my bed. Her wings spread out so far that they touched both walls.

'Are you an angel?' I asked.

Angels were something we had learned about at school. A teacher described them as beautiful beings whom we see during our darkest hours. I recognised similarities between this lady and the drawings of divine beings in my school-books.

'If that's what you want to believe, then yes. I'm an angel,' she replied

Her voice sounded soft and reminded me of Mum's. The answer was confusing, but I wasn't ready to pursue it. Just being near her made me feel safe. I didn't care about the details.

'What's your name?' I said, hoping for a more direct answer.

'Aria.'

I was sure I'd heard that before.

'Aria, is… is this my fault?'

'Of course not,' she replied, sounding amused that I would even think such a thing. 'It has nothing to do with you.'

'But why is Dad doing this? Is he still angry because his mum died?'

'Dean. You need to understand something. Your dad, he's sick.'

'Sick?' hearing the word hurt my head. Was that the only reason he's been acting this way?

'He's been sick for a very long time but hides it. His mum dying, well, that brought the sickness out.'

'But he's hurting *my* mum. And that hurts me,' my voice started cracking. 'It's not fair. I don't care what's wrong with him. Make him stop, please.'

Why isn't he getting help if he's ill, I thought? And what kind of sickness makes you beat and terrorise your wife and child?

'I wish I could, Dean. You just have to be strong. You have to be strong for your mum. Don't worry; I'll always be here to help you.'

'P-promise?' I struggle to push the word out.

'Promise,' she says with a radiant smile. 'No matter how bad things get from now on, I'll be here. Doesn't that make you feel better?'

'Yes. Yes, it does. Thank you, Aria.'

'I'll never leave you. And I'll never change. We'll always be friends.'

I buried myself between her open arms, wanting the feeling to last forever. The embrace muted the world even as the volume beyond my door increased. Her wings wrapped around my body, the sobs dissipating. The next thing I knew, I was waking up the following day.

That was many weeks ago, and while Aria has kept her promise, I remain a shell of my former self. I sit here now at my birthday party in a Costa del Sol bar, surrounded by school friends and Mum, who's wearing dark sunglasses to hide her bruises. Dad tells me to make a wish before blowing out the candles on the birthday cake. I close my eyes and pray for the only thing in the world I genuinely desire. I wish with all my heart for things to go back to normal.

February 12, 1990

My wish never came true. After almost two years and despite Aria's presence, I've forgotten what it's like to not live in constant fear. Fear that dinner would be cold. Fear that he'd accuse my mother of looking at another man. Fear of the tiniest thing that could send him into a rage. And the greatest fear of all, that one day he would kill her, either accidentally or on purpose.

A large number of women who become victims of domestic abuse don't seek help. Like Mum, they're often too afraid of what the perpetrator will do if exposed, or they are gaslighted into believing it's their fault. Her situation is made worse by living in a foreign country with no family and few friends. She's also terrified of what could happen to me. My father's psychological problems are getting worse, and there's no telling what he might do if pushed. My mother is a hostage in her own home.

The dream of Spain is turning into a nightmare elsewhere, too. Both parents' businesses are failing while my school fees mount. Times are hard, and a move back to England seems inevitable. The prospect sounds great to me; Mum would be near her family, and we'd no longer contend with a language barrier. But returning to the UK would be the catalyst that turned Dad into a true monster.

CHAPTER TWO

ENGLAND

September 1, 1990

We're back in North East England after seven years. Huge debts and no money to pay them saw us make a quick getaway from Spain. A series of hazy flashes are the only memories I have of this cold country. I recall being happy. My father was still the man who could do no wrong.

Mum and Dad owed my school thousands in term fees and didn't want me telling friends about our intention to abscond. That last Friday was difficult, walking out of the school gates with my best mates just like every day before it, but this was my secret goodbye. Despite never telling them about my troubles, I felt as if they knew something was wrong. I'd grown to rely on the normality they instilled in me, which made hiding our impending fleeing even more challenging. I wondered if they suspected, if they could tell something was amiss when my voice wobbled as I muttered 'see you tomorrow,' knowing that I'd never see them again.

We're now residing in the same small ex-mining town where my dad's brother lives. A cold and unfriendly place made up of industrial units, houses with flat roofs, and farms. There's a semi-permanent smell in the air that reminds me of manure mixed with gasoline.

Comprehensive school in England is a shock. My private education in Spain consisted of corporal punishment and military-style discipline; I once received ten smacks over the hand with a ruler for talking in class. On my first day at Sandham Hall, I witnessed a pupil hit a teacher in the face with a book and go unpunished.

As if I don't have enough to worry about at home, I now sport the kind of acne you see in medical books. Posh-sounding, spot-riddled, introverted new kids are not popular at rough schools in working-class areas of England.

Mum being close to her family again is a relief. I optimistically hope the fresh start will change Dad, that perhaps coming back to his roots might see him revert to the person I knew before that night. Instead, he views the move as a failure on his part, inciting more anger and resentment. But it's his paranoia that's becoming the most significant danger. Dad has always been overly paranoid, but his behaviour has reached a point where he's convinced people are out to get him. He believes those in certain professions – police, doctors, bank managers – are part of a conspiracy and can't be trusted. If my mum breaches the subject of him talking to a professional about these mental issues, she is beaten and accused of being another person who wants him locked away. Throughout his entire life, Dad never once accepted that he needed help, no matter how many of us begged him to seek it.

The more I wish to escape my existence, the more Aria visits. We talk about my parents, school, everything, and nothing. Her assurances keep me going even though I struggle to believe some of them. She stops me from losing all hope.

When I first met Aria, I didn't tell anyone as I thought Dad would find out and blame Mum. The main reason I keep quiet now is a fear of being committed. I still don't know what this person only I can see *really* is, but I genuinely feel that life wouldn't be worth living without her, so she stays. An angel, a figment of a child's imagination, a symptom of an illness inherited from my father. I don't care. All that matters is that we're together.

November 8, 1990

We've been in the UK for a few months now. It's a surprise if a single day passes without Dad throwing a violent tantrum of some kind. As much as she tries to hold it together for my sake, the toll is showing on Mum. She still refuses to leave, but there's only so much one person can endure.

A lack of money means our new home is a real fixer-upper. It seems the extra pressure of trying to make this place liveable is wearing down my mother in ways we can't see. Today is another spent worrying about bills, her husband, the house, and me, an endless onslaught of stress that finally bursts the seams.

Just as Mum enters hour three of wallpaper stripping, she calmly puts down her scraper and asks, 'Where am I?'

It's surprising how easily our minds crack when we can no longer cope. People experience breakdowns differently. In Mum's case, she went back to a time when life was good. A time when her spouse was the same man she married.

It doesn't take long for the paramedics to arrive. They ask her a few questions, including the year and where she is.

'Spain... 1987,' comes the reply.

Dad sits opposite her at the living room table, looking worried as he puffs away on a cigarette. I wonder if the concern is for her or over people discovering his role in all this.

Watching the medical team check Mum's blood pressure brings a mixture of fear and anger. Aria, appearing outside the confines of my bedroom for the first time, stands in the middle of a dingy living room, its half-stripped walls and missing carpet adding to the bleak atmosphere, juxtaposing her perfection. She doesn't speak, but there's a look on her face, the kind you give a friend who's just lost someone close. An expression that tries to say, 'sorry for your loss' and 'I'm here for you.' I stare at the angel for a few seconds before nodding a wordless understanding.

Dad and I wait by Mum's bedside in the hospital later that evening. Doctors call it a 'stress-induced anxiety attack' brought on by the pressures of the move and renovation, though that's only a tiny part of what caused the 'confusion.' Mum's now regained her memory of those missing years. I wonder if that's a good thing.

Dad is trying to confirm the diagnosis.

'Aye, she's been struggling these last few months. We had to move back to England from abroad. Stress has been a lot for her, especially with all the work we've been doing on the house,' he tells the hospital staff, failing to mention the almost daily physical and psychological abuse he dishes out. We're told she needs to stay a few nights for observation.

You can never identify an abuser by their outward appearance. Many come across as friendly or charming, rarely giving any hints of the horrendous acts they inflict. Dad has many friends who care about him, none of whom suspect this jovial, middle-aged man is hurting us in such awful ways.

Once he finishes blaming everything but himself for Mum's breakdown, he puts a hand on her arm.

'We'll have you out of here soon enough, love.'

The insincerity makes me want to vomit.

It's late evening when we arrive home. This will be the first night I've spent alone with Dad. To the best of my knowledge, the pain he's afflicted on me in the past has never gone beyond the verbal and mental. Still, I worry that not being able to exert his usual control over Mum will cause him to direct his physical anger elsewhere.

Some time ago, I asked Aria what I should do if he ever hit me.

'Don't fight back, or your mum will suffer for it,' she said.

I can see her point. The few times I stood up to him in the past resulted in more intense abuse for my mother, extra punishment for 'turning the boy against me.'

Things seem to be going okay tonight, though. Dad's wearing his regular façade of normality, and I'm starting to feel relieved about not having to deal with one of his episodes. But I've learned to spot the signs after so many years of constant outbursts: the exasperated sighs that arrive for no reason, muttered curses, cutlery that gets slammed in the drawer.

We're sitting watching television, Dad on the sofa and me in the armchair on the other side of the room. It's like the calm before the storm, a noticeable change in air pressure. I know what's coming; I've seen it hundreds of times before.

I can't remember what was on TV at the time. Doubtlessly the usual crap that populated British television in the early nineties. Dad grabs the control from his lap without any sound or emotion and points it at the television, using his other hand to hit the off switch in an almost theatrical manner.

'Bastard TV,' he exclaims.

After throwing the control on the floor without enough power to break it, he stands up and starts pacing in the middle of the room, letting out more of those deep sighs I've come to despise.

'I bet your mum's filling those doctors' heads with lies. Just remember, son, don't believe anything they say. I've always looked after you. People are only ever out for themselves; they'll do anything to get what they want, anything. And I'll tell you this: women – they're the bloody worst of them all. They'll lie through their teeth without batting an eyelid. The great manipulators.'

The words tear through my resolve. After everything he's put us through, after spending years listening enviously as my friends talk about their fathers with admiration, hearing his views proves too much.

'You're the liar,' I say in a low growl.

The snarl that had been reserved solely for my mother is now aimed at me. He moves quickly. Fear leaps from my stomach to chest. The back of his hand comes out of nowhere, connecting hard with my face. I hear the slapping noise before feeling the hot sting.

Hate is pretty much the only thing I've felt towards my dad for a long time, but this, this is something else. A raging poison like never before, an urge to hurt him violently. I keep my head turned to one side, nails digging into my thighs to distract from the burning. My breath quickens, blood rushes in my ears. No matter how much it hurts, no matter how angry I get, I'm not giving him the satisfaction of seeing me cry.

'DON'T EVER TALK TO ME LIKE THAT AGAIN, YOU LITTLE BASTARD,' he screams.

Now I know. I know precisely what every day is like for Mum. The pain, anger, and humiliation that comes from someone having total control over you.

I'm unusually big for a kid coming up on eleven, the result of puberty arriving at a very early age – also the cause of my bad acne. The growth spurt means I'm built like a young teen. Dad, on the other hand, is a fifty-one-year-old who's smoked 60-a-day for forty years. He may still be stronger than me, but at this moment, I'm ready to fight until my dying breath.

I turn to look at him, making sure he can see the rage in my dry eyes. There's an expression of confusion as if he's struggling to understand what's happening. I lean forward, ready to get up and rush him, but I can't move – something is stopping me. It's Aria. Her hand on my shoulder, holding me in place with a vice-like grip.

'No,' she says ever so softly.

It's only now that the tears arrive.

'This is your bloody mother's fault,' Dad grumbles, sensing my changing stance. 'I'll make sure to let her know,' he adds, before walking back to the chair, picking up the remote on his way.

November 9, 1990

I spent most of last night talking to Aria from my bed, making sure to speak quietly.

'Is he really my dad?' I asked, hoping she'd tell me I was adopted or something along those lines.

'Yes, sorry.'

'I'd feel a lot better if he weren't. Then we wouldn't be related, and my real dad could be someone nice, not like him.'

'Nobody gets to choose their parents, Dean.'

'So, I'm just unlucky?'

'Look at it this way: if none of this happened, if he'd never changed and were just like all of your friends' dads, you would have never met me.'

Strangely, this made me feel a little better. I'm now closer to Aria than anyone, even my mum. The idea of being alone again, a life without her, is terrifying. But would I give up the angel at the cost of having a normal father?

'Yeah, I guess. I just wish he could be normal, and we were still friends.'

'We can't have everything,' she replied. 'I know you're in pain. I can feel it as well, you know, every minute of every day: the fear and uncertainty of what's waiting for you at home; the constant sickness; never being able to concentrate; scared of the future. What's happening to you, Dean, to your mum, it will all make sense one day.'

It's an accurate description of my constant state of mind but no real answer, as usual.

'I don't get it. Why can't you tell me now?'

'It's... complicated. And not easy for you to understand just yet. Honestly, it will become clearer as you get older.'

The subject made my head hurt, so we started talking about school, games, and even girls – a topic that had never been broached before. All the things that boys my age talk about, though not usually to imaginary beings.

We're picking Mum up from the hospital today. The lack of sleep causes me to nod off during the journey, the stony silence making it harder to stay awake. I mustn't have said more than five words to Dad since he struck me. I'll have to pretend to be okay once we arrive, else it'll be Mum who suffers. I'm thankful that while the backhander did sting, it didn't leave a noticeable mark.

There's both relief and tension as we pull into the car park and make our way through the hospital's wards. Mum is visibly happy when we arrive at her section. She asks if things have been okay.

'Yeah, good,' I say, hoping that the quiver in my voice isn't apparent.

The doctor explains that we must keep her calm and stress-free or face a relapse. I struggle to hold a neutral expression as he talks, knowing such things are impossible.

I get the feeling Dad is pretending last night never happened. It's evident that Mum notices his subdued behaviour during the ride home, but she knows better than to delve deeper. He asks about the hospital stay, analysing each answer as if it has a hundred hidden meanings. Mum's apprehensive, of course, waiting for the sharp tones and cutting remarks that usually follow a 'wrong' answer, yet they never arrive. Has he learned his lesson? Even after everything he's done, was raising a hand to his child a step too far?

December 31, 1990

It's been almost two months since Dad hit me, during which time he hasn't shown any signs of aggression. That's not stopped me from being on edge every day, as usual, but as much as I expect it, the violence never comes.

Aria's been missing since our last conversation. I can't help thinking about what she said, about the choice between having a normal father or seeing her.

It's New Year's Eve, so often a time for fresh optimism. Dare I hope that our lives are changing? Maybe 1992 will be when everything finally goes back to normal. Perhaps Dad's backhand was the best thing ever to happen to this family.

We're travelling to my aunt and uncle's home to see in the new year. Ray is outgoing, funny, and kind, making it even harder to believe he's Dad's brother. While my father puts on his personality camouflage in public, Mum assures me that his sibling is a good human being. People say I'm just like Ray, which makes me happier than they know.

We order taxis on the rare occasions that Dad drinks these days. The prospect of him getting drunk used to fill us with dread, but after several incident-free weeks, we genuinely believe he won't go off the rails tonight. The positive feelings from one of the most uneventful Christmases in years still linger, and a family gathering sounds like a fun-filled affair.

I'd forgotten what it was like to be carefree, to not feel that ever-present gnawing sensation deep in my chest. Tonight, I remember what it is to be a kid again. Everyone's happy. The house is filled with laughter from relatives of all ages as we play games and tell stories. Something happens a few hours into the party that I haven't seen in years: Mum and Dad joking and dancing with each other like a couple who are still in love after many decades of marriage. I smile from across the room, deciding that as sad as never seeing Aria again would be, a normal dad and happy mum *is* the better option.

Everyone sings Auld Lang Syne when the clock strikes midnight. An hour later, just as I'm getting sleepy, our return taxi arrives. Dad chats merrily with the driver while Mum and I sit in the back, my head slumped on her arm. It's been a long time since she looked so at ease. I feel like this has been one of the best nights of my life. Journey over, I wish my parents a happy new year before going upstairs to bed. The duvet's hug warms me, contentment filling my body.

My dreams didn't start unpleasantly, but that changes when I experience the phenomenon of sounds influencing what we see in our sleep, like hearing thunder and dreaming of lightning.

A face appears. It's not Aria, as I first thought; it's Mum. She's screaming, a deafening, ear-piercing screech that engulfs my mind. The shock wakes me, but I still hear it, as if I've dragged a nightmare into the physical world. It takes a few seconds for my brain to acknowledge my waking state. The noise is real; I've heard it many times before. I don't instantly assume Dad is the cause, a futile hope that he hasn't gone back to his old ways. He's been so normal lately, and my parents seemed happy earlier.

I run downstairs, the sound growing louder with each step. Extended screaming that drowns out the shouting underneath. A familiar sensation rises in my stomach, the same one from all those years ago in Spain. I reach the living room entrance.

Mum sits at the dining table. Dad stands nearby. Her face is bloodied and swollen, eyes puffed out, teeth stained red. He stops shouting something about another man from the party when I walk in.

'LOOK WHAT YOU'VE FUCKING DONE NOW!' he screams, pointing in my direction. A series of blows land on the side of Mum's face, her arms doing little to stop the fists. Names get hurled that no child should hear their father call their mother.

My first thought is to attack, but even amid such chaos, I know Mum would suffer more for such an act of defiance. Instead, I instinctively force myself between them, wrapping myself around her to take the impact of the punches. Dad accidentally lands a haymaker on the back of my head. He's shocked into stopping, like a rowdy drunk that suddenly sobers up when the police approach.

I keep hugging Mum, my skull throbbing horribly. Everything seems to stand still, the silence of the night broken only by Dad's laboured breaths and her sobbing. He walks out of the room without saying a word. It's over.

January 1, 1991

Mum and I stayed on the sofa after Dad left. The combination of shock, tears, and the fear he'd return kept us awake most of the night. We didn't say much to each other, apart from my assurances that I was okay. Despite the severity of her injuries, there's a silent understanding that a hospital visit would mean more made-up stories about falling down stairs and the increased chance of another beating.

We hear footsteps around 8 am – much later than the hour he usually rises. I feel the terror once again, making me grip Mum's hand tighter. The noise of water entering a kettle emanates from the kitchen. How can this mundane act of normalcy come from the same person who pulverised his wife in front of his son only a few hours ago?

Dad walks through the door holding a plate of scrambled eggs and a cup of coffee. He flashes an emotionless glance at Mum's swollen, damaged face before taking a seat at the table. Nothing will be said about what happened. Mum ushers me out of the room so she can clean herself up. We must now act as if last night was a figment of our collective imagination.

I feel devoid of hope as I close my bedroom door, like this hell will never end. No help, no respite, no escape until he finally kills one of us. Climbing under my bed-sheets, I imagine sinking into an ocean, the water filling my lungs as I drift into peaceful darkness. No more pain, no more suffering, the suffocating worry finally slackening. Twelve years old is no age to be thinking about suicide.

I wasn't surprised to find Aria sitting nearby after a few minutes of tears. Looking at her makes me realise the sheer horror and absurdity of this moment. I sit up and hug my guardian, begging her to take me away.

'Is that what you really want, Dean?'

'I… I can't live like this anymore. Every time I think things are getting better, he does it again. I hate him. I hate my life. I just want to die. Nothing could be worse than this.' I have to force the words out between my cries.

'And leave your mum? You know what he'll do; he'll blame her, make her suffer even more. She'll believe him, of course. Imagine the pain of thinking you killed your only child, the one thing that keeps your mother going.'

'I… I….'

Dad can be as vicious with his words as he is with his hands. There's no doubt he'd convince Mum she caused my death.

'No. I would never do that. Never leave her alone. I'm sorry.'

'I know, Dean. You're strong and brave and would do anything to protect your mum. I can't stop him, but I'll always be here when you need me,' she says, rubbing the back of my still throbbing head.

'I don't know what I'd do without you,' I say.

CHAPTER THREE

ATTEMPTED MURDER BY VAN DAMME

January 6, 1991

A.M.

Like most children, I dread going back to school after the holidays – an event that's particularly daunting for me. Not only do I worry about lessons, homework, and the bad kids, but I'm also preoccupied with what might be happening at home. I genuinely expect to find Mum dead one day, killed by her husband during one of his fits of rage. It's this constant pressure that makes a troubled child even worse.

Break times bring welcome relief, a chance to talk with friends and briefly block out the worst possible scenarios. We all gather in the yard once the bell rings to talk about Christmas presents and have a laugh, something I've not done for a while.

It's freezing today, so cold that the rain-filled long-jump pits near where we congregate have layers of ice floating on their surfaces. Some bad boys from our year have decided to abandon the area behind the P.E. building where they surreptitiously smoke to play with the frozen water, pulling blocks from the small pools and throwing them at each other.

We have our backs to the commotion. I'm wary but confident they won't risk doing anything to a big group of us, even though we're all near the bottom of a school hierarchy that goes: bad lads, cool kids, funny ones, non-descript types, nerds, those who are different in some way, and the total losers. My friends and I all straddle the line between the last and penultimate categories as we're not smart enough to be considered nerds.

Listening to one of my mates talk about Red Dwarf, our favourite TV show, my confidence in our safety proves misplaced. A smashing noise, a flash of white light, intense pain through my whole head. It's all I can do to stop myself from falling over. Glen, one of those kids who's more a bully's sycophantic sidekick than a bully himself, had walked up behind me and brought a sheet of ice down on my skull.

The feeling is awful, like hot waves pulsing from crown to neck – it landed in the exact spot as Dad's fist – yet the only thing I can focus on is Glen's high-pitch laughter.

'Hahaha! Did that hurt, pizza face?' he sneers, exposing a set of prominent gums that look out of place against his baby-like beige teeth.

Fury overrides rational thought. I lunge without thinking, colliding with the smaller, skinnier boy, my attack lifting us both off the ground. We crash down hard near a rainwater-filled pit where the ice either never formed or has been harvested. The impact winds Glen. I quickly scramble to my feet and grab his arm, dragging him along the ground until his head hovers above the freezing water. Still lying on his back, I straddle him, my hands wrapping around his thin throat, giving me the leverage to force his head back until it's completely submerged.

The panic and confusion in Glen's eyes are clear even while he thrashes wildly and air bubbles escape from his mouth. It's not my fellow pupil's terrified face looking back at me; it's Dad's. He's under the water for just a few seconds before his friends come crashing into my side, knocking me over.

All the noise attracted a teacher who is now frantically trying to separate the two groups. Glen coughs and splutters and cries, his blue face soaking wet, snot running out of his nose. Consequences are coming, but it's not my punishment that worries me.

P.M.

37

Glen's history and my incident-free background ensure I avoid the worst-case outcome of expulsion. It also helps that his friends are hazy about what happened; these kids never grass, no matter the circumstances. Combined with my own mates' testimonies about how I was attacked with a block of ice and merely defended myself, I'm given little more than a slap on the wrist for what could be considered attempted murder. The school does, however, send me home early with a letter.

During the short walk back, I feel like the envelope carries a death sentence for my mum, and possibly me. Throwing it away and waiting until 3:15 is a tempting idea, but I know that no matter how badly Dad reacts now, it'd be ten times worse if he discovered any deception.

My parents are in when I arrive around mid-afternoon. Dad never let my mother go anywhere without him.

'What are you doing back?' he asks in a way that mostly sounds like surprise.

I explain what happened and hand over the letter, bringing up Glen's reputation without detailing how I tried to drown him.

Mum's on my side

'It sounds like you had no choice,' she says. 'He could have killed you.'

It was the other way around, of course. Dad stands in place, choosing not to reveal his reaction just yet. His gaze falls back on the note, studying it like a puzzle.

'If it was his fault, why'd they send you home?' there's an almost satisfied tone to the question as if he's pleased to have caught me out. There's only one place this is leading.

'They sent us both home, Dad.'

'Well, that makes no sense. Are you sure you're not lying? I'll phone the school, and if they tell me it was you....'

'I swear it's the truth. Phone them,' I hear the pleading in my voice.

He looks me straight in the eyes. There's a sickly burning at the back of my throat.

'Well, you must've done something to make him want to hit you first,' he sneers. 'Get to your room.'

'But he smashed a block of ice over my head for no reason! Why am I being told off?'

'I'll show you bloody told off if you don't get to your room, NOW!'

I don't want him to see how much his accusation hurts. The insinuation that I provoked Glen, the same justification he uses for battering Mum. It makes me want to tell the truth, that as I tried to end that boy's life, it was Dad's face I saw under the water. I slowly walk up the stairs, crushed.

'This is your bloody fault,' I hear him tell Mum. 'You're never on my side, and he hates me for disciplining him. You love making me the bad guy, don't you, eh?'

Hearing Dad's anger pointed at Mum because of my actions is the worst punishment of all, despite anticipating this reaction. I sit on the bed, crying at the noises downstairs. Aria wraps an arm around my shoulders.

'I nearly killed Glen. I know he's a prick and all, but I nearly fucking killed him. What's wrong with me?' I ask.

'Dean, you didn't *want* to kill him, did you?

'No, of course not. I just… I just couldn't control it. Like, I knew it wasn't Dad, but I wanted it to be. It's hard to explain.'

'No, I understand. There's nothing wrong with you, honestly. But you need to keep your temper under control, or else you might really kill someone.'

'I'd fucking kill him. I'd kill Dad.'

There's a long silence. The idea that she might condone such action makes me feel a bit happier.

'Maybe you'll get the chance one day.'

January 9, 1991.

The incident with Glen has been a constant topic of conversation in the classroom, especially among my friends who, while far from tough, were quick to pile in when I became outnumbered.

'Dean, will you try to drown me if I ask to borrow your pen?' asks Kieran, whom I consider closest out of everyone. We all laugh, though I doubt Glen's group are doing the same. I passed some of them in the hall earlier, and although no words were spoken, their longing for retribution is obvious.

We play football in the yard at lunchtime, avoiding the long-jump pits by sticking to the fields further away. With 12:30 approaching, we grab our bags and walk down the grassy bank to the school blocks. Kieran and I are talking about video games when I notice someone walking toward us.

Richard Madson has a notorious reputation: expulsion, arrests, punching a teacher. Despite being one of the shortest kids in the year, people are afraid of him; there are rumours that he's genuinely crazy and always carries a knife. Madson wasn't in school on the day of the fight, which is good as Glenn is one of his many hangers-on.

'Deano,' he says with a smirk, his mouth already showing signs of smoking too much.

'Madson,' I reply.

'Hear you think you're a hard fucker now.'

'Nah, I don't think that.'

'Aye? Then why did you try to kill my mate? You must think you're a right hard bastard, eh? Think you could kill me, Deano?'

I look at Madson. He's only around five foot tall, stocky, with a mop of greasy, dirty blonde hair. His face doesn't look like it belongs to a 13-year-old. The ruddiness and nose like a squashed tomato wouldn't appear out of place on an old man. This is obviously a trap – an attempt at goading me into fighting. Like most bullies, he's a coward, so I can either expect a blade to appear or, more likely, his friends to come running from behind a school block the moment things kick-off.

'What do you want, Madson?'

'Well, Deano, I want to know how fucking hard you are. So, come on then, show me. You spotty twat.'

I feel anger well up in me, the same I felt with Glen, with Dad; the same heat that warms my neck, the same adrenalin tremors in my hands. But I know that if I throw a punch, not only will his gang have reason to jump me, but it'll also mean getting sent home again and dealing with my father's wrath.

'Just leave us alone,' I say irritably.

Kieran and I try to walk past, but he puts a hand on my chest.

'You can leave now, but you'll fucking pay for what you did.'

I might avoid confrontation today, but what about tomorrow or the day after that? I already spend most school hours worrying about my home life. I couldn't deal with the constant threat of being beaten half to death as well.

An idea forms, though it could backfire terribly. Being a young teen, one of my favourite movies is the 1980s martial arts flick Kickboxer, starring the great (to me) Jean Claude van Damme. There's a scene where he tries to kick down a bamboo tree with his shin, failing miserably until the stereotypical 'master' character offers some motivation, reminding Jean that the antagonist crippled his brother. It's all very cheesy but left an impression at the time.

'Come on then, Madson,' I tell him, gesturing towards the P.E. block.

'Good boy,' he whispers.

We make our way toward the building in silence, Kieran following behind.

The grassy decline levels out as we approach the vast structure. I wonder if Madson's crew is watching somewhere, waiting for me to strike first. We reach the block's outer perimeter: a waist-high wooden fence consisting of a single length of wood running parallel to the ground, supported by vertical posts planted every few feet.

I turn to face him.

'Mind if I warm up first?'

'Eh, the fuck you gannin on about, Deano?'

My blazer comes off. Shirt cuffs unbuttoned. Madson's looking around as if he's searching for someone. A few kids walking back to their classes notice us and stop to watch.

In addition to being big for my age, I have these weird, Popeye-style forearms that appear stuffed with playdough. They seem so out of place that many people comment on them. While I'm not stupid enough to try and knock this fence down with my shin, Van Damme-style, I'm hoping it will break before my lower arm does.

I drop to my knees, close to one of the posts. Madson looks wholly bewildered. I stretch out my right arm, make a fist, and slam my forearm into the wood. A stinging pain shoots from wrist to jaw, but the fence barely wobbles. Too late to stop now. I conjure my hate, my anger. The surroundings fade away as Dad comes into focus. My arm's retracted and swung again, this time with added speed and power. The post groans in its foundations, helping me ignore the numbness that's spreading across my entire right side. There's another slam, and another, and another, the gap between strikes shortening. I'm lost in my mind, the world slipping away. All sensation has disappeared from the tips of my fingers to my shoulder blade. Only when I hear my name do I snap out of the trance.

What appears to be half the school has formed a circle around me, most of them shouting and cheering. Blood trickles onto the grass from where the skin's peeled off my arm. It's certainly not on the same bone-exposed level as my martial arts hero, but it looks convincing enough to have done the job. The voice calling me belongs to Mr Padgham, easily my favourite teacher.

'Come on now, Dean, you're going to cause a bloody riot,' he says matter-of-factly.

His calm reaction to what must be a very surreal sight is typical of the man. Padgham's a teacher who tries to be friends with his pupils, and I suspect he knows my family issues. He also makes English one of the few subjects I enjoy.

Rather than going to the principal first, something any other staff member would have done, Padgham escorts me to the tiny medical room so the school nurse can check my self-inflicted injuries.

'Dean here's had a bit of an accident. He fell down the hill and caught his arm on a rock,' he tells the stone-faced woman.

'I'll clean it up and get a bandage – doesn't look like anything's broken. Do you want to inform the parents or shall I, Mr Padgham?' she asks.

'I'll let them know, Mrs Cook. It's no problem.'

'Very good. Just wait here while I get some wrappings, please.'

Sitting on an old table that doubles as an emergency bed, I stare at my bloodied limb.

'I'll just tell your parents the truth, son. That you had a fall.'

'Thanks, sir.'

The post never broke. I'm not sure if it was even remotely damaged, but my stunt served its purpose. Madson and his friends were nowhere to be found when I left the nurse's office and never bothered us again. His 'crazy' reputation had now passed to me.

April 6, 1991

It's been three months since I tried to murder someone and break a fence with my arm. Most of the school believes I have genuine mental problems, which, in addition to probably being accurate, is no bad thing – nobody wants to mess with the dodgy kid in case he goes psycho again. It's made life slightly more bearable, and my friends appreciate being 'protected' through association.

The worst parts of existence remain unchanged. I've been extra careful not to antagonise Dad since the day I was sent home, but he seems to delight in a new form of psychological torture. The source of his temper tantrums is now his evening meal. This routine involves Mum serving dinner, him playing with the food, nibbling at it, making an exaggerated face of disgust, then pushing the plate away before stating, 'If that's my tea, I'm not looking forward to supper.' I still shudder when recalling those words.

There are times when Dad forces my mother to eat what's left. Refusing isn't an option, and the single time she said it tasted okay led to a beating for 'calling him a liar.' Now, she just sheepishly chews, apologising for being a terrible cook and wife. This plays out the same way at least twice per week, usually while I sit at the dinner table. Occasionally, he throws the plate on the floor, giving her a contemptuous look of disgust while she cleans it.

'If you learned how to make the fucking thing right, I wouldn't have to do this.'

Always Mum's fault, never his.

I know what would come from my verbal or physical intervention, so I look away as he goes through the motions of humiliating her. I've learned tricks to stop myself from showing emotion, such as biting down hard on my tongue and focusing on the pain. I no longer hate Dad; it has moved to another level. Imagining his death is one of the few things that makes me happy. I've even started to feel anger towards myself for sharing his DNA. How could I ever have come from that bastard?

It's early evening. Dad has again decided that dinner isn't up to standard after taking one mouthful and spitting it out, letting the fork fall from his hand and clatter loudly on the plate. The noise makes me jump.

'Bob...,' Mum cries. There's a begging tone in her voice that makes him angrier. He grabs the plate and smacks it into her face, food-first, not hard enough to smash but with enough force to send vegetables and bits of meat flying everywhere. She screams in shock, staggering backwards.

I stare at the woman who gave birth to me, watching gravy drip from her hair, listening to the stifled sobs, my mind's door straining against the weight of the scene. My legs start shaking, followed by a familiar ringing in the ears. I grip the large pint glass half-filled with water that accompanies my every meal, knowing that lunging forward and ramming it into his neck from a position across the table could end all this permanently. It would take him by surprise. Surely my young age would keep me out of jail. Mum would make sure the police knew he deserved it. Extenuating circumstances and all that.

I stand up, holding the glass tightly. Dad's now reading his newspaper if nothing happened. Is this the opportunity Aria mentioned? I'm glued to the spot, staring at his bald head and red face. Mum, busy cleaning herself in the kitchen, doesn't notice what's going on. His eyes dart from the page to me.

'What?' he snaps, seemingly oblivious to my whitening knuckles.

'… Nothing.'

Why can't I do this? Is it the knowledge of what murdering my father would do to Mum? Is it the fear that I'll mess it up and he'll kill me in self-defence? I place the glass back down, walk around the table, and head to the kitchen, making sure not to make eye contact. The loathing now directed at my failings. Mum stops wiping food from her clothes with a kitchen towel so she can hug me tight.

'I'm sorry, Dean.'

I can't understand why she's apologising when I'm the one who should be sorry.

A few hours later, I'm once again looking for answers from someone only I can see.

'Was it you, Aria? Did you stop me again?'

'Despite what you believe, I can't actually stop you from doing anything, sweetheart. Not really. I can only offer... guidance. It's up to you whether you follow it.'

'I wish I'd rammed that glass into him. He fucking deserves it.'

'People rarely get what they deserve, as you'll discover. Life can be very, very shitty. Bad things happen to good people, and vice versa, all the time.'

Aria has changed over the last few years, though not physically. Her vocabulary and personality are different. She's even started dropping in the occasional piece of profanity.

'Will it always be this way?'

'No, Dean. Honestly, one day he'll be gone, and both your mum and you will be free. All this horror, all this pain, it will feel like a dream you can't quite remember.'

'How could I ever forget this?' I spit out the question, insulted at such a claim.

'Your memories of these moments will fade without ever really going away. They'll leave a mark that moulds you into the man you'll become. What sort of man, well, that's up to you.'

'Why do you never give me a normal answer?'

'I don't have them all.'

CHAPTER FOUR

FLEETING HAPPINESS

May 10, 1994

A.M.

Time moves slowly when you're young. The last couple of years dragged by, filled with days that varied from bearable to horrendous. I stayed quiet about Aria throughout it all. My invisible angel remaining the only person I can confide in, the only one I talk to about what's happening and how it affects me. But things aren't improving; they're getting worse.

While some days are better than others, a week never passes without at least one incident. The constant stress affects my body, etching a hardness onto my fifteen-year-old face that enables me to buy alcohol without being asked for ID.

It's a typical Tuesday, sitting in French class at around 11.15, my mind only half on the teacher's words. Mr Holmes is a stern educator who may not have been the most popular but can coax the best out of his pupils. On this occasion, however, I'm nodding off as he talks about conjugating verbs. My eyelids droop just as the door opens at the back of the classroom. Even before I turn around, Mr Old, my head of year, speaks.

'Excuse me, Mr Holmes. Do you mind if I borrow Dean for a minute?'

I don't initially register my name.

'Of course, Mr Old. Off you go, Dean.'

Wobbly legs struggle to move me from the chair. A familiar spinning in the lower stomach spreads to my chest, beads of sweat form on a tingling brow. Mr Old wears the expression of a doctor about to tell a patient some life-altering news. The eyes of the class are on me.

I wonder if she's dead.

The teacher's voice drops to a low whisper once we move into the privacy of the corridor.

'Dean, I've just had a call.'

Everything feels very dream-like.

'Your Mum is coming to pick you up. She'll be here any minute.'

The relief at hearing she's still alive is almost too much to take. Mr Old puts a hand on my arm, giving me a nod. I have a feeling that, like Mr Padgham, he knows what's really going on. A school these days might involve social services in such circumstances, suspected or otherwise, but things were different back then.

Various possibilities invade my thoughts while waiting outside the block. Has she killed him? Will Mum and I make a getaway back to Spain, Dad's undiscovered body rotting in the house? As much as I want him gone, the idea of her potential incarceration makes me feel ill. Maybe he's died of natural causes. I hang on to the happiness that possibility brings.

My mother walks around the corner. Even from this distance and with dark glasses on, the damage is apparent.

P.M.

We're at my aunt's. It turns out Dad woke up in a terrible mood this morning. After deciding breakfast wasn't to his liking, he once again rammed the plate into Mum's face. This time, though, perhaps because I wasn't there, it connected with enough force to smash.

The threat of Dad's retaliation had stopped Mum from running away during all the years of abuse, but this pushed her over the edge. She'd endured more brutal, prolonged attacks in the past, yet none as potentially lethal. Mum quietly sneaked out of the house an hour after the incident with nothing but a handbag while Dad showered. Making her way to my school on foot after using a payphone to

56

call ahead, she collected me before we took a taxi to her sister's home about 20 miles away.

The ride was long and silent. The driver occasionally glanced in the rear-view mirror at the poorly covered gash in Mum's face. There's pity in his eyes. I've seen it before, usually on the faces of people who say: 'I would like to help, really, but I just can't risk getting involved.'

I try to imagine Dad's reaction when he got out of the shower and realised his wife was gone. It's beautiful to think that his anger quickly turned to the kind of panic and despair he always instilled in us, though I doubt it happened that way. He's probably convinced she's run off with the bloke next door.

My aunt greeted Mum with a massive hug. I hear them both talking about Dad, trying to keep their voices low for my sake.

Everything about this feels different, more real. Apart from Mum's previous visible damage, long brushed off as accidental to those who ask, our suffering has always been secret, hidden from the world. It's now being forced out into the open – people are discussing Dad's violence. Sometimes, while talking to Aria, a theory would pop into my head: maybe none of this is real. Perhaps I'm locked up in an institution somewhere, my whole existence playing out as one long delusion.

The rest of the day is spent with my cousins – two boys around my age. We play on their Sega Mega Drive, talking as if nothing's amiss. I can tell they're under orders from my aunt not to ask why I'm here. Video games are one of my few escapes. It's not just that they're fun, it's the way they immerse me so deeply that, for a short time, I forget about all my problems; Dad, life, the constant stress, it all washes away when I become someone different, an avatar that is strong and in control.

Despite the distraction of trying to pull each other's spines out in Mortal Kombat, I can't help but wonder how long we'll be staying here? I've no idea what happens next. My hope is that we'll never go back, even if it means leaving behind another school and set of friends.

The living room sofa bed comes out once the clock hits ten. Aria always appears following trauma, so her absence is surprising.

Lying on that tiny, comfy mattress, wrapped in a sleeping bag while staring at a ceiling stained yellow by cigarette smoke, it hits me: I don't have to worry about Mum

being attacked tonight. It's been years since I slept so peace-
fully.

May 17, 1994

We've been here a week. It's decided that the best
option is to stay off school for a while, leaving mum and me
to wander the city during the days and spend evenings with
her sister's family. I can't remember the last time I was this
happy. I play with my cousins once they get home, just like
an average, carefree kid. Living out the rest of my childhood
here is a wonderful fantasy, but it seems the price is no more
visits from Aria, whom I've still not seen since our arrival.
The possibility of switching to my cousins' school is becoming more appealing, too.

I've already learned that wishes don't always come
true. Mum, while safe, is struggling with day-to-day living
costs. Dad had controlled both their finances, a way of tightening his control over her. The money she escaped with is
dwindling and taking the cash Olive keeps offering isn't an
option in my mother's eyes. There's also the problem of
switching me to a packed school in the middle of a term.

For reasons unknown, Mum has agreed to meet Dad
tomorrow in a public place to talk things out. I later discover

that Dad had been phoning my aunt, begging for his wife to come back and swearing he was 'okay' now. Maybe it's the fear of how a single, jobless, homeless woman in her fifties would manage with a teenage child, or perhaps it's the worry over what to do about my school and the disruption it's causing me. She might even think, or hope, that he really has changed this time, that things will be different. Whichever way she rationalises it, the decision is like a stone hand crushing my heart.

May 18, 1994

I watch Mum walk out of the door on her way to meet Dad. The turmoil our lives face if she decides to leave him forever is obvious, yet it's a thousand times preferable to the alternative. I play Mega Drive games while waiting for her return, finding it impossible to focus. I don't care about existing off baked beans and not getting a single GCSE; it would be better than having to face that monster again.

I glance anxiously at the time. There's been no word from Mum in the three hours since she left, leaving me imagining the worst just as the key enter the lock. She enters the living room, wearing a smile that reminds me of the one Mr Old sported last week.

'It's okay, son,' she says. 'We're going home. Everything will be fine from now on. You'll get to see all your friends again. Your dad's better now. He won't do anything to upset us again.'

I don't know whether Mum genuinely believes it or if she's trying to convince herself. Things won't be okay. He'll probably seem like a different man at first, just like before, but old habits die hard.

We hug. Instead of the usual happiness, all I feel is the joy I've experienced these last few days evaporate.

June 1, 1994

Coming home means telling friends that my absence was due to some unspecified death in the family. They seem dubious, especially after seeing Mr Old drag me out of class, but don't inquire further.

Everything seems okay right now, just as I predicted. In his attempts at repentance, my father remains on his best behaviour – cheerful, happy, non-aggressive. It doesn't fool me. I noticed Dad muttering during dinner recently while playing with his food. He eventually got up and silently scraped the remainder of his plate into the bin before sitting down to chat with Mum as if they were the most average couple in the world.

I know he's struggling to control himself. The tension is visibly growing every day, given away by the pulsing veins in his head, clenched fists, and twitching eyes. Something will push him over the edge, and he won't be able to contain it any longer. I'm afraid for Mum, and myself, because when he lets out all that pent-up wrath, there's only one place it'll land.

One positive is that I've seen Aria every night since our return. I understand better how her appearances correlate with my state of mind. I rarely see her when I'm at peace, only during times of stress, which is paradoxical as her presence always cheers me up. Our conversations this week have mostly revolved around what's coming. Every passing hour brings Dad's inevitable meltdown closer. The threat has become the first thing I think about upon waking and my last thought before falling asleep, like discovering an asteroid will soon collide with earth but not knowing when.

'He'll be even worse this time, and Mum might not be able to get away. I fucking hate living like this. Why did she come back?' I ask the angel.

'You can't blame her, Dean. She didn't have much choice. No home, no money, no job, what could she have done? She couldn't just switch you to a new school at the drop of a hat.'

'We'd have managed. Anything would have been better than being back here, with him.'

'Your Mum only wants what's best for you. She still blames herself for all this and doesn't want to turn your life upside down again. She really thinks he's changed this time.'

'It's all bullshit. He'll go back to his old ways.'

'Yeah, I know. Do you remember all those years ago, when I told you he was ill?'

'Yeah.'

'He's getting worse.'

'It's obvious, isn't it? Mum's asked him to get help before, but that just feeds his anger. He thinks everyone is out to get him.'

'That's part of the illness, believing the world's the enemy. He's convinced it's your mum who makes him do those... things.'

'So what, Aria? I don't care if it's not his fault,' I protest, raising my voice. 'He makes our lives fucking awful.'

I pause for a long time, drawing breath before I ask the next question.

'Will I ever be like him?'

'In some ways, yes; you are his son. But it's your choice whether you turn out *exactly* like him.'

August 13, 1994

It's been nearly three months since we returned. Dad still hasn't had any outbursts, though there were moments I expected one, especially during mealtimes, yet nothing ever materialised. Could I have been wrong? Did the shock of us leaving really cause him to change? I've become more at ease as the uneventful days pass, allowing me to enjoy the school summer holidays more than in previous years.

Mum and Dad are out shopping, as per the usual Saturday routine, while I'm home alone and bored, having completed my entire collection of video games several times over. There isn't that much to do in the house during pre-internet days. All my friends are away, leaving me to flick through a gaming magazine idly. I notice a picture of a reader's bedroom, part of a regular feature in which young people send photos of their 'dens.' This one has posters covering the walls, a stark contrast to my bare room. All I have to look at is bland, dark blue wallpaper that would definitely benefit from a few images breaking up the monotony.

I go through my back catalogue of mags to find some cool pull-outs, removing any that catch my eye: Mario, Wing Commander, Street Fighter, all classics of the day. The search for Blu Tack, however, is less successful, leaving Sellotape as the only option. A roll has sat untouched in the kitchen drawer since Christmas, so it's not as if anyone will object.

I stand back to admire my work after sticking up nine different A4-sized sheets. They make me want to boot up my computer and play something. All in all, I feel pretty good about things right now, that childlike optimism making a rare appearance.

The positive feelings are still present when my parents return. I rush down to meet them, pulling Mum's hand and demanding they see my room's new look.

'Oh wow!,' Mum says. I can hear the slight exaggeration in her voice as she tries to sound impressed, an effort I appreciate. She loves seeing me excited and behaving like a normal schoolboy.

Dad stays silent, moving closer to one of the posters while I excitedly tell Mum about each game adorning the walls. Maybe it's the title itself – Star Wars: TIE Fighter – that's attracted his attention, though I don't ever recall him mentioning an interest in the franchise. No – he's inspecting the tape.

'Don't tell me you used Sellotape on these?,' he interrupts.

'Y-yes. I couldn't find any Blu Tack,' I stutter, unsure why he's asking. It's been in a drawer for eight months. He can't be angry that I used some, surely?

He works his fingernail under the tape and viciously yanks it upwards, taking the wallpaper with it.

'JESUS! YOU'VE RUINED THIS FUCKING ROOM,' he screams, ripping the rest of the poster off in one violent movement.

Despite knowing his capricious nature all too well, Dad's reaction shakes me to the core. Seeing him revert to this behaviour just when I thought he was changing is almost as devastating as that terrible New Year's Eve. All the bottled-up anger, unleashed by something so trivial. The shock of blinking from happiness to horror is something I've experienced before, but this time it was different; this time, it was entirely my fault.

'GET THEM DOWN!,' he screams at Mum. I can already tell he's looking for ways to blame her.

'Bob,' she says in that familiar way I hoped never to hear again.

'DON'T. FUCKING DON'T,' he barks. 'THIS IS YOU! RUNNING OFF AND DOING WHATEVER YOU WANT, GALLIVANTING AROUND. NO FUCKING WONDER HE THINKS SHIT LIKE THIS IS OKAY.'

Tears well in my eyes. I knew the resentment he felt toward us for leaving had been building and that something would eventually open the floodgates, letting it all spill out. But I never thought I'd be the cause, and with something as innocuous as Sellotape.

'NOW LOOK WHAT YOU'VE DONE,' he screams, pointing at me. I bite down hard on my tongue, trying to focus on the pain in a desperate attempt to hide any emotional response.

'Don't cry. Don't cry. Don't cry,' I repeat silently.

Dad rips the other posters down. It's as if he wants the damage to be as extensive as possible to justify his outrage. I stand in the middle of the room, watching Mum struggle as she tries to remove some tape gently. The coppery taste of blood filling my mouth.

The final poster is torn away and thrown at Mum. The way it limply spins and falls short might have made me laugh in another situation. It just makes him angrier. He storms out of the room, his broken wife following close behind.

'It's okay,' she mouths to me.

No, things are far from okay, and she doubtlessly knows it.

The shouting continues downstairs. Dad again shifts from blaming Mum for the posters to berating her for the brief stint at her sister's. I'm rooted to the spot with my jaw clenched tight, breathing becoming erratic. There's a panicky feeling that I'm going to pass out. It takes a massive effort to snap out of the trance and run down the stairs. Dad's in the middle of a rant that's about to become physical when I burst through the living room door. He turns, the hate on my face eliciting shock on his.

'Don't! Don't you fucking look at me like that, lad,' he says with implied threat rather than volume. 'Blame your cunt of a mother for this.'

'FUCK YOU,' I scream.

It's not as if I've never said that word myself – it's a popular term in the schoolyard – but hearing Dad use it to describe Mum is too much. I charge. He grabs my arms, holding them above my body. Instinctively, I throw a headbutt. Having no idea how to execute one, I aim for his forehead rather than his nose. It probably hurts me more than him, though the blow causes Dad to reel backwards. Mum shouts for us to stop, but adrenalin pushes me forward.

Despite my increasing size, I'm still a teen fighting a grown man. A surprise cross connects squarely with my left eye socket and temple. My legs turn to jelly and give way. The last thing I hear is the panic in Mum's voice as everything goes black.

August 14, 1994

I've no idea where I am, how I got here, or what happened. My head pounds, making it difficult to put together the blurry pieces. I'm in my bed. Checking the clock, I see it's almost 8 am. How have I been asleep for so long? Aria stands in the corner, wearing an expression I've never seen on her before: disappointment. The world spins when I sit up.

'I warned you, Dean. I warned you not to fight back.'

Hearing her scold me for the first time hurts as much as the headache.

'I can't... What happened?'

'You headbutted him, remember? That wasn't a good idea, especially as you planted it in the wrong place.'

It's coming back now, like the hazy memory of a drunken night that slowly returns. The wallpaper, that word, the punch. Did I go to the hospital?

'You... you heard what he said, what he called her. I should have killed him,' I groan.

She solemnly shakes her head – another first.

'You can't be controlled by your emotions the way he is. It'll only make things worse. You have to think. Fighting him will just bring more suffering to you both, and you can't always be there to protect your mother.'

I try to put the rest of the pieces together just as the door opens. The relief at seeing Mum walk into the room is overwhelming, ending the gnawing fear that she bore the consequences of my actions. Her face bears no cuts, bruises, or scratches, which is both surprising and welcome.

'Oh, thank God you're up. We were worried for a while there.'

'Mum, what happened?'

'Are you feeling okay, Dean?'

'I just…yeah. I'm okay. What, what happened?' I repeat.

Mum explains that Dad was filled with remorse after hitting me, blaming it on everything from her, obviously, to him not feeling very well. She called an ambulance, telling them I'd slipped on the carpet and landed on my face. As much as Mum wanted to reveal the truth, she feared what Dad would do if threatened by the law.

'Don't worry, though. I said he'd have to kill me before raising his hands to you again.'

I know she's trying to comfort me, yet I do believe Dad's capable of murder.

It turns out that I'd been taken to hospital and diagnosed with a mild concussion. Not mild enough that I could remember even being there, it seems. They recommended overnight observation, but Dad insisted home was the best place for me, no doubt terrified that I would tell someone how I really ended up with a black eye. It was late when we got back, and with my mind still in a fog, I went straight to bed.

'Thank you, Dean. Thank you for trying to protect me. But please, don't fight him again. Your Dad loves us, you know. It's just that he's... he's not well, you know? And won't get any help. But honestly, he wouldn't dare do that again. He feels terrible for it. I've told him he's in the last chance saloon with us.'

How many times have I heard that he's not well? Those words make me just as angry now as when Aria first said them. Why is nobody to blame for the misery he inflicts on us?

'That's how he shows his love, by hitting us? I hope he dies,' I spit. Mum looks more sad than shocked.

'I'm sorry we put you through all this.'

I don't reply, not even to ask why she said 'we.'

September 7, 1995

It's been over a year since Dad knocked me out. His attack proved to be another incident that scared him into a period of near normalcy, one that didn't last – just like every other time. The moments of aggression arrived incrementally, leading to the point where his violence and irrational behaviour once again became the status quo. While his actions continue to leave physical and psychological scars, we've grown accustomed to such horrors. It's as if we accept that he'll never change – better to just live with it than trying to escape and risk making things worse.

Aria remains the only one I can talk to about my home life. I listened to her advice; no matter how much provocation Dad dishes out, fighting him is out of the question. His paranoid delusions have worsened, become more unhinged, and the physicality of his rage fits make you forget he's an unhealthy man approaching 60.

Sometimes, as I sit speaking to a woman with wings who only I can see, I return to the theory that she is the manifestation of my own mental illness. Maybe this is what she meant about me being like him in some ways. 'Crazy people don't know they're crazy,' I keep telling myself. Anyway, conversing with invisible angels is better than the alternative.

'Aria, am I ill, too?'

'Of course not. Why do you ask?'

'Well, most kids stop seeing imaginary friends by the time they're my age.'

'I'd like to think I'm more than just an imaginary friend.'

'But only I can see you, and you're, like, an angel, so you're imaginary, obviously.'

'And a friend,' she adds with a smile. 'Huh, then maybe I am. Or maybe you're imagining all of this. Maybe this is all a dream.'

'It's not a very good dream, is it.'

'Haha, no, not really. Like I keep telling you, it'll be over one day. Don't forget that you'll be old enough to escape him eventually.'

I never think about the future. Being in constant fear of what tomorrow will bring does that to a person. Dad could have an uncontrolled episode at any moment and kill us both, so why be concerned about the next year or decade?

I used to play a game when I was younger. Every day when I got back from school, I'd sit on the edge of my bed, take off my shoes, and try to throw them into a small gap between the chest of drawers and the wall. The target was around seven or eight feet away and about two feet wide. The idea was that if either shoe landed in the right spot, the next day wouldn't be as awful as the current one; this was the extent of my future planning. Funnily enough, at least one shoe always landed, though it rarely meant a better tomorrow. But I kept playing, not wanting to tempt fate

CHAPTER FIVE

THE ROAD TO FREEDOM

December 4, 1995

My seventeenth birthday. Mum gives me a gift that will eventually change both our lives forever: driving lesson vouchers. Having a car is something I've never given much thought to, partly because I'm worried about being far away from what's happening at home, but I like the idea of avoiding the twenty-minute walk to college every day. My GCSE grades were far from exemplary, which didn't come as a surprise, meaning my choice of post-school education was limited to the local community college.

As I stare at those pieces of paper offering half-price tuition, an idea forms; if I ever get a car, maybe Mum and I could escape. Dad never lets her leave his side for a second these days, but should the opportunity present itself for both of us to make a quick getaway, we could go somewhere he wouldn't dare look. Suddenly, I feel something I'd almost forgot: hope.

April 17, 1996

Despite the combined distractions of Dad, college, and England's terrible winter months, I'm ready to take my driving test today. Everyone goes into their exam hoping to pass, but I feel the extra added pressure of knowing what doing so would mean.

Mum embraces me as I leave, wishing all the luck in the world. Dad advises against killing the instructor when I crash. Failing a mock test before tackling the real thing does nothing to calm my jangling nerves.

Changing into the test car, I notice the assessor seems friendly, helping me feel a little more at ease. I try to clear my mind of everything as we pull away from the centre, focusing solely on the next hour.

The initial 15 minutes and that all-important first manoeuvre go well. As I pull up to a red light and indicate to go right, my concentration starts to lapse as fantasies of leaving Dad prove a distraction. I accelerate once the light turns green, completely forgetting to give way to oncoming traffic. I hammer the brakes. While this stops me from colliding into a car moving in the opposite direction, I'm left stranded at an awkward angle in the middle of the road. I've failed. It feels like forever before a gap opens so I can finally end this misery. The only consolation is that I don't have to worry about messing up the rest of the test; I've already let myself down.

The remainder of the exam passes quickly – not being concerned about failing improves my driving. Still, the anticipation of my uselessness being verbally confirmed makes me queasy.

'Just pull over wherever it's safe to do so and turn off the engine, please,' my examiner says in a very official manner.

I can picture Dad's response. He kept telling me I was stupid to think I'd succeed.

'Well, Mr Graham, that's your test over, and I'm very pleased to tell you that you have passed.'

A friend once advised me to deal with difficult situations by focusing on my happiest memories. I have few to draw from, but recalling the exact moment that sentence left the assessor's lips will forever be a mental morphine shot. My head drops onto the steering wheel, the mixture of shock, relief, and joy proving too much. It's the first time I've ever cried with happiness. Even the tester, who had no doubt seen various reactions during his years, seems surprised.

'Errmm… are you okay?' he asks.

'I'm… amazing. Thank you. Thank you so much. I thought I'd failed at those lights!.'

'No, that was just a minor error for positioning – your only one. Well done.'

As my instructor drives me home, I sit in the passenger seat and stare out the window, listening to Oasis' 'Wonderwall' playing on the radio. I'm filled with joy. A feeling that the future, which up until now seemed utterly bleak, might not be so grim. The sun warms my face, and I smile.

I walk through the door faking a sad expression.

'Oh, son. Did it not go well?' Mum asks.

My morose features morph into a massive grin.

'I PASSED!' I shout, throwing my arms in the air. It's now my mother's turn to shed tears of happiness, another sight I'm not used to seeing.

Dad says one thing.

'Huh, can't believe you managed it. That test must be a piece of piss these days.'

May 17, 1996

I'm halfway through a college computing course. It's a subject I've always been interested in and, despite the class containing some people who picked it as a last resort rather than get a job, it's enjoyable. What I don't like, however, is the part-time evening sociology class I take alongside it. I only opted for this extra A/S-level hoping it would help me get into university, should I choose the option, but it's not what I imagined – tons of homework, boring, and nobody seems to like the teacher. As such, my friend and I have skipped several classes. We could just drop out, but I know what Dad would say about that.

As a result of our actions, the lecturer has taken it upon herself to phone our parents and inform them of our absences – I don't know if this is college protocol or just because she dislikes us. My classmate's mum and dad simply ask why he didn't just quit, whereas my father sees this as another sign of my disrespect. As always, Mum is the one who suffers. Dad screams at me for leaving, saying I'll be lucky to get a job sweeping streets, a phrase he's used many times to describe my prospects. I try to explain that I dislike the course and that it barely counts towards university entrance, but he doesn't care about facts.

Dad's stopped raising his fists to Mum in front of me, possibly due to my rapidly growing size. He saves the physical stuff for the times I'm not at home. I'll come back from college or sleeping at a friend's place to find her with bruises and welts. When I ask, she regurgitates the same excuses repeated by so many domestic violence victims: it's not his fault, I'm just as much to blame, things will only get worse if you try to help, I'll be okay. Her promise of Dad being on a final warning is now long forgotten.

Life gets even worse after the call, the frequency of the tantrums, psychological abuse, and sudden bruises increasing. The worst part is, like the poster incident, it was my decisions that led to this state. It was me who skipped the classes, and I should have known what would happen.

Most of my friends have already picked which university they're aiming to attend next year, whereas I face a dilemma. The freedom and independence of living away from home sound fantastic and being far from Dad is a fantasy I've harboured for years, but it also means he will be alone with Mum permanently.

'I don't want to stay here forever, but I don't want to leave Mum alone with him,' I explain to Aria.

'I know, but your mum wants you to go. She thinks everything will have been worth it if you get an education and make something of your life. If you prove him wrong.'

I've talked to Mum about university and my fear of her being isolated with Dad. The response is always the same.

'Don't let that bastard ruin your future, Dean. You go to university and get yourself a great job. Don't be like him. I'll be fine, I promise. The thought of you with initials after your name would get me through anything,' she'd say with a beaming smile of pride.

'Why don't you just leave as well, Mum? I could drive you to aunt Olive's. You'd never have to see him again,' was my usual response.

'Dean, I'm far too old to be running away and starting my life over from scratch. Anyway, you know how he'd react if I did that. Don't you worry, son, I can give as good as I get,' she would reply.

I always swore not to leave Mum at the mercy of Dad's wrath, but she's made it obvious she'll blame herself if I choose to stay rather than continue my studies in a big city. As I've already discovered, the knowledge that you're responsible for a loved one's pain is so much worse than experiencing any yourself.

'I understand what Mum wants, Aria, and why, but what if he really hurts her badly while I'm not here? What if he kills her? I couldn't live with myself.'

'You can't think that way. You can't keep living in fear of the what if.'

July 24, 1996

Dad is in hospital. Mum rang in a panicked state around two in the afternoon on a day I finished college early. They'd been walking around a local shopping centre when he fell to the ground after complaining of feeling ill.

'What's wrong with him?' I ask.

'Doctors think it's diabetes. Both his brothers have it, you know, but they're quite overweight. He said he's been peeing loads recently and drinking gallons of water. They said his blood sugar must have been sky high for ages; the hospital gave him insulin. Say he's lucky not to have gone into a coma. He's going to have to inject himself for the rest of his life.'

'So, how will it affect him, other than injecting?' I ask, not knowing anything about the condition other than the passing mention in a school biology lesson.

'They're pretty sure it's type 2, like Ray and Norman, so it's not as bad as the other kind, apparently. He'll still have to make a few changes. No more smoking, for a start.'

That'll put him in an even better mood.

'And he's supposed to improve his diet. Cut down on sugar and fatty things. Look after his heart.'

'Is he going to be... okay, you know?'

'Well, they have to do a load of tests to make sure his kidneys and heart are undamaged, but he should be alright. A lot of people have diabetes, you know. He gets this little machine for testing his blood, and as long as it's within a certain range, he's okay. I think that's how it works. I was a bit flustered when they explained it.'

'What happens now?'

'They'll be watching him for a while, want him to stay in overnight, but you know what he's like. Said he'd come back in tomorrow instead.'

'Yeah, I do know what he's like.'

Dad doubtlessly believes that leaving Mum alone for the night will result in her sneaking off.

'Are *you* okay, Mum?'

'Yes, I'm okay now. It was just a bit of a shock, that's all. We'll get a taxi back and pick the car up tomorrow.'

'Okay, see you later.'

'See you later, Dean. I love you.'

She never says that at the end of phone calls.

'I… errr… love you too, Mum.'

Diabetes, I struggle to remember what my teacher said about the disease. Something to do with the pancreas? Dad's brother, Ray, always seems totally fine; he drinks booze, eats whatever he wants, always laughing. Maybe it's not even that bad. I'm surprised because Dad is pretty skinny, and I thought only overweight people got it. The talk of him in a coma brings a little satisfaction; yeah, I'm glad he's got it.

'Is that how you really feel?'

Aria stands nearby, wings folded behind her body to fit in the small landing at the bottom of the stairs.

'Yes, I do. It's a shame he didn't fucking die, but hopefully this will finish him off. As if he's going to stop smoking and eating fried pork sandwiches.'

'You don't seem convinced it's what you want.'

'What the fuck are you talking about? I've wished he were dead for years, and now it might happen. So yeah, I'm pretty convinced. A hundred fucking per cent.'

I've never been this angry at her.

'Look, Aria, I know you're trying to get me to accept that on some level, there's a part of me that still loves him, that he's still my dad despite everything. So let me set you right: No, there isn't. Fuck him. He deserves everything he gets and worse.'

And with that, she's gone.

There's a strange atmosphere when my parents finally return. Dad looks dishevelled, though I'm more stunned by how happy he seems to see me.

'Alight, Dean? Sorry, we might have given you a scare there. I got one myself, haha.'

'Alight, Dad. Yeah, canny shocking. You okay?'

'Aye, son. I'm alright.'

Son, there's a word I haven't heard him utter in a while. He must have had a real fright.

'I'll be injecting myself a few times each day from now on. Said if I don't, I could have me feet amputated, could even go blind. I'd rather be bloody dead than blind.

Norman and Ray seem to manage okay. Mind you, neither of them smoke, so I'll be knocking that on the head. Doctors said it's the worst thing a diabetic can do. Aye, could have been a lot worse. Reckon I've had it for a long time without even knowing.'

I can't remember him speaking to me this earnestly in the past.

'Anyway, give us a hug. Was worried for a while there that I would never see you again.'

His voice quivers as the words come out. Dad grabs me, and I put my arms around him in a very awkward manner. I'm pretty sure it wasn't even this decade when we were last this close physically, other than when fighting.

'I love you, son.'

'I-I love you, too, Dad,' I reply, not really believing the words.

October 7, 1996

Dad isn't managing his diabetes well. He's already suffered several hypoglycaemic attacks, a result of taking too much insulin. By not balancing the amount he injects with the carbohydrates he consumes, his glucose levels drop dangerously. Hypos, as they're called, are often compared to being very drunk but without the fun element. People start slurring and act confused, emotional, and erratic. They also shake, sweat, and struggle to move. Should the levels go even lower, diabetics can pass out and risk slipping into a coma, leading to death.

Dad's typical response to a hypo is to start crying. It's weird to see, especially after all the times he brought mum and me to tears. My mother has to stuff glucose tablets into his mouth when he gets this bad to raise his sugars. I watch her sometimes, shoving them down his throat as he drools and cries and calls her names, saving the life of a man who's tortured her for over a decade, and I wonder why she does it – probably the same reason she's forgiven him so often.

December 4, 1996

It's my eighteenth birthday, the day I officially become an adult. Thanks to living in constant stress, the secret smoking habit I've picked up, being overweight, binge drinking, and a horrendous mullet, I look like a 40-year-old roadie for a seventies rock band.

I've no happy memories from previous birthdays, and I wasn't really expecting much today. Cards and gifts wait downstairs from family and friends, but there's no present from my parents on display.

'Happy birthday, son,' says Mum.

'Aye, you're supposed to be an adult now, so hurry up and earn your keep, haha,' Dad's way of taking the shine off anything: comments that only he finds funny.

'Thanks,' I say, opening my cards. I'm pleased to find money in some of them. A few of my presents are bottles of vodka, which I can now enjoy legally. I've unwrapped everything, but there's still one notable absence.

'Let's go and get our present, then,' Mum tells me in an excited tone.

The three of us leave the house and head toward Dad's council-rented garage about 100 feet away. He's acting surprisingly normal, putting in extra effort for my birthday, perhaps.

Despite all the signs, I still don't believe it will be a car. The lessons were one thing, but an actual vehicle that mum and I could potentially escape in – no way Dad would allow that. My expectation had been for me to save up enough money and buy a banger in a few years.

'Go on then, open it,' an excited smile spreads across Mum's face as she hands me the garage keys. The last time I saw her so happy was when I passed my test.

I lift the door and see my present. It's a tiny, boxy, red car that's about fifteen years old. I've not even heard of the manufacturer, but it doesn't matter. It's a car. It's *my* car. I'm as overwhelmed as I am surprised.

'Oh my God! Thank you so much! I can't believe it,' I gush.

'Aye, you've your uncle Norman to thank, belonged to your cousin. He got a new one, so we got this for a steal. Now I won't have to give you lifts everywhere, and you can find a bloody job with it, ha,' says Dad.

February 20, 1997

Another Christmas comes and goes. More cutting re-marks from my father about presents and their cost never affected me, but there are times his passive-aggressiveness leads to something worse when I'm not home. The holidays pass slowly, probably because I keep wishing they would end. Dad's rarely good during this time of year – barring my birthday – usually a result of excessive alcohol – his diabetic team's recommendation to cut back falling on deaf ears. He did quit smoking, which has made his temper even viler. At one point, my conviction that he was planning to hurt Mum stopped me from setting foot outside the house for almost a week, causing my friends to think I'd gone into hiding.

The constant worry about leaving my parents alone helps make up my mind. Despite it going against her wishes, I tell Mum that university just isn't for me, and maybe I can get a local job instead, live at home for a while longer. I'd even start paying rent to keep Dad happy. She cries when I explain my plan.

'Dean, I've told you before, I don't care what happens to me. You're the only thing that matters. I know you haven't had the happiest childhood, and I'm sorry for that. But we got through it together. If you don't make the most of your opportunities now, then it might have all been for nothing.'

'All for nothing.' Those words cut deep. It's a lot to process, but it helps me understand what my actions mean to her. Against my better judgement, I decide to apply for a university place tomorrow, but I'll choose somewhere close to home as a compromise.

CHAPTER SIX

GOODBYE

October 2, 1997

I picked a university in the same city where my aunt lives, just a short drive from home. It only took a few days here to realise I'm unhappy.

If growing up with a violent, abusive father wasn't enough to turn me into an introvert, the bad acne that's somehow getting worse as I age intensifies my shyness. This place illustrates how I can only make new friends by using my current ones as a crutch, drawing confidence from their proximity. Alone and without the familiarity of others, I'm a mess.

Whenever talking to someone new, I visualise myself outside of the conversation, like a stranger watching it from somewhere nearby. I see the person looking at me with a mixture of disgust and pity; I imagine the negative emotions they must be struggling to hide. Jesus, my ineptitude is sickening. I long to bury my insecurities so I can act and think like a normal human being.

I feared that being away from Dad would mean fewer visits from Aria, but whether it's because of my low mood or concern about what might be going on at home, we still speak regularly. Appearances are confined to my student accommodation's bedroom, thankfully; the sight of me talking to myself would be the final straw for my already concerned housemates, who probably think I'm as a mass-shooter in the making.

'Have I done the right thing?' I ask her one Saturday night, sitting by myself while other students revel in town.

'You're making your mother happy, so I'd say you made the correct decision, yes.'

'I just wish I could get along with people. They must wonder how I even got into this place. They look at me like I'm stupid.'

'You're the only one who believes that, Dean. Remember what Mum said: you shouldn't let him ruin your life.'

'It might be a bit late.'

I despise my thought process and this defeatist attitude.

'Don't say that.'

'Yeah, I know. I'll get through it. Anyway, fuck these fucking… snobs.'

'Maybe they think you're the snob. It is you who barely speaks to anyone and then acts all weird when you do.'

'Ha, maybe. I'll try to be more normal.'

'Not coming across as a serial killer would probably make you more popular, yes.'

'Very funny.'

November 8, 1997

Two months at university have seen things turn around. Taking Aria's advice, I came out of my shell and made some friends, all thanks to alcohol. Booze was, and in most cases still is, an integral part of life for British students. I remember being hesitant to try it for the first time as a 16-year-old at college, given my dad's history with the bottle, but I love how being drunk eliminates my hang-ups and helps me forget about the past. The way it changes me into someone else, a confident, funny, outgoing person. And getting *very* drunk turns me into an absolute party monster who makes everyone laugh – a feeling I adore.

Being Saturday, I'm driving home to visit Mum. I usually stay with my parents until the evening before heading back and getting semi-drunk in preparation for hitting the town. Dad rarely leaves Mum's side while I'm there, though I take advantage of his trips to the toilet to ask how he's behaving.

'I'm okay, Dean. Honestly. I can handle him. I'm just over the moon that you're doing so well,' is her usual line. I only believe the last part, though she bears no bruises, at least none I can see.

It's a typically grim November day in England. The iron-coloured skies leak rain, and the cold is extreme enough to see your breath, adding to the heavy atmosphere of depression. I pull up in the square next to Dad's car at around 12.30 in the afternoon.

The winter air nips my face when I step out and walk towards the old place. The street's unusual design means there's another house between my parents' address and where I park, making it a 30-second stroll to the front door. As I approach, a faint sound rises. Familiar but difficult to place.

I'm in front of the closed gate and fence that tower above my head before I finally place the noise. It's a combination of Dad's shouts and Mum's hysterical crying, emanating clearly from the front yard.

It's been over twenty years since that day, yet I can still picture what lay before me upon opening the gate. Mum, close to 60 years old, down on her hands and knees at the top of the path. An overturned refuse bin next to her, its contents spread across the ground. Dad stands nearby, screams bursting from his red face. He rants like a madman.

Neither parent reacts as I approach. Mum picks through the bin's disgusting innards, moving around wet kitchen towels, rotten food, and dirty packaging like she's searching for something, gagging at the vile smell that cuts the icy air.

'What… what's happening?' I ask, not aiming the question at either of them. Against all logic and reason, I hope for a rational explanation.

'Ask your fucking mother,' Dad says before storming into the house.

I help Mum up from the ground. She's uncontrollably crying as I lead her into the downstairs bathroom to get cleaned up.

'He… He said I'm trying to kill him; thinks I've been putting poison tablets in his food. I swore I'd never do that, but he made me search the whole house for them. Said I must have thrown them in the bin. He tipped it over and told me to go through it, or else he'd kill me.'

I'm struggling to take this in. There have been plenty of occasions when Dad acted psychotic, but not on such an extreme level. My hands start shaking in a delayed response. I need to get a grip.

'Will you be okay for a second. I need to use the other bathroom,' I say. Mum nods, choking back the tears and wiping grime from her face with a damp towel.

Going straight up the stairs to avoid the living room where Dad's watching the news, I struggle with each step like an old man, legs carrying the weight of lead while my mind bolts from one thought to another, making me feel like I'm about to empty my churning guts. Pulling myself along using the banister helps me reach the upper floor.

Turning left and walking towards the upstairs toilet takes me past my parents' bedroom. Their inward-opening door is ajar, leaving a slight gap. I can see pieces of perfectly cut wood protruding into the air like they're somehow attached to the back of the door itself. Stepping inside reveals four brand-new planks, the kind you would buy from a hardware store, nailed to the rear, each one sticking out beyond the edge.

'What the hell?'

Closing the modified fitting confirms the planks' purpose; they seal the room from the inside. Small holes populate the sections that cover the wall, a result of nails inserted and removed repeatedly. It reminds me of a zombie film in which people board themselves indoors to keep out the undead.

A hammer and box of nails on the bedside cabinet confirm that Dad's paranoid delusions are out of control. There's a strong smell in here: urine. A walk to Mum's side of the bed reveals the source as a bucket half-filled with piss, my father's way of allowing his wife to relieve herself while imprisoned.

These revelations – his madness, her torture – prove too much. All semblance of control lost, I race into the bathroom, the stench still burning my nostrils, and throw up.

Bile burns the back of my throat when I return to Mum, who's now standing in the hallway looking a bit more composed.

'What the fuck, Mum? Why's he got your bedroom door nailed shut? And that bucket.'

A look of shame passes over her face.

'He's... he's just going through a bad time right now. He thought I was leaving the house after we'd gone to bed to see the bloke next door, so now he nails us in.'

The idea that my mum is having an affair with the married 27-year-old neighbour who she barely acknowledges would almost be funny in other circumstances.

'Are you fucking kidding me?' I don't like swearing in front of her, but it's hard to show any restraint right now.

'He'll have calmed down now. Just let me speak to him, please. I'll be okay, I promise. Look, just get yourself back to uni and come over tomorrow when he's better. I'll let you know what happens. And don't worry, I'll be okay.'

'Okay! He thinks you're trying to poison him! He threatened to kill you! And what about the bedroom?'

'I think his blood sugars have been off a lot recently. He's not himself when that happens.'

'What are you talking about? I'm pretty sure diabetes doesn't turn people into raving lunatics. It doesn't explain the ten years before his diagnosis, does it? He wasn't diabetic when he was beating you half to death every week. Why are you defending him?'

'I know, Dean. I'm sorry. I just... he's not well.'

'Fucking hell! How many times have I heard that line? He should get help if he's not well.'

'He won't accept help. You know that. What else can I do?'

'Mum, let me drive you to Olive's, please,' I hope mentioning her sister will jog some sense into my mother, but she seems to shudder at the idea.

'That's not a good idea, Dean. You don't know what he might do, and honestly, I think he'll be okay once he's eaten. I'm begging you, don't do anything. I'll sort it out, honestly.'

I hate that I'm feeling this way towards her. Why won't she leave? Why is she sticking up for him? How can she still love him after everything? I don't understand.

It breaks my heart to know that short of picking her up and carrying her out, there's no way I'll get Mum to come with me. I reluctantly do as she asks, knowing that facing him myself will result in me murdering the prick. Holding back the tears, we hug. I silently pray it won't be our last.

'Please be careful, Mum. And if anything happens, just run next door and tell them to call the police.'

'I'll be okay, I promise. See you tomorrow. Love you.'

'Love you too.'

I walk out the door in a daze, struggling to focus on a single thought for more than a couple of seconds. Fighting off tears becomes impossible once in the car. The urge to run back and grab Mum is overwhelming, but I know what that outcome will be, especially now that I can't sneak her out without Dad noticing. I think about fighting him, just going in there and knocking him out, but her words still ring in my ears: 'You don't know what he might do.'

I pull away from the street, replaying everything, convincing myself that I should have done something differently. The frustration at how Mum can make excuses for that bastard drives me crazy. The more I think about what I witnessed, the more the back of my neck and face heat up, despite being in a bitterly cold car with broken heaters.

It's fifteen minutes into my journey when I notice my cloudy breath filling up the vehicle, pouring out of me like a steam train. Short, sharp gasps of air come in rapid succession, but no matter how hard I focus, a regular breathing pattern won't return. I'm hyperventilating. It feels like too much blood is pumping into my head, and even the worst hangover never made my mouth this dry. Gripping the wheel tightly, I try to ignore the panic stemming from my narrowing vision. An eternity passes.

'Come on. Nearly there, nearly there,' I repeat.

It takes an ungodly force of will to stay conscious while navigating the busy city roads. The bucket and the overturned bin branded into my memory alongside the smell of urine and vomit. Pins and needles spread across my face, working their way down my neck, torso, and legs. A cyclist screams expletives when the car misses him by inches.

There's the street! I turn without slowing, tyres screaming as my shitty old Seat Ibiza skids into the wrong lane before mounting the curb and coming to a stop. I struggle out of the seatbelt, still taking quick, desperate breathes, crawl outside and stagger to the front door, grateful that it's unlocked. Stepping inside is like passing an invisible finish line. My legs give up, and I hit the ground – darkness. I think of Dad. What will he do to Mum if I die?

'Dean. Dean, mate. What's the matter? You're not pissed already, are you?'

'Is he on medication? He's never mentioned 'owt to me.'

'Me neither. Looks like he's had a fit or something. DEAN! YOU ALRIGHT, MATE?'

Is this a dream? The voices drift through a dense haze. I recognise them as belonging to two of my flatmates,

104

Paul and Andrew. Although my eyes remain shut, I can tell the pair are standing over me, discussing what to do.

'Dean. DEAN. You okay, mate?' the concern in Andrew's voice is touching. He's a few years older than me, and like everyone I've met here, talking to him was a struggle initially. But thanks to the social lubricant that is alcohol, our shared love of geek culture and rock music – two things that cemented my status as a loser at school – has brought us close.

The dry nothingness sitting in my throat prevents me from replying. My body has shut down, another defence mechanism against the real world.

'We should call an ambulance,' I hear Paul say. He was Andrew's mate long before they left a local pit village for university. The three of us have become friends in the short time we've lived together.

The mention of an ambulance sends a thought into my swirling head, a brief moment of lucidity. If I end up in the hospital, then somebody – the doctors, university, or a friend –will inform my parents, and I know who'll get the blame. My eyes open instinctively, followed by a sound forced through my throat with a herculean effort.

'Noo…,' it's all I can manage.

'No? To an ambulance? Eh? Ha'way, man, you soft shite. Let's get him off the floor,' says Paul.

They pick me up, positioning my arms around their necks. My feet dangle above the ground as I'm carried along the corridor. Andrew is six-foot-one, while Paul is a monstrous 6 foot, 7 inches – almost an entire foot bigger than me. Ironically, I used to be considered tall for a schoolkid because my growth spurt ended when I was about 12. I've only grown about an inch during the last six years. Most people I towered over at school now look down on me in the literal sense. Early puberty has a lot to answer for.

After flopping my limp body onto the sofa, Paul moves into the kitchen section at the back of the sitting room to make coffee. Andrew sits in the chair opposite.

'Mate, I really think we should call someone. It looked like you were fucking dead for a bit there.'

Andy's a typical student stereotype: skinny, stubbly, pasty, and hair reaching halfway down his back. I appreciate how much he cares. It's not something I expect from people.

'No, mate, please. I'll be okay, honestly.'

I sound like my mum.

'What's the matter?' Paul shouts from across the room as he fills the cup. 'Is there something wrong with you? Like, medically?'

Yeah, doubtlessly.

'Nah, mate. It's... I'm....'

Should I make something up? It might be the easier option.

Virtually every day of the last decade has been spent dealing with Dad. Apart from Aria, and on rare occasions, my mother, I've never spoken to anyone about him – the real him –yet I *want* to tell my new friends the truth. There's a connection between us, one that's strengthened by our living arrangements. They already feel like the brothers I've always wanted.

Everything comes spilling out: Dad, Mum, the violence, the pain. The only part I leave out is my invisible, winged confidant as talking about her might push their limits of understanding

Recounting the entirety of my life to real people for the first time is surreal. I've taught myself not to think about the past too much as dealing with the present's horrors is hard enough. Explaining the things Dad did over the years is like a floodgate opening, releasing the suppressed emotions

I've bottled up. It's like reliving all those events again. My attempt at not getting overly emotional fails terribly. I appreciate that Paul and Andrew don't appear embarrassed. Their mouths drop open, and their heads shake at some moments, but they never seem uncomfortable.

After what feels like ages, getting through three cigarettes and two coffees, I conclude with the events of earlier today and subsequent hyperventilation. They now agree that calling an ambulance would be a bad idea.

'Jesus, mate,' says Paul. 'Maybe you should go back home now instead of tomorrow. You don't know what he'll do to her tonight. I'll come with you if you want.'

The statement makes me feel bad for ever thinking these two took a disliking to me.

A moment of clarity arrives, no doubt brought on by recounting everything; he's right: I can't wait until tomorrow, no matter what Mum said. And while I appreciate Paul's offer, the presence of a blonde crew cut-sporting giant who resembles a James Bond henchman would exacerbate the situation.

'Thanks, mate. Aye, I'll go back as soon as my head's on straight. Cheers for the offer but I think it'd be better if I go alone. You don't know how he'll react if I turn up with someone.'

'Just be careful. And let us know if you need anything,' adds Andrew.

We talk more about the past while waiting for my dizziness to stop. It's weird to think that right here, right now, at one of the worst points in my life, opening up about Dad is proving an amazingly liberating experience. The idea of discussing him had always filled me with fear; not only did I worry that people might judge me, but I also believed he could find out I'd been revealing his secrets. I set off home again after about fifteen minutes, happy that nobody stole my unlocked car.

The journey is spent mentally planning what to do upon arrival. Is confronting him head-on the best option, risking later repercussions, or should I make an excuse for my return and secretly convince Mum to sneak away with me?

Discovering the contents of the now-upright bin are back where they belong comes as a relief. I open the house door, still lacking a solid plan.

Silence. Even the TV is off. Dad's car is in the usual spot, indicating they're both here. A feeling of dread rises as

I run through different scenarios. Has he sealed them both inside the bedroom again? Peering upstairs, I see that the door's still open. What's going on? They never sit in the living room without the television blaring.

The ominous silence is broken only by my boots connecting with the kitchen linoleum. I picture what waits for me in the living room; one dead body, maybe two, an empty room covered in blood.

I instinctively hold my breath while inching inside. Dad's feet come into view – he's lying on the floor. A tingle shoots through my spine a second before I see him twitch. He often naps in this position, lower half on the carpet and his torso resting against the sofa's base. It allows him to trap Mum as she sits directly behind, one leg on either side of his body, making it almost impossible for her to move without waking the captor. I've seen this scene plenty of times before, but instead of watching TV, as usual, Mum's head is slumped down. Is she asleep as well?

'Mum?' I whisper.

She slowly looks up at me. He's left marks on her countless times; this, though, this is the worst I've ever seen. Both eyes are black and so severely swollen that they're little more than slits. Scratches, cuts, and smaller bruises cover her face. Dried blood flakes off her lips and nostrils, a clump of hair is missing, and an ear still bleeds, likely due to an earring being torn out. Tears squeeze through the tiny gaps when she sees me. I feel Aria's presence.

'It's time, Dean. You know what to do,' the angel says.

It takes everything I have not to stamp on Dad's head until it pops like a melon. No, this will hurt more. I quietly edge toward Mum. Without saying a word, I grab both hands and use them to lift her off the sofa silently and into a standing position, ensuring not to disturb the sleeping monster below. If he does wake, one of us will die. I don't know if it's fate or luck, but somehow Mum manages to pass over his body without him stirring. We quickly move out of the living room and tiptoe through the kitchen before walking out the front door together for the last time.

CHAPTER SEVEN

STUDENT LIFE IS A KILLER

November 9, 1997

Although I begged her to let me drive to a hospital, Mum insisted we go straight to my aunt's. The horror on Olive's face was evident when we walked through the door but attempts at getting her sister to a doctor proved just as fruitless as my begging. Calling the police was another option Mum talks us out of, warning it would push him even further over the edge. She swears she'll never go back; he'll never hurt her again.

I decide to sleep at my aunt's to be near Mum. I don't doubt Dad knows where we are, but I'm confident he wouldn't dare turn up. Despite his issues, he remains afraid of both authority and my mother's extended, hardened family.

It's 1 AM. I'm back on the same sofa bed I'd occupied just a few years ago. Staring at the ceiling, which now has even more yellow smoke stains, I realise that a life without fear and worry has become a completely unfamiliar concept. I've become so used to always being on edge that their absence is almost frightening. All the horrors he committed start playing back in my mind. By not being constantly preoccupied with the present, am I left to dwell on the past?

'Is it over?' I ask, hoping Aria is listening.

'For your mum, yes,' she replies.

'What about me?'

'You'll still have to face him, Dean. Confront the things he's done.'

'No, fuck that. I never want to see him again. I hope he dies regretting everything he put us through.'

'Why would he feel regret when he thinks he's blameless?'

'How many times, Aria? How many times did we beg him to get help? He went fucking crazy if we even suggested it. Anyway, he always managed to act normal outside the house, trick people into thinking he wasn't a fucking lunatic.'

'You know you can't leave it like this.'

'Why not?'

'It will eat you up inside. You need to know the truth. All of it.'

'No. Fuck him. It's over.'

She doesn't respond.

Morning. I have no idea where I am when my eyes open. The memory of yesterday starts returning upon hearing Mum and Olive talking in the kitchen. She's laughing. Not the nervous, forced laugh I've heard so many times before – a laugh without joy – but a natural, heartfelt sound. A noise made by someone who isn't afraid. Last night's trepidation about dealing with a life free of pain is fading. All I feel right now is happiness, the kind I never expected to experience again.

December 25, 1997

It's our first Christmas without him. I've been staying at my university digs, though the last few days were spent at my aunt's, helping get everything ready for the big day. Dad's dislike of and paranoia towards other people meant this occasion had almost always been just the three of us, and it came with the underlying threat that he could explode at any minute. But life is different now. A family he'd kept me apart from for years, all gathered together. About 15 of us sit around the table, laughing and joking. I've never seen my mum without the weight of the world crushing her. I had no idea this was what a real family celebration is like; it makes me sad to think of what I've missed out on during my childhood.

With Mum living off the state and me relying on student loans to survive, we barely have a few pounds between us, but that doesn't matter in the slightest. It's still the best Christmas I've ever had and one I'll never forget.

October 10, 1998

I returned to university for a second year. Dad's been out of our lives since the day we left, though friends who still live in his town tell me he's been asking around about Mum and me.

Most of 1998 has felt like a new beginning. I wanted to be as carefree and happy as the other students, and for a while, I was. Andrew and Paul were ecstatic to hear about Mum's escape, and the three of us continue to grow closer.

Despite everything going well, I know something isn't right. I'd become so accustomed to the daily misery of my old life that I rarely experienced other emotions, and that can make them frightening. Now that the suffocating fog has lifted, I can't stop thinking about the past, analysing it, replaying all those moments. It's awful and upsetting, but my brain keeps defaulting to those worst memories when it's not engaged.

There are other warning signs. Binge drinking certainly isn't an unusual characteristic for a student. In my case, however, I've reached a point where blacking out is the norm for a night in town. Even though I hate the taste of alcohol, being drunk has become my favourite pastime. I still love what it gives me – confidence, popularity, the ability to make people laugh – but I now appreciate how it shuts out the dark thoughts, stops the feelings of self-loathing. Not only am I drinking vast quantities several nights of the week, but I've also started mixing it with drugs such as speed and ephedrine – easy to find on-campus – thereby enhancing and lengthening the experience.

Friends' advice to slow down goes ignored. I know something is changing inside me. It feels like a cancer within my body. At a time of life when I should be at my physical peak, I've become an overweight, near-alcoholic who smokes 30 cigarettes a day. My shambolic state has earned me a semi-jokey nickname among my friends: Dean Forty. At nineteen, I can pass for a forty-year-old, and a very unhealthy one at that.

It's hard to dispute the name. I've started to resemble a fatter version of TV detective Columbo, and the mixture of powerful acne antibiotics I've taken for years, near two decades of stress, and hereditary factors mean my hairline is receding at a drastic rate for a teen.

My appearance is another thing that makes me even less willing to approach girls. It's also why I think nothing of acting like a tit on nights out; I'm never going to attract anyone, so I may as well have a good time while amusing others with my drunken shenanigans. Sometimes people laugh at me rather than with me, but I don't care. All that matters is that they like me.

My flatmates and I have decided to hold a big house party tonight. Wanting to make it extra memorable for the attendees, I've spent a chunk of my student loan on alcohol, high-grade speed, and cannabis.

I start the night with homemade cocktails. A line of amphetamine is snorted every hour or so to stop me from slowing down, meaning I can move onto the straight vodka without blacking out too early. The combination works well; I don't lose consciousness until around 4.30 am – a personal record.

October 11, 1998

Terrible hangovers have become a depressingly regular fact of life, but they all pale in comparison to what I'm feeling right now. In addition to the pounding confusion, churning guts, and taste of vomit, there's blinding pain coming from my left armpit. As per usual, my current location and the previous night's events are a mystery. When my eyes finally open like a new-born kitten's, they revealed that I'm in a bathroom. It is *my* tiny bathroom, so things could be worse.

Something that comes as no surprise is how intoxicated I still feel. It's that post-night out drunkenness – far from enjoyable and usually mixed with the debilitating effects of a hangover. Is this even my own vomit I'm tasting? My brain and bowels feel like they belong to someone else. I try to move.

'Arrgh! Jesus! Wha… What the fuck?'

How am I only now realising that I'm on my knees, stuck in the tight gap between wall and toilet? I doubt I could have been here long, even though my legs have gone dead. I can't understand how the top half of my body has remained upright in an almost praying position.

It turns out the discomfort in my armpit originates from a metal toilet roll holder that's screwed into the brick at around waist height. The pointed end has somehow pierced both my shirt and flesh, embedding itself within my ample man boob. I must have come into the room to relieve myself or, more likely, throw up, and started passing out before slumping against the wall, my body sliding down its surface as consciousness ebbed away. My body presumably descended at such an awkward angle that the end of the U-shaped metal bar used to hold loo paper worked its way into my armpit and beneath the skin, leaving me hanging like a piece of meat in an abattoir.

'This could only happen to me,' is my first thought.

I try to stand, feet slipping on what could be any number of liquids covering the floor. Nobody responds to my screams of pain as the foreign object works its way deeper inside. Pressing my foot against the toilet, I manage to push myself up the damp wall slightly. It feels like the holder has penetrated my flesh by just an inch or so, but it's not leaving without a fight. Moving brings waves of pain that emanate from the entry point. I wonder if cutting back on the booze would be a sensible plan.

'Just like... pulling off a plaster,' I slur to myself.

Placing my free hand against the wall, foot still pressed to the toilet's base, I take a deep breath, ready to launch myself up and back on the exhale.

There's a wet popping noise as the thin, cylindrical metal exits, a sound akin to pulling the plug from a sink filled with a splash of water. I scream. The pain is so bad that I'm sure I'll throw up. The inertia sends me backwards, shoes once again skidding on the alcohol/piss/vomit/blood. I meet the opposite wall with force so strong it shakes the whole room. Sliding down into a sitting position, legs apart, head down, and blood trickling from my armpit, the threat of vomiting becomes a reality just before the door opens.

'Fuck Me! It's Dean Forty,' yells Andrew. 'I think he's dead.'

November 15, 1998

Like many men, I've decided the best way to address the terrifying symptoms my body is throwing at me is to ignore them and hope they go away. Halloween and Bonfire night were excuses to drink so much that I came close to alcohol poisoning, and the monstrous hangovers that followed consisted of more vomiting. Nothing too unusual there, apart from the traces of blood in what I expelled.

Today, though, I'm neither drunk nor hungover. Following my third meal of beans on toast this week, I start to feel an awful burning sensation at the top of my stomach that reaches into my throat. It's grinding and relentless as if I'd swallowed shards of hot glass. The pain is so bad that I try to numb it with a mixture of vodka and orange juice. Unsurprisingly, a combination of alcohol and acidic fruit is of little help.

Lying in the foetal position on my bed, writhing in pain and convinced that I'm dying, Aria appears. Her visits are few and far between these days, possibly resulting from my mind being fogged continuously by substances.

'You really need to see a doctor,' she says, and without even a hello.

'Thank you for such sage advice.'

'Now, now. I'm only thinking of you, as always.'

'Not seen you much recently, Aria. Been anywhere nice?'

'You'd don't seem to need me very often these days.'

'Yeah, life's a bed of fucking roses right now.'

'I think you've found other ways to deal with your problems,' she says, looking at the collection of empty bottles strewn around the room, all different shapes and colours, spread across tables and floor like garish decorations.

'Is this it?' I ask, ignoring the comment. 'I finally get away from him, and now I'm dying?'

'I'm sure you're not dying, drama queen. You're just living life in the fast lane a bit too often. It's not healthy. I'd have thought vomiting blood was an indication of that.'

'Yeah, but people love me when I'm drunk. And it stops me from thinking… bad thoughts, about the past.'

'I told you that dealing with this wasn't going to be easy. You look like hell, by the way.'

'Cheers. It's why girls find me so irresistible.'

I start laughing, despite the agony. Aria joins in. I wonder what Dad's doing now, whether he's given up trying to contact us or is plotting something else. Before drifting off to sleep, I decide to call a doctor in the morning.

December 4, 1998

Twenty years old today. I recently received a welcome early birthday present: I haven't got stomach cancer.

A hospital visit revealed that the pain and blood-filled vomit is the result of a peptic ulcer. While discovering I'm not dying came as a relief, I feel like the diagnosis confirms the theory that I'm a dishevelled middle-aged man onto his third divorce and struggling with a stress-induced drinking problem. I've also been informed that my blood pressure is high, and I have an elevated white blood cell count, neither of which comes as much of a shock.

January 25, 1999

University isn't going well. While drinking heavily and acting like a clown helps me make friends, the subsequent ill-health, hangovers, and post-boozing bouts of depression are hardly conducive to passing exams. Many lectures are missed because I'm too sick to attend. Now, I'm paying the price: an appointment with the course head to discuss my attendance.

Sitting in his stuffy office makes me feel even worse. It's brutally hot, and my stomach is playing up again.

'Your attendance is below 50 per cent, Mr Graham. Anything under that threshold means we have to investigate.' I feel like he's repeated that line a thousand times.

'Well, I've been having health issues,' I protest, but the words feel like a feeble excuse.

'Ah, yes. I see from your doctor's letter that you have an ulcer. Does it still cause problems?'

'Errmm... well, yeah. It hurts now and again. It can make me feel pretty sick. I'm on medication for it, still.'

'I don't mean to sound callous, Mr Graham, but it doesn't seem to be the kind of illness that would explain you missing half the term,' he says, his attempt at not sounding callous failing terribly.

'We may have to look at taking back your student grant. A more extreme measure might be expulsion, but it shouldn't come to that, hopefully.'

Both those threats fill me with dread. Paying back my student grant would be impossible, seeing as I spent it all and have no job. There's also the thought of how being kicked out of university would disappoint Mum after everything it took to get here. Was Dad right? Am I a failure who'll never amount to anything? His favourite line rings through my head: 'Don't worry, son. The world will always need street sweepers, haha.'

In my panic, I say something unexpected.

'There… there are other, extenuating circumstances.'

'Oh?'

I can hear the scepticism in his voice.

'I, errmm… I've had some problems with my father in the past. We're estranged. He was… he was very abusive. I do sometimes feel like it still affects my day-to-day life.'

I'm not lying but bringing this up sickens me. Other than Paul, Andrew, and Aria, I've avoided talking about my past to anyone. It feels like my blaming him just confirms that Dad's still controlling my life, years after I last saw the man.

'Really!'

The lecturer's demeanour changes completely, body language moving from defensive crossed arms to hands palms-up on the desk, like he's offering me a hug.

'Dean, (it's no longer 'Mr Graham') we take the mental health of our students very seriously. You should have mentioned this earlier. I imagine it must be challenging to talk about. I'm going to refer you to our counsellor. She'll be able to assess you. We'll sort everything out, don't worry. And I'm sorry for… all this.'

While relieved that the threat of expulsion has lessened, the thought of talking to a mental health professional is scary. I'd always assumed they'd never be able to help me, or maybe even make things worse, so I'm not particularly enthralled at the prospect of revealing all to a total stranger. Still, it's better than the alternative.

February 3, 1999

It doesn't take long for my appointment to arrive. I'm surprised to find that the psychologist is young, perhaps only six or seven years older than me, which adds to my nerves. I worry she'll think I'm weak, soft. Tell me to pull myself together, and that other people have it much worse. And will she believe I'm really twenty?

'Hi, Dean. I'm Jane,' she starts. I can already feel myself going red. Maybe expulsion would have been the better option.

'Errmm… hi,' I reply, hoping the discomfort I feel isn't obvious in my voice.

'So, you've been referred to me because your tutor believes you may have extenuating circumstances as to why you've been struggling on your course. Could you elaborate?'

'Well, I… errmm… I had what I suppose you'd call a bit of a difficult childhood because of my dad. My Mum and I only recently got away from him, and I feel like the effects of what he did are only hitting me now. Like, I'm only just starting to deal with the errmm… the trauma.'

'That's understandable. I'm sorry to hear it. Can you tell me about how you've been coping?'

'Well, I sometimes feel like there's like a black hole inside me, and every day a little bit more of the person I am disappears into it. I don't know; it's hard to explain. It's as if my mind won't accept that I should be happy now, I think. I can't stop dwelling on the past and wondering why he did the things he did. It eats me up inside, you know? I find it hard to deal with everyday stuff. I don't even like talking to people when I'm sober – getting blind drunk definitely helps keep me sane.'

'Are you able to talk about some of these things he did?'

It's the question I was dreading. I take a deep breath and start at the beginning.

'Well, it all began when I was nine. We lived in Spain….'

I tell her everything about that night, the moment I saw the father I loved turn into the man I grew to hate. I tell her about the violence we experienced over the years. The times he hit me, locking Mum in the bedroom, making her look through the bin for poison, all of it. Saying all this aloud, going into even more detail than I did with my flatmates, the emotions I felt at the time come flooding back, causing me to breathe heavily, unable to stop. There's a desperate battle for air that refuses to fill my lungs. I'll pass out at any second. I'm hyperventilating again, yet all I can think about is how embarrassing this must be for Jane.

'Are you okay, Dean?'

'Not… really…,' I splutter, gasping between words. The counsellor jumps up, grabbing a paper bag from the cupboard – this must happen regularly. She hands it to me, calmly explaining to take slow, controlled breaths into the opening. My breathing returns to normal after a few minutes. Not blacking out and hitting the floor is a relief, but I wonder how much uglier I must look with tears streaming down my red, puffy face.

'Thank you. Sorry about that.'

'Dean, you've got no reason to be sorry. What you've been through was… horrible… and it's doubtlessly left some deep scars. But I do wonder if there's something you're leaving out.'

Aria? is she talking about Aria?

'What do you mean?'

'Dean, there's a common phenomenon among people who experience trauma at a young age. It's essentially a mind's defence mechanism, blocking out memories that are so bad, you can't cope with them.'

I don't like where this is going.

'With your permission. I'd like to try a form of hypnosis on you.'

I'm very hesitant. Jane's theory is something I'd never even considered. The things I do remember are bad enough. What could be so much worse that I've erased it completely?

'Honestly, it's an excellent way to discover repressed memories, from which point we can deal with them,' she says, noticing my reluctance.

'Well, if you think it will help.'

I'm sure I only agree to this because of my eagerness to please.

'Yes, I really do. Now, please relax and concentrate on the sound of my voice. Close your eyes and try to re-member that first night in Spain when you were nine, and your dad changed. Picture yourself in your bed. Think of how the sheets felt and what you could smell in the air.'

It takes a couple of minutes before anything happens. The more I relax into the memory, the clearer it becomes.

'I… remember. The covers were starchy, uncomfort-able. They were damp in parts from my sweat. It was so hot. It was always hot over there. Mum was wearing her usual perfume, smelt like lavender and lilacs. Dad… I could smell his BO cutting through the aftershave. San Miguel, the beer he drank, it stank – on his breath.'

'What happened after he stopped hitting your mum and sat on the bed with you, Dean? What did he do?'

Even in my semi-hypnotised state, I realise what she's implying. It can't be true. Mum was virtually incapaci-tated at the time, yes, but he wasn't like that – isn't like that. He's a paranoid schizophrenic who put us through hell. The kind of abuse she's suggesting seems impossible. It's a sce-nario that had never once crossed my mind in all these years.

'Dean. What happened?'

'The bear,' I mutter.

'What bear?'

'He told me about a bear. Everyone was scared of it, but he said I didn't need to be scared. I... I couldn't understand what he meant. Then... then he....'

'Then what? What did he do?'

The memory fades, slipping through fingers like sand. All I can see is the light, the beautiful light that filled the room when she appeared.

'The light. It was Aria. Aria saved me.'

'Aria? Who's Aria? Saved you from what? Dean?'

Hearing someone else say her name snaps me back to reality.

'Sorry. I-I need to stop now.'

'That's okay, Dean. But can you tell me who Aria is?'

'I'm, errrmm... I'm not sure, really. Sorry. Could we talk about it another time, please? This has all been quite intense.'

'Of course. Whenever you're ready, and don't worry about the course, I'll write a letter to the administrators explaining the situation. I must be honest with you: I'm concerned that you're repressing a lot and not dealing with what happened. You seem to be using physical and mental crutches to get by. It's not healthy. That barrier you've created inside your head will only last so long. If, or when, it breaks, what you're feeling now could become ten times worse.'

Great, something else to look forward to.

February 4, 1999

I hardly slept last night. Jane's suggestion bounced around my head, keeping my brain ticking. Is Aria really a defence mechanism created by my mind? Did I invent her to protect me from the truth? Mum would have killed her husband if she suspected he'd ever done those… things, but would she have even known?

Hopes that seeing a counsellor might improve my mental state have been well and truly dashed – visiting Jane has left me feeling worse. I want to speak to Aria, ask her what really happened that night. But calling out her name, concentrating, begging, none of it works.

February 22, 1999

It's been almost two weeks since the session. University is finally off my back about missing lessons, thankfully, but that's of little consolation after Jane's words left me an utter train wreck. She's alone in her office when I turn up unannounced.

'Dean! Hi, I was wondering when I might see you again. Are you here to book another appointment?'

Is it me or my story that makes her remember my name? My paranoid side starts pushing the theory that she's only taken an interest for personal gain. I can see the research paper now: repressed childhood sexual abuse manifests as an imaginary friend, or something like that.

'Hi, Jane. Thanks for writing the letter. It helped. But I'm actually here to tell you I won't be coming back for any more sessions, at least not for a while. No offence to you at all; I just don't think I'm ready for this yet. I need some time to sort my head out on my own, decide what to do next. You've given me a lot to think about. Thanks.'

'I understand, Dean. But I do strongly advise that you come back as soon as you feel able. And don't you dare think about dropping out,' she says with a smile.

'Nah, I would never drop out. My Mum would kill me.'

'Ha, mums can be scary. I'll write another letter explaining the situation to your course tutor, ask him to give you some leeway.'

'That's great. Thanks again, appreciate it.'

February 23, 1999

My certainty that stopping counselling was the right decision is waning already. All I want to do is put my past behind me and start fresh, but it's easier said than done, and the idea that I'm embracing ignorance weighs heavily. There's only one thing for it: get my shit together, stop the drink and drugs, and focus on my health, both mental and physical. I can do this.

February 27, 1999

Standing in a pub at four in the afternoon, I throw back the sixth pint of the day while contemplating my breath-taking lack of willpower. Resisting my vices lasted one week; Paul's offer to 'get the drinks in' was all it took to break the promise made to myself. I want to point the finger at Aria, whose absence has been felt heavily at a difficult time, but then I've always blamed my problems on other people, real or otherwise.

I love being around Paul. While I have to be blind drunk before talking with any kind of confidence, everyone is attracted to his natural charisma, wit, and imposing stature. He still offers to 'help' with my dad, which I take to mean in a mafia-style way. I've revealed a lot to my friend but haven't mentioned what Jane said, and Aria remains my secret alone.

I'm pretty drunk now, though, which means I'm talking too much.

'You know, Uni made me go and see a counsellor,' I suddenly blurt out for no reason.

'Aye? What for?'

'They were going to throw me off the course 'cos I was missing too many lectures. Told them I was having mental issues from what happened with my dad.'

'Haha, nice job, fella, got away with that one.'

I laugh a bit and say nothing.

'It's not true, is it?' he asks. The smile's still on his face, but there's a hint of concern in his voice. The 1990s were when men were 'expected to be men,' especially in this part of the world, and Paul is the epitome of that. He doesn't believe blokes should talk about their feelings, or have emotions at all. His solution to most things is to punch them in the face.

'Well, I mean… Nah, probably not. But, ermm… the woman they made me see did say something I'd never… considered.'

'Aye? What?'

'Well, she thinks I might be blocking out stuff he did to me. Like, really bad stuff. You know?'

The smile drops from his face.

'Fucking hell, mate. Did that actually happen? Honestly, I'll fucking kill him if it did.'

'That's the thing – I don't know. I don't think I want to know. The thought's been doing my head in these last few weeks. It's hard to believe he could have done this shit, and I've no memory of it. It would probably explain a lot, mind.'

'Like?'

'Like why I'm a bit fucked in the head. Talking to people who aren't there, ha.'

He laughs, assuming I'm joking.

'So, what do you want to do about it?'

'It's the past now. I'm sick of it, dragging me down and ruling my life. Time to put it all behind me, forget about it, and move on. Fuck it. Let's gets absolutely arseholed and share a wrap of whizz.'

February 28, 1999

Hangovers bring plenty of unpleasant symptoms: vomiting, nausea, headaches, regret. I find extreme depression is the worst sign of a good night out. Waking in my own bed and not hanging from a toilet roll holder brings relief, but I feel atrocious, and not just mentally. My ulcer still gives me an occasional reminder that it's there, a pain exacerbated by the copious amounts of alcohol and drugs I consume. Every part of my body hurts, and I feel so fucking low.

The misery is swallowing me this morning, like a vast emptiness pulling my soul inside and extinguishing any flickering lights of optimism. I can't cope with my studies, yet I'm terrified at the idea of quitting university. And despite my best efforts to let go, the past still haunts me.

The hangover bubbles my darkest fears to the surface. What kind of future would I have as a uni dropout with serious mental issues? The scenario makes me sick with worry, inducing suicidal feelings. The only reason I don't obsess over it is my preoccupation with an even more terrifying thought: ending up precisely like Dad.

I'd read somewhere that severe mental issues such as schizophrenia can skip a generation. Instead of doing more research – not an easy task in days before the internet was easily accessible – I've taken this as gospel. As such, I decided a while ago that having children would be selfish and unfair to them. Many people my age swear they'll never become parents, only to end up as great mums and dads years later. My decision, however, doesn't come from a desire to party until I drop; I'd just hate for Dad's problems to pass on to his grandchildren.

I'm more concerned about my well-being right now. Aria is a creation of my mind, not an actual angel, this I've long known, but I've started noticing more worrying signs of mental instability, such as a quick temper, increasing paranoia, and jealousy. Hurting another human being remains a repulsive thought – I still have the occasional nightmare about nearly killing Glenn – but it's as if Dad's worst traits are appearing in me. I would rather die than become the man

I despise, and today, deep in a hangover-induced pit of despair, I'm contemplating ways of achieving that aim.

Movies suggest cutting your wrists in a hot bath is popular. I'd choose it over jumping off a building or hanging as they seem like the worst ways to off yourself. Maybe a cocaine overdose would be the best option, but that would cost money I don't have.

I try to push the misery to one side by recalling last night. It's incredibly hazy. Paul ended up going home with a girl, that much I can remember. I hope for his sake he avoided the notorious 'whizz dick' effect brought on by amphetamine consumption. Sadly, being a chunky pisshead who looks twice his actual age doesn't make me an appealing prospect to ladies. Even if someone's beer goggles were thick enough, I'd worry about any potential partners uncovering my issues.

I throw my feet over the edge of the bed, using their weight to rock into a sitting position. There's a flash of light behind my eyes that intensifies an already blinding headache. Small pockets of memory keep popping into existence, including Paul chatting up that first-year student and me dancing like a lunatic before being dragged out of somewhere by bouncers. I struggle to recall more sordid details when I notice my mattress seems damp. How much did I sweat in the night? That seems like an awful lot of perspiration. I lean over the large, dark patch, confirming my suspicions: I've graduated to wetting the bed. Maybe I am crazy; I'm pretty sure it's a symptom.

I stagger to the toilet, falling to my knees once I reach the bowl to once again pray before the porcelain god. A memory of getting into a 'who can gargle tequila longest' competition with Paul makes me empty my guts. It's mostly blood. Maybe I won't have to go through the trouble of killing myself. I crawl back into bed while lamenting the student union bar's 'one pound per pint' deal.

June 21, 1999

I'm still alive, but my mind and body falling apart have made classes less of a priority. It's reached the point where I never think about the next day and live every moment as if it were my last, though this is less inspirational than it sounds. It's more 'get fucked up as fast as possible all the time.'

The better news is that I'm allowed to repeat the year – a necessity, given how much of the course I've missed. I even get a new grant and loan. More hospital visits combined with Jane's recommendations were enough to convince the university that I deserve another chance.

I try to convince myself that things will be different this time around if only I can overcome my self-destructive nature. It's so bad that I try to avoid moments where my mind might stray – doing something monotonous or boring triggers the worst memories and potential scenarios. I've taken to cleaning my teeth in the living room to watch TV throughout the two-minute process, which hasn't gone down well with my flatmates. Even taking a piss, when it's not in my bed, is becoming arduous. I find myself counting aloud or singing the theme song to Friends as a way of distracting myself while emptying my bladder.

September 10, 1999

Paul, Andrew, and I have decided to leave our awful, cramped student accommodation and rent a house together from a private landlord. We get on brilliantly and want somewhere with more space, so the move makes sense. It's a four-bedroom end-terrace residence. On our first day, we discover a message carved into a window frame by the previous occupant. It reads: 'THIS HOUSE IS FUCKING FREEZING IN WINTER.'

'Soft bastards,' Paul remarks.

September 20, 1999

I'll be 21 In three months. It shames me to say that I've never had a real girlfriend. While I'm far from attractive, much of this stems from my fear of the inevitable rejection should I ever speak to a girl while sober. Aria's lengthy absence has made me realise that being alone can make a bad situation worse. I long for someone to love, someone to take away the pain.

September 22, 1999

There's a nice girl on my course called Michelle who doesn't seem to flinch in my presence. A hint of an accent makes me think she may be an exchange student, French, perhaps. I felt queasy nerves when speaking to her for lesson-related reasons in the past. She has the most amazing long dark hair, brown eyes you could get lost in, and a dragon tattoo on the outside of her calf. But it's the way she's so outgoing and full of life, always happy and laughing, that I find attractive – nothing like the sober version of me.

I decide to speak to Michelle while our class waits in the corridor for the lecturer to arrive. People have split into groups, talking about the course. I feel tolerated by these other students, rather than welcome, like an oddity. I don't blame them, though; my crippling shyness and inability to talk to people makes me come across as aloof at best and a total twat at worst. If only I could get them to come on a night out with me.

Michelle's leaning on the wall, looking at some notes. I take a deep breath and walk over, wishing I'd drank just a little bit of vodka this morning.

'Errr… Hey, M-Michelle,' I stutter. At this point, I just hope she doesn't scream and run away.

'Oh, hi, errrmm… sorry.'

'Dean. It's Dean,' I tell her.

This is going only marginally worse than I anticipated. My heart pounds as anxiety starts to pull me into a despair whirlpool. The main goal now is to avoid any further humiliation.

'God, sorry. Of course. My head's all over the place right now. So much shit to remember.'

'Ha, That's okay. I can relate.'

Okay, trying to ask someone who doesn't remember my name on a date isn't a good idea, but it would still be nice to have at least one friend on this course.

'Sooo… how are you finding it all?'

'Yeah, it's great. Everyone is so nice and friendly. It must be a bit weird for you, I imagine, yeah?'

I freeze. What does she mean? Repeating a year isn't that unusual.

'Errrmmmm… weird?'

'Oh, like, coming back into education and all that.'

The penny drops. She thinks I'm a mature student. The only way this situation could get any worse is if my trousers suddenly fell around my ankles. Michelle realises that she's made a faux pas, probably from the devasted look on my face

'Oh, Jesus. I'm so, so sorry. I thought you were, like… you know, older than us.'

'Haha! That's okay. I get it all the time. I had a hard paper round,' I joke, not wanting her to see my heart tearing in two.

'Ha. Honestly, though, I didn't mean to insult you. I bet it was great never being ID'd when you were younger.'

Hearing her laugh is lovely, though I still feel like I've taken a blow to the gut. Is this how people see me? Do the other students act weirdly because they think I'm in my 30s and not just one year older than most of them? I can feel my face burning up with embarrassment. All I want to do is get out of here.

'Yup, I've literally never been asked for ID. This face does have its advantages,' I say, murdering the possibility of any romantic connection even further, were such a thing possible.

'Anyway, just going to check my emails before we go in,' I lie.

'Better hurry. You know what he's like if someone's late,' Michelle says with a smile. It's genuine, but not in the way I would have wished. I wonder if anyone will ever show me a smile filled with love and desire. A young man trapped in an old body, that's how I feel. Disgusted with myself and full of self-loathing.

'I will, thanks,' I tell her.

I make my way to the computer section of the library and stroll straight past, moving through the building's exit and toward my car. Closing the door alleviates some of the pain, locking out the world.

The short drive home is completed on autopilot while humming loudly – my go-to self-distraction technique. Paul and Andrew are out, thank God, so I don't get any shit for taking the only drink left in the house, three-quarters of a bottle of Bailey's, into my bedroom at 10:15 in the morning and closing the door.

September 29, 1999

I haven't been to university for a week, a result of my deteriorating mental state and wanting to avoid Michelle. Paul and Andrew know I'm repeating the year and would kill me if they discovered I'm missing classes again, so I've been leaving the house every morning as usual. Instead of driving across the bridge to campus, I head for the nearby car park and wander into town. About an hour later, long enough for them to have left, I come home, usually with some cheap alcohol.

Today, though, I've decided to return to my course before this routine becomes too difficult to break; they might send me back to a counsellor at this rate. The lecturers themselves never enquire about absences unless it's been an excessive amount of time, but I'm not sure what excuse to give Michelle for 'nipping off to my check emails' and disappearing for a week. She didn't even remember my name, so maybe she'll have forgotten what happened. I realise that's just wishful thinking when she scurries over after I arrive in class.

'Dean! Where have you been? What happened?'

Usually, I would have been happy that she's taking an interest and recalls who I am. Now, however, I'm faced with having to lie again. It's not something I want to do, but telling the truth, that I'd went home and drank heavily for a week because she assumed I was a mature student, wouldn't go down well.

'Oh, hi, Michelle. Yeah, had a bit of family emergency,' I say, trying not to show my disdain for bullshitting.

'Oh no. Is everything okay?'

There's concern in her voice. I know she has zero interest in me but looking into those incredible eyes gives me a rare feeling of warmth, a sensation I wish I could experience more often.

'Yeah, it's all sorted now. Thanks for asking. Families, eh?,' I smile.

'God, tell me about it, ha. Glad you're okay, mate.'

Hearing the word 'mate' brings me back down to earth. It feels like it's there to cement my permanent position in the friend zone, which I suppose is still better than my regular spot in the no-friends zone.

December 31, 1999

New Year's Eve 1999 – the dawn of a millennium. Unfortunately for me, my situation hasn't improved. If anything, it's got worse. It's rare for a few hours to pass without me thinking about Dad, wondering what he's doing, whether he's repentant.

I also find myself dwelling more on the counsellor's words. Did my father really abuse me in ways I don't know? It's hard to believe, yet I've got an overwhelming urge to confront him about it. Aria hasn't appeared in months, and I know the reason is related to Jane's theory. I wonder if my brain is conspiring to shield me from the truth, though it's unclear if the angel will have answers.

While I spend most days quite drunk, this is one occasion when it's socially acceptable to drink until passing out. It's also an excuse for me to embrace the excess even more.

Paul, Andrew, and I start drinking at 10:30 am. That's early even by my standards, so I hope the wrap of speed I managed to procure keeps me going for the next fifteen or more hours. We're planning on going for food around mid-afternoon and saving the amphetamines for the evening, by which point I should be more pissed than usual.

The physician Gabor Maté, an expert on the relationship between past trauma and addiction, claims there's no such thing as an addictive personality. He believes addiction originates from a need to address deep-seated issues from our past and that the control, peace, and happiness these substances provide act as an escape from emotional distress. It's a theory that certainly applies to me. I love getting drunk and taking drugs. I adore the freedom, confidence, and blissful release, despite being aware of the short- and long-term damage.

We've been knocking them back for just under four hours. It's already looking like another New Year's Eve where I'll blackout before midnight. There have been countless drinking sessions during which I've promised to pace myself, but alcohol gets thrown down my throat like it's a race every single time. We're currently in a greasy takeaway after bar hopping. An oily burger helps focus my vision but isn't doing anything for guts that still cause problems. I choke it down, feeling the discomfort as it squirms through my pipes like lukewarm lead. With my friends' pizzas long gone, we head to the next establishment.

It only takes two more hours before I'm kneeling on the piss-soaked floor of a pub toilet, puking into a bowl. The burning sensation as it blasts out is agonising, though my only concern is to avoid getting any on my clothes. Even the lumpy vomit's red colour doesn't register – just cider and black mixed with tomato sauce, surely. It's time for the speed.

Remaining on my knees, I remove the tiny, carefully folded piece of paper from a pocket, open it up, and lay my tongue across its contents. The familiar bitterness is there, along with the taste of crushed Aspirin used to bulk it out. I greedily swallow most of the drug before a terrible realisation hits me: Paul's paid for half and expects his fair share.

He's a friend, but one with a reputation for going a bit psycho when the red mist descends. Worried that I might get beaten for my overeagerness, I pull out a coin and scrape some plaster from between the filthy toilet wall tiles, mixing it with what little white powder remains. Even my heavily drunken mind and rapidly spreading euphoria doesn't stop me from feeling terrible about this action. Still, it's better than a broken nose.

January 1, 2000

I'm staring at an unfamiliar ceiling. Having no clue where I am or what happened the previous night isn't a new phenomenon – anything else would be a bit weird at this point, frankly. The millimetre-thin carpet I'm lying on offers no protection against the hard, cold floor beneath. My mouth has the bone-dryness I've experienced a hundred times before, making the familiar taste of vomit and bile all the more pronounced.

There's a stiffness in my neck that makes me wince when craning my head to one side. I've never been in this room before. The mess, stubbed out joints, and empty pizza boxes suggest it's a student house. At least I haven't been abducted. There's a couch near me with someone asleep on it, their size 14 feet hanging over the end and massive head dwarfing the tiny pillow. It's Paul.

You'd think I'd have learned not to sit up quickly in these situations, but no. The sudden jerking motion causes a fight between my stomach wanting to expel its contents and my will to keep them down. I'm also noticing how cold it is in here. The leather jacket I left the house with is nowhere to be seen, neither is my Nokia phone. That makes three coats and two mobiles I've lost on nights out over the last 12 months.

Experiencing a drunken blackout after taking speed requires a heroic amount of alcohol, explaining the pins and needles surging from the top of my head to my toes. I use a deep, slow breathing technique to stop myself from being sick. At this exact moment, I genuinely believe I'd kill a person for some water. Incredibly, as if the gods themselves were listening, I see a glass of clear liquid next to my leg. My drunken self often leaves water on the bedside table for when I wake up half-paralysed and parched. Assuming I'd repeated this act in a stranger's house, I grab the glass and swallow a massive mouthful, only tasting the pure vodka as it travels down my throat. I throw up all over myself, lie back down, and close my eyes.

'Dean. Dean! Look at the state of ya, haha. Ya daft twat. Come on, mate. It's time to leave,' Paul says, his voice croaking from the cigarettes and toilet-wall plaster. I've no idea how long has passed since I defiled my shirt.

'Err... aye. Where are we?' I ask, hoping it's not too far from home.

'It's me mate John's place. Take it you can't remember, soft arse. Mind, I hoyed up as well – sure that speed must have been dodgy. Churned my guts up something rotten.'

It turned out that despite being the biggest party night most people will experience in their lifetimes, no bar or nightclub was willing to let us in after a certain point last night, the consequences of being blind drunk, high, and smelling of piss and vomit. Paul knew someone from his media course holding a house party, so the three of us invited ourselves over.

Paul explains that I passed out on the floor not long after arriving, the sheer amount of alcohol and several joints counteracting the speed's effects. I have no recollection of midnight, but at least I never pissed myself again.

The physical pain is amplified tenfold when I learn it's a 30-minute walk back home. The odds of getting a taxi today are about the same as a lottery win, so we've no choice but to make the journey on foot. Andrew, who somehow never seems to get hangovers, woke up early and made the journey hours ago, leaving Paul and me to brave the freezing weather.

I've experienced hangovers in extremes of hot and cold before, and while the heat and dryness that comes with the former do worsen symptoms, it's still the lesser of two evils. The shivering and headache that are part of the post-drinking experience are intensified by cold, as is the tingling – a warning sign that another bout of vomiting is on its way.

As we stagger out of the house, stepping over a couple of strangers sleeping on the hallway floor, the icy wind hits like a hammer, entering my ears, freezing my eyeballs, and chewing up my soul. I gasp in shock, forcing the freezing air into my smoke-scarred lungs. I'm sure the only reason I'm not throwing up is that there's nothing left to come out.

Every step sends a painful vibration through my entire body, while the speed comedown and near-zero temperatures make me shiver so violently that my teeth audibly chatter. It might be half an hour, but it's the longest walk of my life, made all the worse by the short-sleeved shirt and thin jeans. I repeatedly stop to pull myself together, listening to Paul complain about the takeaways being closed on New Year's Day. The man is an animal. The tingling in my numb face is a brutal contrast to the burning in my stomach. I swear never to drink again.

We finally make it home by around one. Not emptying my guts, bowels, or bladder during the journey is a bonus, though it still took almost twice as long as usual. We open the door to find Andrew happily watching TV in his dressing gown and drinking a cup of coffee. I, on the other hand, look like an unhealthy corpse. Dragging my broken body upstairs to the bedroom, I yank off my boots, drink a gallon of water, and bury myself under the covers without undressing. It'll be 18 hours before I wake up.

February 20, 2000

Even in the throes of agony and mental despair, I knew quitting booze was always going to be a challenge. I did try, but the absence of its numbing effect was strongly felt. I lasted about ten days before saying 'fuck it' to the 'New Year, new me' lies we all tell ourselves. New year, worse me, it seems. And falling off the wagon means indulging in a vice even harder.

I haven't been to university since the Christmas holidays. More absences during the last term meant I was already way behind and catching up became an impossible task that increased the pressure and anxiety. Time off over the holidays did bring some much-needed relief, but the thought of returning to that stress and misery became all-consuming, so I decided against it.

I now spend every day drinking in the house instead of going to classes, feeding my depression spiral. The previous pattern of deception is repeated: Paul and Andrew see me leave each morning, not realising that I return to an empty house soon after they depart. When they get home, I explain away my obvious intoxication by lying about 'popping to the pub after class.'

It's been almost six weeks since uni restarted. I've passed the point of no return, but all I worry about is how this will affect my student grants and loans. With no job, they're my only means of survival, and alcohol isn't free.

March 8, 2000

Despite not wanting to let down Mum, I couldn't face going back to my studies. The thought of being berated by lecturers, students looking at me like an outcast, failing to catch up with others, and repeating the year for a second time proving too much.

I head to the uni campus, my first visit since December, to inform the admin office of my decision. They say I'll receive a letter in the next few weeks telling me if I need to repay anything, which I most definitely will, and I've already spent virtually all of a grant meant to last until Summer. I'm not too worried as this feels like a 'blood from a stone' situation. The one bit of good news is that the rent has been paid in advance, giving me until the end of July before being made homeless.

CHAPTER EIGHT

PATRICIDE

March 15, 2000

Instead of doing the sensible thing and holding on to
what little money is in the bank, I've been pissing it away on
drink and skanky drugs, and my credit cards are close to
their limits after using them repeatedly for food and car ex-
penses. Telling Mum about dropping out of education is another huge concern. I usually visit her at least once a week at
Olive's, but I've not been totally honest about university
life, naturally, though I'm ready to come clean.

I'm so distracted during the short drive to my aunt's
that I struggle to remember the way. I keep thinking about
how escaping Dad was the best thing that ever happened,
how it's all I ever wished for, but I'm so scared by what's
ahead, especially the prospect of having nowhere to live.
How will I get a job? I've done little more than some summer work and part-time shelf stacking. And where is Aria in
all this? It's been over a year since I last saw her. Even before my one and only psychiatrist appointment, the angel's
visits were becoming less frequent.

I enter one of the city's more deprived areas, drive
into the cul-de-sac, and pull up outside the row of terraced
houses. The garden's slightly overgrown and littered with
random objects: a rusting bike, an ancient manual
lawnmower, an old mattress lying against the fence. Despite

my current sombre mood, the happy memories this place holds makes me smile. I remember that first Christmas without him when we never stopped laughing, and the future felt so bright. Life rarely turns out the way we hope.

'Hello? Anyone home?' I shout as I walk through the unlocked door. The house has an unusual design, with a small toilet immediately to my left and the kitchen on the right.

'Hiya, Dean,' Mum replies with her usual enthusiasm. 'You alright?'

'Aye, canny,' I pull out a chair from under a large wooden table that's been here since the 1980s.

'Olive at work?'

'Yeah, I've just been down the town and tidying up here. Did I tell you that she's trying to get me in doing some waitressing work with her? I might actually get a proper job for the first time in years, and I'm a pensioner, ha.'

'That's brilliant, Mum. I'm over the moon for you.'

'Aww… thanks, son.'

'Mum, I need to talk to you about something.'

'What is it?' a concerned look appears on her face.

'It's university, Mum. I'm... it's....'

I don't know where to start or what to say.

'Dean, you can tell me anything. It's okay,' she says, putting a hand on my arm.

I take a deep breath, trying to steady myself.

'Okay. It's just that I'm struggling with... everything, really. I know how much me going to uni means to you, but honestly, I'm having an awful time. I've fallen so far behind with my work, and I just can't seem to... concentrate. And I know it's my choice, but the lifestyle, it's... it's not good for me. I hate saying this, but I'm not happy there anymore. I think I'd be better off with a job. I'm so, so sorry.'

Her expression remains unchanged. I'm half expecting to see tears.

'Dean, you never have to say sorry. You know I want you to go to uni and have a good career, I still do, but nothing is more important to me than your happiness. You had an awful childhood –I feel guilty for it, I do – and you deserve to be happy finally. You're my son, and I love you more than anything in the world. I'll support you no matter what you choose. Anyway, you could always go back in a few years when you're ready and finish the course.'

I struggle to keep my emotions in check.

'Thanks, Mum. I will make you proud one day. I promise,' I stand up and hug her.

'I AM proud of you, Dean. I wouldn't be here now if it weren't for you. You're the best son anyone could wish for.'

March 17, 2000

Mum taking my decision to leave university so well makes things easier, allowing me to focus on the other pressing issues: money is fast running out, my credit card debt is building, and I need a job. Ignoring the problem will leave me with nowhere to live in a few months. Mum said I'm welcome to stay at Olive's for a while. I appreciate the offer, but my aunt's three-bedroom house is already home to four grown adults – both my cousins, now in their 20s, aren't in a hurry to leave home, and I don't want to add to the burden.

As soon I've had a big blowout this weekend, I'm going to pull myself together, get organised, and find a job. Mum's right: nothing is stopping me from returning to uni in a few years to finish my course. I'll probably be okay by then. After all, I can't even remember the last time I saw Aria. Maybe it's a sign that my mental health is improving.

March 20, 2000

Monday. I've always noticed that the second day of a two-day hangover is when the depression and anxiety hit hardest. Last Saturday was another in an endless line that involved me blacking out at around 11 pm. The only reason I crawled out of my pit yesterday was to expel fluids from various orifices violently. Today consists of sweaty, panicky feelings brought on by terror-inducing scenarios of never being able to find a job, sleeping on the streets, and turning into the failure Dad always said I would become.

July 18, 2000

Despite sending out what feels like hundreds of application forms, I've not received anything more encouraging than 'we'll keep your name on record.' Has anyone ever got a job from a company that kept them on record? I somehow doubt it.

I'll be evicted from the flat in one week. If that prospect isn't bad enough, my credit card is over its £2,000 threshold, and I'm way beyond my bank's overdraft limit. I've had to borrow money just to keep my car running and food in the fridge. Turning to Mum for help isn't an option – even though she wouldn't refuse me her last penny, there's no way I'd put on her again. Making matters even worse is my expensive car insurance expiring in a few months, and no vehicle means even less chance of finding work.

Paul and Andrew have invited me to a night in the town. While I'd usually jump at the chance to bury my head in some alcohol-soaked sand, my bank isn't allowing me to withdraw any more cash. They both offer to pay, but I can't bear the idea of more mooching, and God knows when I'd be able to pay them back, so I'm left at home with the TV for company.

A new program called Big Brother starts on Channel 4 tonight. Andrew said I could have what's left of his vodka, which is one offer I wasn't going to turn down. About half the bottle remains, good for a few glasses mixed with some dirt cheap 'lemonade' that lacks any suggestion of lemon in its taste.

Years before it became a TV staple, the idea of watching a show about people doing nothing was bizarre. It's compelling, car-crash television, despite each burning throatful of the awful drink making it harder to concentrate

165

on the screen. I start imaging how I'd be introduced as a contestant:

'This is Dean. He's semi-alcoholic, unemployed, and has severe issues after suffering years of mental, physical, and possibly even sexual abuse at the hands of his father. He's also just twenty-one years old – if you can believe it.'

I start laughing aloud to myself. How did I get here? From the most fantastic day to facing homelessness in just a couple of years, and with nobody to blame but myself. What am I going to do? What options do I have?

'You could always go back.'

I slowly turn my head to face her through a fog of drunken haziness.

'Where… where the fuck have you been?'

Aria sits in the armchair that only Paul is allowed to use. Wings folded behind her back, blonde tresses falling over her shoulders, wearing the same white robe as always. Ageless. Blemishless. The ugliness of the world never mirrored on her perfect features.

'I've not been anywhere. I'm always here when you need me.'

'Really? Have you seen the fucking disaster my life has become? I'm going to be living in my car next week. Well, until they take it off me. So yeah, I'd say I need you. I've needed you for a long fucking time. Since… since….'

'Since Jane suggested he abused you?'

Why am I surprised she knows? It's not like I can keep secrets from her. Can she keep them from me?

'It's fucking bullshit. I… he couldn't have done anything like that. Why weren't you here? Why couldn't you have told me the truth?'

'Would you really want to know?'

I sit silently for a minute before my eyes drop to a hole in the floor. I think about its creation: the three of us had come back drunk from a night on the town when I flopped onto the old sofa, close to passing out. All seventeen stones of Paul then decided to dive on top of me for a laugh, at which point Andrew climbed atop the coffee table and jumped on the pair of us, like Hulk Hogan flying off the top turnbuckle. His landing caused the furniture's leg to pierce the floorboard. I don't think I'd ever laughed so much in my life.

'Okay. Maybe… maybe I didn't really want to know. But I do now – I think. Fuck. So, is it true?'

'Dean. I can't tell you.'

'Oh, you are fucking kidding me. Why not?'

'Because whatever I say would make no difference. There's only one way to find out the truth and keep a roof over your head; you have to go back to him.'

'Him? What are you talking about?'

'You'll soon have nowhere to live. You want to know what happened, so why not go and stay with your dad?'

My mouth falls open.

'Are... are you fucking insane?'

'Think about it – your mum won't be there for him to hurt. It's certainly not as if he could physically harm you now; you'd finally have power over him. And if you want to know... everything... this is the only way to be certain. As soon as a job and somewhere to live is lined up, fuck off and leave him to die alone.'

'I... I don't know.'

Although the idea of seeing Dad again fills me with disgust and fear, Aria makes a compelling argument. I've never been one for pragmatic solutions that ignore emotions, but the constant uncertainty I've been living with is killing me. I must know if Jane was right. Without Mum there, I can ask Dad anything, find out why he did the things he did. Just stay with him until I get sorted, yeah. Fuck him. This is actually like a punishment for the bastard.

I'd always believed I would never speak to or see my father again. I finish the rest of the vodka and decide to call him tomorrow.

July 19, 2000

I was drunk enough not to hear Paul and Andrew when they got back last night. They're both sleeping off their hangovers while I sit in my bedroom, staring at the phone. I've been rehearsing this for hours but still don't know what to say, how he'll react, or if it's even a good idea. My nerves are jangling, and it's not just the cheap vodka and lemonade's fault. How long have I sat motionless now, looking straight through my Nokia's 3310's monochrome screen?

Right when I'm about to put the phone down and abandon the whole plan, I rapidly type my former home's number and hit dial. The sweat on my brow and hand tremors come from more than just the hangover. I listen to the tone, fighting the overwhelming urge to hang up. The possibility he might be out somewhere is a relief; I'd have more time to think about this. Maybe I should hang up and…

'Hello.'

Hearing his voice for the first time in years makes my arm hairs stand on end. It's shocking how normal he sounds. I wasn't expecting him to answer in tears or anything, but there was a pleasant, almost happy tone in his voice. I open my mouth, but no sound comes out.

'Hello?' he asks again, more curious than annoyed.

'Hello… Dad. It's… errmm… me. It's Dean.'

'Dean?' his voice changes when he says my name like he's both surprised and about to cry.

'Yeah. Listen, I want to talk to you – just me, not Mum. I don't want us even to mention her. Understand?'

'I've missed you so much, son,' he says, voice breaking.

'Is it okay for me to come over tomorrow, about 12?' I ask, ignoring his comment.

'Of course! I would love to see you.'

'Okay. I'll be over then.'

'Have you been okay?'

'Errmm… yeah. I'll explain everything tomorrow, okay?'

'Okay, son. Thank you. I love you.'

'Okay, bye.'

A huge sigh. Meeting him so soon hadn't been part of the plan. I had hoped to put it off until I was literally out on the streets but fumbled under pressure. It irritated me to hear him say 'I love you' as if it was a get-out clause. I no longer remember expressing the same sentiment to him. There was a conspicuous lack of an apology on his part, too, not that I expected one.

July 20, 2000

I've kept news of the visit to myself – best if Mum and my friends stay blissfully ignorant. I'm unsure how others might feel about me going back, no matter my motivations, and there's always the chance I might end up walking away after a few minutes in his company.

Every time I try to imagine how this will play out, every time I visualize speaking to him, a blinding headache intervenes. Fail to plan, and you plan to fail, so they say, but this isn't something I can prepare for.

It's uncomfortably hot today. The stifling, sticky heat is one of several reasons I'm glad I never drank last night.

Sitting in the tiny, cemented back yard of our student house, I light a cigarette bummed from Paul and inhale deeply, holding the warm smoke in my lungs for a few seconds before letting it out through my mouth and nose. Dad smoked 60 a day for about 40 years before becoming one of those vehement anti-smokers following his diabetes diagnosis. Knowing how angry he'd be at my habit makes me smirk. I check the kitchen wall clock through the window. It's eleven – time to go.

I'm waiting in the car, not wanting to arrive too early and risk making myself look eager. Am I doing the right thing? The sound of the engine jumping to life brings a sharp stabbing pain to my chest. I make a mental note not to start hyperventilating again and set off on a trip I never expected to repeat.

Journeys you don't want to make always pass the fastest. Little has changed in this small town during the near-three years I've been away. There are few happy memories in this shithole.

I pull into my old street. Dad's car isn't here. Parked in his usual spot is a sporty white number that might have looked impressive when it launched in the late 80s. I know straight away that it's his, a late-life crisis for a man desperate to find a woman who knows nothing about his past.

My efforts not to stare at the house fail as I approach. It's like the physical embodiment of all we endured: the violence, the misery, the insanity; this isn't the best frame of mind for facing him. Stepping through the gate surfaces memories of that last day. I picture Mum on her knees, picking through rubbish strewn across the floor, Dad standing over her. The phantom smell of the overturned bin's contents is still detectable when I knock on the door. What am I doing?

He looks smaller. It's the first thing I think when Dad answers. Has he shrunk, or have I grown? I remember how intimidating this man looked when I was young and how afraid I was of him. Today, right now, he resembles a sad old gent. Balder, more ruddy faced, with the same Cuban heels he always wore to add a couple of inches to his height.

'Oh, son. It's great to see you,' he croaks.

I can see he's welling up. Dad moves in for a hug, but my body language clarifies that's not going to happen.

'Hi, Dad. Err… you okay?'

'Well, not too great, to be honest. Bloody diabetes, eh? Come on in.'

I follow him into the place that was once my home. It's horrendous. Dad had always been meticulous when it came to cleaning, making sure Mum and I knew when our efforts weren't up to his standards – another way of exerting control over us – so to see it like this takes my breath away. Dirty clothes lie in piles on the filthy hallway carpet; an awful stench emanates from the nearby toilet.

We move into the kitchen. It looks as if it's never been cleaned since the day Mum and I left all those years ago: the floor is sticky and covered in bits of food; the sink is overflowing with dirty cutlery; there are dead flies on the windowsill, with those still clinging to life dragging themselves between the corpses. Everything looks wet and diseased. There's a gag-inducing waft of rot permeating the room alongside the scent of a recently dispersed air freshener,

'Not had much of a chance to clean up, I'm afraid,' Dad says, noticing the look on my face as I glance around the house.

'It's okay. You should see my place.'

'Haha, I bet,' I feel like there's some resentment in his voice, as if this mess isn't his fault, whereas I choose to live in filth.

The living room is just as bad, a mixture of discarded clothing, floor debris, and wall stains. Dad gestures to the chair where I sat and watched him hurt my mother on so many occasions.

'So, how have you been, Dean?'

'Good, yeah,' I lie. 'Uni's going well.'

'That's great, son. I'm very proud,' the word bringing an involuntary twitch to my face. 'And, errmm… is your mum okay?'

'She's fine, Dad. But I told you, I don't want to talk about her.'

'I just want to know that she's okay,' he says with the tiniest hint of irritation.

'Like I said, she's doing well. But if you keep asking about her, I'm leaving.'

'Okay, son. I'm sorry. I wouldn't want that.'

I take a deep breath and swallow, trying to blank out every bad thing he's ever done.

'Dad, I need to ask a favour. My landlord's changing the rent agreement, so we can't stay in our digs over the summer holidays anymore. I was wondering, would I be able to crash here for a few weeks?'

I know I'm not going back to uni in September, but I'm sure I'll have found a job and a place of my own by then.

'Of course, son. That would be great, wonderful.'

I feel like telling him this is something I do out of necessity.

'Cool. I'll move my stuff in soon.'

'Do you need a hand?'

'No, thanks. It's not as if I have much.'

'Aye, most of it's still in your room, I think.'

I wonder if that's a reference to us leaving so abruptly – a subject we're both avoiding.

'Mind If I take a look at the place?'

'Your room? It's still yours – you don't have to ask, heh.'

'Thanks.'

I get up and leave him there with a smile on his face that makes me feel guilty. I still wonder if I'm betraying my mum – and myself. I try to remember that I'm also doing this to get answers.

The landing at the top of the stairs has the same hoarder-style look that matches the rest of the house. There are so many clothes, magazines, and dirty plates on the ground that it's hard to tell the carpet's colour. Trepidation fills me upon approaching my old room, the closed door adding to my feeling of dread. I take another deep breath, grab the handle, and push down.

It's immaculate. The bedsheets look fresh and are set out with military precision, complementing a floor that's been hoovered and shampooed so much it could pass as new. There isn't a speck of dust to be seen. The window glass is spotless, and everything smells fresh. The disparity between this area and the rest of the house is jarring. The pristine carpet and incredible cleanliness suggest this wasn't accomplished in one day; the upkeep has been going on for a long time. He kept my room in perfect condition while the rest of the house fell to pieces, waiting for his son to return. Even after all his horrific acts, both known and suspected, Dad kept this a shrine. I don't know how to feel.

July 27, 2000

Compulsive liars all have the same problem: remembering which lie goes with which person. A week at my dad's has seen me tell my housemates that I'm living with Mum, my mum that I'm still in my student house, and the few locals I remained friends with that I'm just here during the summer holidays, which is the closest lie to the truth.

Dad still thinks I'm going back to university in September. He doesn't know the exact term dates, so I've got around seven or eight weeks to find a job and somewhere to rent. I haven't thought about the important things, such as money for a deposit, the time it takes to get a first pay packet, and everything else related to renting, but I'll cross those bridges when I come to them.

I've avoided Dad during the day by hanging around my old college with friends who either never left the place or have nothing else to do. We pass the time skating and rollerblading around the car park. I know I should be looking for work but hanging around others of a similar age whose lives also haven't panned out the way they hoped makes me feel better, but not in a schadenfreude way. Laughing in the sun, smoking when you're too young to worry about its effects, it's these things that make me forget about my situation and a future that's looking increasingly bleak.

Something else I still haven't dealt with is talking to Dad about the past. Broaching the subject of why a parent inflicted years of mental and physical torture on their spouse and son isn't easy, and then there's the sexual abuse question. Like my other problems, I decided to put it on the back burner for now.

August 4, 2000

Another week gone. I can tell how much Dad wants to quiz me about Mum. He's grown bolder with each passing day, occasionally dropping her name into a conversation before asking a seemingly innocent question regarding her wellbeing. Each time comes a reminder that I will not talk about her. Each time he takes my refusal slightly worse than the last one.

I often stay late at a friend's place on Friday nights. Arriving back at Dad's around 10:30 pm, I'm relieved to find he's still at the pub, though he'll be back soon. My hopes of being able to cook supper, eat it, and go to bed before his return prove futile when the door crashes open a few minutes later.

'Alright, laddy?' he shouts. It's the first time I've seen him drunk in years. With Mum safely elsewhere, I'm not afraid of what he might do. Even with that 'crazy-person strength,' as she used to call it, I doubt he'd get the better of me in a fight. Nevertheless, there's an uneasy feeling gnawing away in my stomach.

'Alright,' I reply.

'Not got any supper on?'

'Nah, I'm not really hungry.'

I'm starving but don't like being around him at the best of times, never mind when he's pissed.

'Shame your mother's not here, eh? She could've stuck a couple of bacon sandwiches on for the men, haha.'

I'm thankful to be watching TV and not looking at him – he'd see the disgust on my face. I bite my tongue and stay silent, not wanting to antagonise Dad into saying anything else.

'Aye, wonder where she is now, maybe cooking something for another fella, eh?'

My fists clench, jaw tightens. Keeping quiet has stopped being an option.

'Well, Dad, for a start, she's not with any 'fella.' I'm pretty sure the years of misery you caused has put her off men forever.'

'Eh, misery? Now you bloody listen to me; we've been married forty years and had some brilliant times. Every couple has their up and downs. She'll tell you herself that she knows how to push my buttons.'

'Push your buttons? Oh, yeah. That's it. That's why Mum deserved to be beaten half to death. Maybe she enjoyed it, eh?' sarcasm's unlikely to help, but emotions have taken control.

'Don't be fucking cheeky. There are things you don't know, believe me. Your uncle Norman? My own Brother? He told me what a good fuck she was.'

I want to kill him – not a new feeling. I could hit him with something, push him through the inner glass doors and tell the police it was self-defence. One conversation with Mum, and her sister, would confirm his violent tendencies to the law.

I stand up. Dad's mouth hangs open, his chest heaving with each heavy, drunken breath. I visualize a haymaker to the throat. He wears a look as if he expects it.

No, not like this; it's too risky. I'm not going to jail for him. There would be too many unanswered questions. He flinches as I storm past and run upstairs to my bedroom. My hands shake with anger, yet I'm half hoping he'll follow me. I want to go back down there and get satisfaction, but I need all the answers first. Then payback.

August 5, 2000

I never heard Dad go to bed last night. In the cold light of day and with emotions cooled, I start thinking about what I should have said and done – leaving the house and sleeping at my friend's might have been a good idea. I'd still have had to come back and face him, of course. I did learn one thing: he still blames Mum entirely for his actions. There's no remorse or regret.

Dad's sitting at the table when I come downstairs. He doesn't look up from his paper as I silently walk past and sit on the sofa to watch the news.

'Want some breakfast?' he asks.

A familiar scenario. It's his 'act like nothing happened' routine. I was always grateful when he did it with Mum – better Dad was non-violent the morning after a night of beating her. I'm not going to forget what he said last night; now just isn't the time to bring it up.

'Anything on the go?' I reply.

'Pork sandwich.'

'Cheers. I'll grab it.'

'I can fix a fresh one up for you if you want.'

This is his way of apologising, making one of his greasy pork sandwiches that would have been rubbed in Mum's face for being so rank. Fucker.

'I'll just have what's left, cheers.'

I feel as if I'm accepting his apology, but I'm not ready to get into it with him again. I need more time to think about what I'm going to say and how to approach this.

He leaves for the kitchen, scraping the rest of the pork from the pan and placing it between two slices of bread.

'There you go. That'll put hairs on your chest, son,' he says with a grin. The words cut into me. The audacity to pretend everything's okay is bad enough, but his witless comments combined with the term 'son' make me shudder. It takes everything I have to stay quiet, managing only a slight nod of acknowledgement.

August 12, 2000

I've come up with a way of avoiding more drunken incidents: ensure Dad is already asleep in bed before I enter the house when returning late. The best way to do this is by parking near the bottom of the street, far enough away that he can't see me from the window, then waiting until the living room light goes off – a sure sign that he's retired for the night. I sneak in about 20 minutes later, by which point he's sleeping. The plan's worked perfectly a few times. Knowing that he's going to the pub, it'll be put into action tonight, too.

The evening's spent at the cinema watching Hollow Man, an 'invisible man' movie that was far from memorable, though anything that gets me out of the house is appreciated. I arrive back around 11:15 after dropping friends off. Pulling up to my usual stakeout spot, I see the light is still on. Time to wind down the window, light up a cigarette, turn on the radio, and wait.

The light's still on 45 minutes later. Dad usually goes to bed within a quarter of an hour of getting home – the length of time it takes to fry and eat the cheap meat he so loves. Staying up this late can only mean one thing: he's drunk again and wants to have another 'talk' about Mum. I still haven't come up with mental bullet points of what I want to say to him, and even if I had, it's not a conversation to have while he's intoxicated. There's no way I'm leaving this car until the light goes out.

August 13, 2000

It's 1:10 AM. I've been waiting almost two hours now. A pile of cigarette butts sits on the road. Getting through so many so fast feels like swallowing a cactus. Despite my discomfort and desert-like thirst, I crave another Regal King Size to calm my nerves and warm me up. How much longer can he stay awake? He's obviously determined to start something.

'I'd give it another half an hour.'

I was looking out the window when Aria's voice came from the passenger seat. The unexpected shock causes me to drop the seventh cigarette of the night into my lap.

'SHIT. FUCK. SHITFUCK,' I yell while frantically try to stop my crotch from igniting.

'Hahaha! Nice one!' she giggles.

I manage to pick up what's left of my ciggy, but the lit tobacco droops limply from the end. It joins the rest of its brothers on the pile.

'Glad you decide to show up now. I've been in this fucking car for two hours.'

Seeing the angel is a relief, though I'd have appreciated her company a lot earlier.

'Well, this is total bullshit, isn't it?' I say, checking for holes in my trousers.

'Certainly is. He must really want to get something off his chest.'

'Great. Maybe he'll fall asleep with the cooker on and burn to death. A fitting preparation for what's awaiting him.'

I pull out another Regal, unsatisfied at not having finished my last smoke.

'Anyway,' I continue, 'I don't want to hear what that old cunt has to say. He'll be pissed up, and I'm not having a repeat of last time. I won't hold back.'

'I know, Dean, but you can't stay here all night.'

The idea of sleeping in my car is genuinely more appealing than facing him right now, but the cold is starting to bite, causing my hands, lips, and nose to lose feeling. I don't want to risk turning on the engine to power the heaters in case he hears and makes a public scene. Am I willing to risk dying of hypothermia rather than going into the house?

'… I know. Fucking… ugh… was this whole thing such a good idea? Coming back to him?'

'You wanted to know the truth.'

'Yeah, he blames Mum. It's not like I didn't already know that. He always said everything was her fault. He still thinks he's done nothing wrong – can you fucking believe it?'

'And the rest?'

'The rest?' I ask, knowing what she means.

'You want the full story, don't you?'

I take a long pause. Do I, though? Are we better off not knowing something from our past if it can damage us in the present? Maybe ignorance really can be bliss.

'I'm not so sure anymore.'

'You really should go in now,' she says. I don't know whether Aria wants me to face him or is just concerned about me freezing to death.

'Yeah. Fuck this. I'm not dying inside a piece of shit car.'

I climb out into the night, experiencing every painful ache and cramp from my uncomfortable wait. The living room is the only illumination in the street, making it look even more ominous as I slowly walk towards the front door. I keep picturing the Exorcist poster, the one with the priest in front of the house.

Tiredness and emotion have turned my mind into mush. Just staying awake is difficult. Desperation for sleep pulses through my body, making formulating a plan impossible.

I quietly slide the key into the door and ease it open. The total silence that greets me brings more apprehension. I imagine Dad sitting with the TV turned off, left with only his paranoid thoughts for company, simmering away and ready to explode as soon as I walk in. I creep down the hallway and into the living room, where the awful reality is revealed.

He's not here.

Whether it was because of too much drink or just a genuine mistake, Dad went to bed without switching off the downstairs lights. Equal parts rage and joy fill me.

'For fuck's sake!' I mutter under my breath, not wanting to wake him.

Did Aria know? Is that why she told me to leave the car? Not that it even matters now. I collapse into bed and fall asleep in seconds.

August 24, 2000

Two things speed up the passage of time: ageing and deadlines. Dad thinks I'm going back to university next month, and I'm still unemployed. While I probably should have sent out more application forms, the total lack of response is deflating. I even applied for a chicken processing factory, for fuck's sake. There's no point looking for somewhere to rent without a job.

It's been nearly two weeks since my determination to avoid a confrontation with my pissed father almost led to my freezing to death. I've managed to avoid any more drunken bust-ups, but I'm no closer to discovering more about the past, either.

Going further into debt has kept me alive while funding the occasional night out. Friends in my uni city have long favoured Thursday as the best weeknight for boozing. One of the big nightclubs keeps it permanently reserved as a student night throughout the year, even when the kids are home for the holidays. As usual, I decide the best way to deal with mounting problems is to drink them away, so a trip to Pzazz is in order later, especially as it's 2-for-1 on alcopops.

I sit in silence opposite Dad, eating the artery-thickening crap he made for dinner. Not having to spend what little money I can acquire on rent or food is appreciated, but it's ironic that after years of beating Mum up for what he deemed bad cooking, Dad is possibly the worst chef I've ever known.

I look at him as he takes a bite into yet another pork sandwich while reading his paper, fantasising about throwing my dinner in his face the way he did to her. Maybe repeat the 'If that's my tea, I'm not looking forward to supper' line that always filled me with terror.

His hand is shaking.

Dad doesn't seem to realise what's happening even as the tremors become more pronounced. Just as I consider asking what's wrong, the sandwich drops from his hand and lands on the carpet with plop, brown sauce flying everywhere.

'Jesus. Oh, Jesus,' he cries, actual tears filling his eyes.

I know what's happening; I've seen it before: he's having a hypoglycaemic attack. There were a few bad ones during my school years, but this one came on very fast. Dad doesn't seem to take his insulin doses very seriously these days. He must have given himself way too much, causing his glucose levels to crash dangerously low.

'Dean. I need my… my tablets.'

I feel nothing toward what's happening in front of my eyes. Dad used to recover from these pretty quickly in the past, the glucose tablets bringing his sugar levels back to normal. I saunter to the kitchen cupboard to retrieve the sweets, return to the living room, and drop them in his shaking hand. He awkwardly forces two square tabs into his mouth.

It's too late. Dad's gone so low that he can't chew properly. The now-crumbling tablets fall from his mouth onto the floor; they were the only ones left in the last pack.

'Shit. Dean, can you… I don't know what…,'

He's slurring now, tears falling down his face.

'What have… I done?'

Still sitting, his head flops onto the plate's edge, sending the other half of the sandwich to join the mush on the floor. Dad's still awake and sobbing but close to passing out. There's no way he'll be able to raise his glucose levels without help. The next step will be a diabetic coma followed by likely death. He needs an ambulance.

A thought pops into my mind, appearing so quickly and unexpectedly that it's as if someone else planted it there. Tonight's plan is to drive to my friends as soon as I finish dinner for pre-night-out drinks. But what if Dad's hypo came on *after* I left? With nobody to help, death would be a near certainty. It could have occurred a few minutes after I walked out of the door. Who could say for sure when it started, officer?

I watch as drool dribbles from a mouth making the occasional gurgling noise. The side of his face is flat on the surface of the plate, arms dangling. Crumbs and specks of food populate his bushy eyebrows and stick to his lips. Helpless. As helpless as I was. As helpless as my mother was. I can see her now, the gravy running down her face, burning and choking her.

Is this what Aria kept talking about, the chance for revenge? All I need to do is leave and pretend nothing happened. He'll be long gone by the time I get back tomorrow morning after sleeping at my mate's. Could I live with myself? I think about everything he did and those things he might have done, pulling open the deepest scars. There's nothing but hate when I look at him. What did he feel when he looked at my battered Mum all those times? Disgust? Loathing? Contempt? Fuck him. It's all been leading up to this instant, a perfect example of karmic justice. I turn around and prepare to walk away.

'ssshh… sss…,' he makes a low-volume hissing.

'sssson… son. Please.'

That word. How many times did hearing it send shudders of revulsion through my body? A reminder that no matter what he did or how much I hate him, I'll always be his offspring, a replica of the thing I despise. Hearing it now, its pleading tone, I wonder if we sounded the same when begging him not to hurt us?

Aria's hand grips mine. Time stops.

'You know what to do, Dean.'

'Why? Why should I help him? He fucking deserves this. This was meant to be.'

'He is still your dad.'

'So what? How's that an excuse? It's even more of a reason to leave. He should have protected me, us, but he made every day a fucking living hell. I'm not normal. I'll never be normal. He took that away from me.'

'Dean, I understand your hate. But if you walk out now, it will stay with you forever. Nothing will ever justify it. The guilt will consume you until there's nothing left. Remember what I said: you aren't the same as him. But this, this is a path that will turn you into your father.'

'I...,' the rest of the words dry up in my mouth.

I can't; it's not right. It's not what I want. We got our revenge the day I took Mum away, condemning him to be alone forever. Looking at Dad now, struggling to cling to life, I have a vision of the man I once loved. The father I knew before that night in Spain.

Time restarts. I pull Dad's head up from the table and rest him in a sitting position. He's only just hanging onto consciousness. I grab the pieces of the broken glucose tablets from the carpet and shove them into my mouth, chewing while making sure not to swallow anything. Squeezing his cheeks so Dad's lips purse, I spit the lumpy concoction into his mouth. It's a risky move as he might not be able to swallow the chunky paste, but it could keep him alive long enough.

'I'm going to call for help, Dad.'

I run through the kitchen to the hall telephone and dial the emergency services. They arrive in ten minutes. Trying to assess him while he's wailing is difficult.

'He seems quite distressed. Did something happen to him recently?' one of the paramedics asks.

'Errmm.... well, his wife left a while back,' I reply, without going into any details.

'Ah, yeah. That'll do it.'

Dad's placed on a trolley. They wheel him into the back of the ambulance and administer a glucagon injection. I sit in the rear cabin of the vehicle next to the medical worker, who praises my quick thinking. It makes me feel awkward.

It's nearly seven. My mate will doubtlessly be calling the house to see where I am; nights out were a pain to organize before the proliferation of mobile phones. Instead of a potentially fun time in Pzazz, I've now got several hours of sitting in a hospital waiting room ahead. I slump forward in the seat and put my head in my hands.

195

'Don't worry, lad,' says the medic, patting me on the back. 'Your dad will be okay.'

'I know. It's just that I was supposed to be going clubbing tonight,' I respond in a gloomy tone.

The look of horror on the guy's face will always stay with me.

August 25, 2000

Many hours after our arrival, the doctors decide to keep Dad in hospital overnight for observation, leaving me to get a taxi back home sometime after one in the morning. I must admit that it's nice to have the house to myself, though missing out on a drinking session is always disappointing.

I collapse into the sitting room chair – shame it's too late to hit the town. My friends must be wondering what happened. Some of them know I'm staying with Dad, and my absence could raise alarm bells.

There's a manga anime on TV called Legend of the Four Kings. It looks good but appears to be in the middle of a series. I stare at the screen, watching the action but not taking anything in, running through the events of the night in my head.

'You know what scares me, Aria? I really was going to walk out. I was going to let him die.'

'I knew you wouldn't. Fantasising about it for years doesn't make pulling the trigger any easier – or more satisfying. I still believe you'd have made the same choice if I hadn't turned up.'

'Yeah, well. I not so sure.'

'Dean. Despite everything, I don't think you're one for patricide.'

'Would it have been patricide? It's not as if I'd have actually killed him myself, is it? That would have been the diabetes, right?.'

'I'm not sure a court would see it that way,' she says with a smile.

I slowly drift off to sleep in the armchair, the sound of dragons and magic infecting my dreams.

September 15, 2000

Dad doesn't remember much of what happened the night he almost died, not that it makes him any less grateful. I've still made sure to avoid any of his potential post-pub rantings, though there's a different shitstorm on the horizon:

he thinks I'm returning to university in the next fortnight, and I've still no job or place to live. I thought I'd have secured an interview from at least one of the positions I applied for. Surely completing part of a degree course is better than not doing one at all, but that might be a view held only by me.

It's Friday night, which means he's at the pub. Being broke has left me at a loose end and stuck in the house while Dad goes out. I consider waiting until about 11 pm then hiding in the car for half an hour but decide against it. He's been on his best behaviour since the hospital incident, having not mentioned Mum once.

'Balls to it,' I say to myself. He'll be okay.

The key scrapes across the door at around 11:30, indicating a level of drunkenness where getting it into the keyhole requires several attempts. The pub's only a five-minute walk down the road, but he still drives there and back. The key finally hits its target. The door swings open as a dreadful sense of déjà vu floods through me.

'Alright, son?'

'Alright,' I say, trying to sound disinterested.

He slumps into the chair opposite the sofa where I'm lying, the booze making his face and bald head even redder than usual. I can smell the larger.

'What you watching?'

'Nowt, really.'

'Ah, good. Means we can have a little chat.'

Fucking hell. Why didn't I wait in the car?

Dad staggers out of the chair and walks toward me, causing my body to go rigid in anticipation of what's about to happen. He reaches out a hand. I hold my breath, only exhaling when he grabs the remote control from my chest to switch off the TV.

'You'll be going back to university soon, and, well, I'm worried you might just forget about me again. I'd hate to think you've been taking advantage of my hospitality.'

I swing my legs over the side of the sofa and sit up straight.

'Was I taking advantage of your hospitality when I saved your life?' I ask, somehow managing to maintain a calm composure despite the provocation.

'Well, I'm grateful, obviously, but I wouldn't expect to have to thank you repeatedly for calling an ambulance in an emergency.'

'Yeah, cool. And I wouldn't expect you to accuse me of 'taking advantage.' I could have easily just stayed with one of my friends, you know,' a total lie, but it's better to let him think otherwise.

'Look, son, all I'm saying is that I don't want to lose touch with you. I just want us all to be a family again: you, me… and your mum.'

I can't decide if this is a symptom of his insanity or the drink. How can he be so deluded?

'Haven't we had this discussion before, Dad? Why the fuck would she come back after what you did to her?'

That's when it slips out.

'Fucking hell. I don't even know why *I* came back, especially after what you did to me.'

'Wha… Dean. I know there… there might have been times when I lost my temper with you, but any father would have done the same – discipline's important. Look at where it got you.'

I somehow manage to ignore the numerous flaws I could have raised with that statement.

'That's not what I'm talking about.'

'Then, what?'

'Dad. I need to know something. Did you ever do anything to me you might... regret deeply. You know? I mean, like, when Mum wasn't there.'

'I don't know what you mean.'

I take a deep breath, wishing I were as drunk as he is.

'I've always had... issues. So, I went to see a counsellor at uni. She suggested that they could be my mind's way of coping with being... abused... when I was a kid.'

His face turns to ash. Mouth hanging open like a fish. Bringing this up while he's drunk was something I hoped to avoid, but it's been put off too long. It's now or never. The silence before he responds seems to go on for an eternity.

'Son. How... how could you think that? I love you more than anything. I'd never... this was your mother, wasn't it?'

'What? Jesus! No! Fucking hell. I just told you who
it was. Is there anything you won't blame Mum for? She
knows nothing about it. She doesn't even know I'm here.'

'Don't lie to me, son. It was her, wasn't it? Poisoning you against me like always. That fucking bitch.'

'What's wrong with you? It's nothing to do with her;
it never is. But you blame her for everything.'

'Bullshit. Why would a stranger make up horrible
lies about me? I've done everything to be a good dad. I'd
never hurt you. I'D NEVER HURT YOU!' he screams at
the top of his voice in a way that sounds like he's trying to
convince himself.

'You did hurt me, Dad. Lots of times.'

'Not... not like that. I'd never.'

'Would you even know if you did? You do... horrible things... then act like they never happened. You think
it's Mum's fault that you nearly killed her all those times?
You need help; we've been telling you for years.'

I can see the tears forming in his eyes. I don't know
whether they're regret or realisation.

'I'm... there's.... there's nothing wrong with me.
Everyone gets angry sometimes. There are things about your

mother you're better off not knowing, you bloody believe me. She's not the innocent angel she pretends to be.'

It's far from the first time he's blamed Mum, but this feels different somehow. This was his chance to repent, to admit his failings, yet the finger points at her, as always. It fills me with despair. Confronting him about what he may or may not have done was incredibly difficult, yet all he does is turn the subject toward Mum's perceived faults. Faults he still believes were so bad that they justified over a decade of constant hell. I give up. I give up on answers, on closure, everything. It all feels pointless now. I doubt he even re-members half the things he's done.

'Look, son. I've had a bit to drink, so I'm not at my best right now. Why don't we talk about this silliness in the morning?'

'Yeah, sure,' I tell him

'That's good. Goodnight, son. Love you.'

'Night.'

Dad gives a slight nod before leaving the room. I didn't know it then, but the next time I'd see him, six years from now, I'd be standing over his dead body.

September 16, 2000

2 AM. I waited an hour after Dad went upstairs before going to my bedroom, though I don't plan on getting any sleep. My few clothes and possessions make packing the travel suitcase quicker than anticipated. I sit on the bed, looking around and wondering if he'll still keep this place in such perfect condition.

'I can't take it anymore, Aria. It's like banging my head against fucking a brick wall. That crazy bastard doesn't seem to know what he did the other day, never mind ten years ago.

'So, you're leaving?''

'What choice do I have? You heard him; he's not going to let me go without a fight. Jesus, he was talking about the three of us being a family again. Can you believe that? Fuck this and fuck him.'

'Regret coming back in the first place?'

I let out a long sigh.

'No, no I don't. I came for answers more than anything else. In a way, I think I got them. I'll never know for certain if he did those… things to me, and he'll *always* blame Mum for what he put us through.'

'Crazy people don't know they're crazy.'

'My favourite phrase. Probably explains me, eh?'

'Doubtlessly.'

Enough time has passed. I slowly open the door and listen intently. Dad's snoring resonates through the house – time to move. Quietly reaching the stairs isn't the hard part; descending them while carrying a case and making no noise is the challenge.

The first few steps are traversed in slow motion, reaching the eighth, about halfway between the upper and ground floors, a silence-splintering creak freezes me to the spot. Dad's snoring stops. The pounding of my heartbeat feels deafening. Should I run back to the bedroom or make a break for the door? My lungs cry for air. What excuse to give if he catches me? The snoring restarts. A slow breath is released, making me want to cough. I must give up cigarettes.

The remainder of the trek to the front entrance continues as noiselessly as possible. The key is turned, handle lowered gently. Here I am again, sneaking out while trying not to wake Dad. History repeating itself. I take one last look inside before closing the door.

'Goodbye,' I whisper, unsure if I'm talking to my father or my former home.

It's almost three in the morning when I arrive at my aunt's. It takes concentration to knock hard enough to wake the inhabitants without alerting the whole street.

'Dean? What's happened?' asks my half-awake cousin

'Alright, Nick. Errmm… it's a long story. Do you mind if I kip here tonight? Don't want to wake Mum.'

'Of course, mate. You don't have to ask – you're family.'

Family, it's still a strange concept. I struggle to feel that relationship with anyone other than Mum, a result of Dad keeping us isolated for so many years, afraid of letting me get to know cousins, aunts, and uncles on her side. Sometimes, in my most paranoid moments, I wonder if they see parts of him in me.

Once again, the sofa bed I've become so familiar with is readied.

Mum comes into the room when the sun rises a few hours later, berating me for not waking her upon arrival.

'Dean? What happened? Are you okay?'

'Mum, I've got some stuff to tell you. Well, a lot of stuff, to be honest.'

I explain everything that's happened over the last few months, including the money troubles, staying with Dad, and wanting to know why he hurt us. I avoid mentioning the abuse theory.

'Oh, Dean. Why the hell didn't you just come here?'

'I guess I didn't want to impose. It's pretty jam-packed in here, and as I said, I thought I'd discover why he was such a bastard for all those years. As if there were a simple explanation behind it, ha. Honestly, Mum, I'm not even sure he knows. He's convinced he was a good husband and father.'

'That does not surprise me one bit. He always said I *made* him do those things, but I can understand you wanting an actual reason, something that explains it all. I just don't think there is one. Anyway, he's out of our lives forever now. I'm just glad you escaped without him realising.'

So am I.

'And what do you mean by impose?' she continues. 'Why would you think that? We'd all rather you'd have stayed here than went to him.' Mum looks out of the window with a look on her face as if she recalls a memory. 'I begged him to get help so many times, Dean, I did. It just made him angrier. If you hadn't taken me out of there… I've no doubt I'd be dead.'

'Yeah, certainly. You know what shocked me most? The house was a total tip, but my bedroom was spotless like he'd been keeping it ready for me coming back.'

'I know he made our lives hell. But he always loved you, as strange as it seems.'

I say nothing.

'I'm just happy you're here now, Dean. Don't worry about university – as long as we're safe, healthy, and together, that's all that matters.'

It's so obvious that leaving Dad has knocked ten years off Mum's age. That expression of permanent worry is gone, and the lack of wrinkles around her bright eyes is conspicuous on someone past retirement age. Many of the medical issues she once faced are now seemingly gone, proof that stress kills. Maybe she's right; perhaps the simpler things in life are all that matter. I lean in and hug her.

'I love you, Mum.'

'I love you, too, son.'

CHAPTER NINE

MR BEAN

October 2, 2000

I've been half expecting Dad to turn up at my aunt's door during the month since I left, ready to drag us back physically, but his fear of Mum's family and the law still outweighs his urge to do something stupid. There have been times when, lying awake at night, I hear a car engine outside that lingers for a little too long. It's already on the move by the time I reach the window. Am I being paranoid, like him?

December 25, 2000

Money, which has been an issue for as long as I can remember, is getting even tighter. I claim jobseeker's allowance, but the £52 per week doesn't go far. My car insurance finally running out made the decision to sell it easier. My cousin's mate paid a generous £150, which went toward bills, food, and debts.

The severity of the situation was illustrated a few weeks ago when Mum and I returned home from a trip to town, only to realise we'd forgotten to pick up her sister's parcel from the post office, as promised. We couldn't scrape together the £1.25 needed for a one-person return bus ticket, so I ended up making the four-mile round trip on foot. We even applied for a crisis loan, which involved a dehumanising process of explaining why we 'struggle to manage our finances,' as the Department of Work and Pensions employee put it. They eventually gave us £20.

As a result of being so broke, we've come to an agreement regarding Christmas: rather than buying each other presents, what little we have will go on the family to say thanks for putting a roof over our heads. Most of the gifts consist of alcohol, making for a fun day. I have to be wary of getting into my usual blackout state when sleeping on somebody else's bed, though. If there's one thing that'll ruin Christmas, it's soiling a relative's furniture.

'Dean, I'm going to get us our own place,' Mum announces as we sit around the dinner table wearing paper hats. 'I've already spoken to the council. They're sorting it out.'

My aunt and cousins seem genuinely disappointed. I enjoy spending time with them but sleeping on a sofa bed and hanging around someone else's house all day takes its toll.

March 20, 2001

I finally entered gainful employment last month, thanks to my former flatmate, Andrew. He's been working at a home and garden retail store for a few years now, slowly climbing his way up to a supervisor position. I still go on an occasional night out with him, Paul, and other friends when funds allow. They knew my situation – living with my aunt and Mum, on the dole, skint, desperate. I was grateful he told me about the shelf-stacker position, even if it is part-time.

I breezed the interview, mainly because Andrew told me what questions to expect and the best responses. I like to think of it as me using my connections rather than cheating. Despite the monotonous routine and minimum wage, work-ing alongside a friend makes it more enjoyable than it should be.

The council finally got back to Mum; we're no longer homeless. Unfortunately, our new residence is in a block of flats occupied almost entirely by people over 70. This isn't how I envisioned spending the prime years of my life.

Living with my mother in a grim building along with the nearly dead isn't ideal, though the most upsetting part of my existence right now is the lack of any romance. I might still be amusing and outgoing when drunk, but years of having my confidence eroded have left the sober me even more terrified of talking to girls, expecting them to reel away in horror as soon as the clumsy words come falling out of my mouth – the experience with Michelle is one I can't forget.

A steady, albeit small, income allows me to do something that helps build self-esteem: joining a gym. It's a dirt-cheap dive; gaffer tape covers the ripped benches, with very few cardio machines and lots of massive weights, but I hope it will stop me from metamorphosing into a shorter version of Tony Soprano. I also like the girl who works there, Lisa. She's about my age and incredibly pretty with dyed red hair. A smile is always flashed in my direction when walking through the door. Seeing her face makes my heart flutter, even though I know being friendly to customers is part of the job. Unfortunately, attempts at small talk range from awkward to embarrassing as I become a Mr Bean-like character in her presence.

Not starting work until five in the afternoon means I can use the gym around noon when it's usually empty. Lisa is taking advantage of the quiet period today by doing a workout of her own.

'Hi, Dean,' she calls out from the squat rack. I remind myself that remembering my name doesn't mean I should start planning our future together, but it still feels nice.

'Hi, Lisa. It's, errmm… quiet today,' I reply, already going red with embarrassment at my terrible conversational skills.

'Yup, just you and me,' she says, exposing a bright white smile that makes me feel so awkward I'm tempted to run back outside. I grin back with an exuberance that makes me look like Jack Nicholson from the Shining, so I scuttle off to the changing room.

Most people don't like talking while working out, giving me an excuse not to shame myself further. The rest of our interactions are limited to the occasional nod and smile when passing. I'm determined, however, to at least say goodbye. I head back toward the changing rooms after 90 minutes of lifting weights, mentally preparing for my feat of bravery. Lisa's on the static bike about 15 feet away. I take a breath.

'See you later, Lisa,' I say, focusing on pronouncing each word clearly without screaming them.

'Bye, Dean,' she replies with a wave.

The joy of performing this simple task is short-lived. Having turned my head to look at my crush while striding across the gym, I miss the changing room entrance by several feet and walk straight into the wall. The rim of my cap squashes down and melds with my face. I stumble backwards, struggling to stay upright. Despite the remarkable amount of pain now surging through me, the only thing I can think is, 'please don't let her have seen that.' I compose myself as best I can and bolt through the door, the sound of Lisa's muffled laughter ringing in my ears. After getting changed, I wait a full 30 minutes for her to return to reception so I can escape without being seen. At one point, I contemplated climbing out the window to avoid detection.

October 5, 2001

My time in what is, essentially, a place where the elderly come to die has thankfully ended. Having not realised the building's true nature, my mum pleaded with the council for somewhere more suitable. The terror I've inflicted on some residents during nights when I return drunk might have helped our cause. On separate occasions, I tried to open the wrong apartment door, vomited in the entrance hall flowerbed, and attempted to scale the outside of the building when I forgot my key.

Our new home is a semi-detached house in a slightly better area of an awful neighbourhood. The good news is that two of the rooms are mine, which means I get my own sofa, TV, bed, and computer – all bought on the cheap. While it's much better than the previous location, I still crave a place of my own and independence. It'll only take another 20 years before that happens.

CHAPTER TEN

OF ALL THE THINGS I HAVE LOST

December 1, 2001

I've not seen Dad in over a year. Memories of the suffering he inflicted fade, but the psychological and emotional damage becomes ever more apparent. I'll be 23 in a few days. If the uni course had gone to plan, my career in the lucrative IT industry would just be starting. Instead, I occupy the spare rooms of my mother's council house and work part-time, filling shelves. But those are the least of my problems. Mentally, I'm falling apart.

In addition to low confidence that's developing into a fear of talking to people, I've started to experience more severe symptoms. There are days when feelings of depression and anxiety are overwhelming, like I'm suffocating in a hole and can't escape, or maybe I just don't want to get out.

It's impossible to imagine any way my life will become worth living. I stay in bed until evenings on days it hits hardest. This can't be depression, surely – depressed people don't go to the gym, do they? But I know Dad experienced something similar. He'd occasionally talk about how pointless and shit everything felt.

This downward spiral brings with it awful feelings of guilt. Mum took the brunt of Dad's violence, yet she's never been happier than right now, so what's wrong with me?

December 4, 2001

Twenty-three. The only thing I'm looking forward to is drinking myself into oblivion come the weekend. Mum surprised me with an unexpected present: a PlayStation 2 and a copy of Grand Theft Auto III. She says the whole family chipped in and that it was 'something I deserved.' There's a much less welcome surprise, too; my dad, presumably in the middle of the night, pushed a letter addressed to me through my aunt's letterbox, not knowing our current address. Olive gave it to my mother.

'I wanted you to have the choice of whether to open it, Dean,' Mum says.

I look at the tiny envelope. It has 'To Dean from Dad' emblazoned on the front. Those words make me feel queasy, adding to an already overwhelming urge to throw it away. But there's an itch at the back of my mind, a curiosity dying to be sated. What if, against all odds and reason, this is a confession of some kind? An admission of guilt? Might there even be an apology that would give Mum and me some closure? Going against my better judgement, I start to unseal it.

The letter contains two £20 notes and a couple of lined paper sheets taken from a small notepad. The scrawled handwriting reads:

Happy Birthday son,

I hope you're doing well and aren't struggling. Sorry you felt you had to run away again. I know we had a bit of a daft argument, but I don't think it was any reason to leave, especially without telling me. I hope that we'll be able to see each other again soon, especially as I've some bad news.

I'm dying, Dean. The doctors told me that my diabetes is getting worse and I'll be on dialysis in a few months. That's end-stage. It won't be long before my kidneys give in and I'm dead. The only thing I want before dying is to see you. I know your mother turned you against me, but you've got to understand there are always two sides to every story. I love you more than anything in the world and would never hurt you. Please come back and see me before it's too late.

Hope you have a great birthday.

Love you,

Dad.

Other than being able to give Mum £40, I utterly regret opening the letter.

December 5, 2001

Staying in bed until 4 pm has become par for the course for non-workdays, with the gym becoming an ever-decreasing priority. The contents of that letter still chew me up. All this time away from him, yet Dad still has power over me.

'Wish I'd just thrown it in the bin,' I say aloud.

'But then you'd have thrown the money away as well.'

Nothing brings Aria out quite like my father.

'Like I care. Though I suppose Mum appreciated it.'

It wasn't easy convincing Mum to take the £40; she insisted I have it. 'Try to imagine it's not from him,' she said, but I'd know. The knowledge would gnaw away at me, the idea he'd be pleased I was spending his birthday gift. I said she should use it to offset some of the financial impact caused by my console. Mum agreed in the end, albeit reluctantly. I never told her what the letter revealed.

'He's lying, you know, about dying. It's just his way of trying to get you back.'

'Honestly, Aria, I kind of hope he's telling the truth, still blaming her on his deathbed. Can you imagine how empty his funeral will be? Bet there'll be, like, five people there.'

'Five! He'd be lucky. And who'd pay for it?' she laughs.

'Maybe the hospital can keep his body for science. Try and find out what was wrong with him,' I say, only half-joking. 'Oh, and by the way: I've not seen you about for a while – again. These visits are getting rarer.'

'Well, maybe it's for the best.'

That comes as a shock

'Eh? What do you mean? I'll always need you.'

'I think you're mixing up need and want. Letting go of me wouldn't be a bad thing, you know. You said it yourself: imaginary friends don't usually last this long. You're supposed to grow by dealing with your issues, not turning to me all the time.'

'This sounds like a breakup.'

'Dean, whether or not you realise it, the reason behind my sporadic visits is that you don't want me here. Dad's not in your life, so what is there to feel bad about?

Right? That's the line you're trying to believe. He's gone. You got your wish after all those years. But it's not fixed everything, has it?'

'Yeah, I know. I can't help it. Wish I could stop feeling this way.'

'I know that nothing brings you true happiness. You feel dirty on the inside. You're so filled with anger and rage and want to just hide from the world. Most of all, you're still petrified of ending up exactly like him.'

'It sounds like I need you more than ever.'

'You must have figured it out by now – I *am* you,' she sighs. 'Do you never think that I only say what you want to hear? You need to deal with your problems, Dean. They won't get better by talking to invisible angels.'

Her words seem to hang in the air.

'Fine… just fuck off then.'

And with that brief interaction, she was gone.

CHAPTER ELEVEN

EMMA

August 9, 2002

A lot has changed in the eight months since I told Aria to fuck off for the first-ever time. As content as I was with my work situation, the few weekly hours on offer and low wages saw me live like a pauper while friends bought homes and holidayed abroad, so I applied for a full-time position elsewhere.

My lack of ambition led me to the exciting world of data entry. Still, it paid slightly better than minimum-wage shelf stacking and offered forty hours per week. Best of all, I didn't have to talk to anyone – not over the phone, not in person, nothing. I never expected to get through the interview process, but thanks to still being slightly drunk from the night before, the talkative, confident, funny version of myself breezed through.

What's even more shocking is that I've now got an actual, real girlfriend. Emma and I became friends when we were 17, which meant talking to her wasn't the terror-inducing feat it usually is with other girls. I always liked her. She's very beautiful and towers above me at a little over six feet – two attributes that make us an unlikely-looking couple.

I started dropping hints of my interest after she broke up with a long-term boyfriend, but the attempts were either overly subtle to the point of going unnoticed or so heavy-handed that she thought I was joking. Emma was worn down eventually (her words), and we got together.

Alcohol is my replacement for Aria when it comes to fighting demons. Emma, who's usually with me when I get blind drunk on nights out, just assumes I like a good time. I can't imagine that she approves, but boys will be boys, I tell her.

My father never sent any more letters. It seems my lack of response sent the right message. A friend who lives near him confirmed my suspicions: not only was Dad alive, but he was spotted gardening.

Aria was right; Dad was never dying. It was just another ruse. I often think about the other things she said, about needing to deal with my shit. Returning to a counsellor had crossed my mind, but the effects of that single session remain hard to shake years later. I didn't want another person poking around inside my head, uncovering darkness that's better off hidden. Anyway, I've got a girlfriend and a real job now. Things can only get better from here.

December 1, 2002

Why did I think a career that involves sitting at a desk eight hours per day hitting the same ten keys wouldn't worsen my mental state? Not having to converse with people does relieve anxiety, that's for sure, but the monotony makes my mind wander, usually to places I'd rather avoid.

In an attempt to make time pass quicker, I split the day into 28 fifteen-minute increments (not including breaks), mentally scratching each one off like a prisoner waiting out their sentence. It amazes me that some people have been working here for thirty years and somehow maintain a chirpy disposition. What's their secret? Drugs? It must be drugs.

The money is helpful, but I'm pissing my wages away on weekend binges and material shit that doesn't make me happy. Hitting the gym has fallen by the wayside, cardio and dumbbells replaced by cocktails and hangovers. At least I don't have to face Lisa anymore.

Emma, my first 'proper' girlfriend, remains a solitary bright spot. She sticks by me, no matter how many times I get fall-over drunk and can't move for the entirety of the next day. We live about 15 miles apart. As she doesn't drive and I work late, meet-ups are limited to weekends at

Mum's. I like that I can easily talk to her and make her laugh, but self-sabotaging thoughts don't disappear: why is she even with someone like me? Am I going to ruin her life like I have mine? Most concerning of all, there are my occasional bouts of unspoken jealousy and suspicion.

March 7, 2003

Life is an unending road of repetition, hammering away at a numerical keypad all day at work then getting blind drunk on the weekend. Bored with watching me act like a clown in pubs and clubs, Emma now stays at my mum's on a Saturday night while I go out drinking with our friends. The only time we spend together is Sunday, the same day I'm so hungover that moving is a challenge. I wonder whether I'm intentionally pushing her away.

Taking Aria's advice and dealing with my problems in a healthy way has proved an impossible task. 'What do I do now?' I sometimes wonder aloud, hoping she'll appear. But no – I'm alone.

I do have strong feelings for Emma. I love how kind and intelligent she is, and I'm very attracted to her, but something stops me from committing. It's as if my mind is telling me I don't deserve this girl. Despite my behaviour,

Emma's happy and fun-loving nature remains, while there are mornings when I wish I hadn't woken up.

November 10, 2003

Work, and in many ways, life, is becoming unbearable. My moods swing from furious internal rages that have no cause to absolute desolation. I think about suicide a lot. The idea of all the pain disappearing is becoming a more attractive option, but the thought of what it would do to my mum and Emma keeps me from doing anything drastic. Thankfully, modern medicine is here to help.

The local doctor's reception is packed with people who look decades older than their actual ages – not that the same description doesn't apply to me. The peeling signs on the grey walls warn of the dangers of smoking and excessive alcohol consumption. I wonder what people like us would have left if these vices were taken away. Bits of conversations are audible between the whooping coughs and sniffs; they mainly consist of patients complaining about their waits.

'Dean Graham to room 3, please,' comes the announcement, forty minutes after my appointment time.

A middle-aged woman greets me inside the small office.

'Hello, Mr Graham. Please, take a seat.'

'Thank you, doctor.'

'So, how are you?'

'Errmm… well… Not great. I've been struggling quite a bit recently. Like, mentally.'

'Right, can you tell me a bit more?'

'Yeah, err…, well. I have mood swings and… I'd call them worrisome thoughts. I just feel like things are getting worse. I had a lot of problems with my dad growing up, and I think there are unresolved issues there.'

'Would you say you feel suicidal at all?'

'Well, I mean, I've not tried to hurt myself, but I do sometimes think about… escaping, I guess.'

'Do you work?'

'I do, yeah.'

'And do you feel it makes your mental state better or worse?'

'Worse, definitely. It's the most boring job in the world, gives me time to dwell on things.'

'Hmmm… yes. Have you tried exercise?'

That seems like a strange question.

'Errmm… no. Well, I used to, but not for a while now. As you can probably tell, ha,' I point at my expanding gut, an attempt at self-deprecating humour that doesn't bring a flicker of a smile.

'Right. I'm going to write you a sick note for four weeks and a repeat prescription for fluoxetine. If at any point you feel like you might hurt yourself, I want you to come back in, and we'll get you an appointment with a counsellor. I also recommend you get some exercise. You'd be surprised how much it helps.'

'Errmm… yeah. Thank you.'

So, I've got antidepressants and four weeks off work. While I'm glad the doctor held back from the counselling option, at least until I've got a razor on my wrist, the outcome's a bit surprising. Maybe she thinks I just want a holiday. And why push exercise so hard? I used to work out regularly and was still miserable. Now I'm both sad and fat.

December 4, 2003

Another year older. Twenty-five is a weird age, still young but not exactly youthful. A time when most people who've got their life together start thinking about kids, marriage, and furthering their careers. By contrast, I live with my mum, remain stuck in the very definition of a dead-end job, and want to leave a girl I could have a real future with because I struggle to connect with other human beings. At least the tablets give me a pleasant, numbing sensation. It's like I still feel depressed but don't care as much. Another bonus is that it now takes half the usual amount of alcohol to get me blackout drunk, saving a fortune.

February 13, 2005

Despite intimacy – something I've long struggled with – ending a long time ago, Emma and I have been together for three years now. Whether it's our genuine friendship, the love we feel for each other, or her hope that I might change, we've held on to a relationship that's obviously doomed.

It's another Sunday spent brutally hungover from a night where my short-term memory stopped working at 11.30 pm. Emma watches TV next to me in my bed, as usual, idly flicking through the channels while I'm wrapped in a duvet by her side, making groaning noises. I wonder about the happy life I deny her: kids, marriage, passion, a partner who's always there and doesn't spend every Sunday in bed. She won't know these things because of me.

'I think we should talk,' I say. Everyone knows what that phrase means. Nobody begins a sentence with it before talking about something banal like plumbing. There's no look of shock or upset on Emma's face, just a solemn nod as if she knows this has been coming for a long time. We both admit to feeling that the relationship should have ended a while ago. There's no finger-pointing, even though it's obvious I'm the one at fault.

I never told Emma the whole story of my childhood. She confesses that what she does know about my past and the antidepressants made her excuse many of my actions. Like most couples whose breakups don't end acrimoniously, we agree to stay friends. She gets a taxi home after we hug for the last time. I slump down on the sofa and switch on the TV, glad for the Flucloxacillin's zombie-like effect. My mind briefly drifts to thoughts of Aria. How many years has it been now since I told her to fuck off? Here I am, alone again, and I deserve it.

CHAPTER TWELVE

DEATH

March 14, 2006

Another useful feature of antidepressant-induced mental fog is that it causes time to pass quickly. Days blend into each other as weeks turn to months without me noticing. It's hard to believe I'm only three years away from thirty yet still reside in my mum's council house, still single, and still slaving away in an awful data entry job, spending every penny on getting wasted come the weekend.

On the other hand, Mum is thriving. She works part-time as a waitress, has loads of friends, and despite approaching 70, has never been healthier. She also wants payback against Dad.

It's been almost a decade since we left him, enough time for the fear that he'll turn up on our doorstep to disappear. There were no more attempts at contact, though a reliable source informs me he's been telling drinkers in the local pub that his wife won the lottery and ran off with another woman. Now, after escaping with nothing, Mum wants her share of the house.

Dad initially refused to sign the divorce papers he received long after Mum left. He eventually relented, likely believing an official separation would keep his ex from her fair share of the marriage assets. Mum had always refused to pursue the matter, fearful of angering Dad further, but that's no longer the case. She instructed a solicitor to start proceedings. Dad can either buy out her half of the house or sell it and split the money 50/50. I can only imagine how he'll react to the letter informing him of this ultimatum.

March 21, 2006

Mum's solicitor phoned. Dad's refused the offer in the strongest possible terms, claiming he paid for the entirety of the house. A complete lie, but we're confident of fighting him in court. If necessary, we're willing to reveal the reasons why we had to run away while he slept.

June 13, 2006

Spending four days in a field and getting off my tits on drink and drugs has left me shattered. The previous weekend was the one thing I look forward to every year: Download Festival, an excuse to overindulge 24/7 while listening to some of my favourite bands. It's become a tradition to attend with Andrew and a few others, a welcome break from the crushing boredom of work.

After several days of living in filth, enduring the worst portable toilets in history and surviving off cigarettes, booze, and burgers, the comforts of home are heavenly. The bath looked like a swamp when I got out yesterday.

I've just woken after sleeping for around 12 hours, resulting in the closest thing possible to a non-alcohol-induced hangover. All the symptoms are there, including grogginess, a sour stomach, and an unpleasant taste in the mouth. Lying in bed at 11:30 am, wishing I'd taken another day off work tomorrow, the phone rings. Mum's out, and while I'd usually ignore it, I know we're expecting more news from the solicitor about the house situation. I stagger downstairs to answer the call.

'Hello?'

'Hello, is that Dean?' says the official voice.

'It is, yeah.'

'Hi, Dean. It's Susan, Betty's solicitor. Is your mum there?'

'She's out right now. Can I take a message?'

'Oh, it's no problem. I just wanted to apologise. I've not been in contact for a while as there's been a lot to sort out.'

'Ermm… yeah, I can imagine,' I reply, assuming she's talking about Dad. He's not actually agreed to our terms, surely?

'Well, yes. When one of the parties dies in situations like these, it can complicate matters.'

'Errmm… sorry?'

Is the pseudo hangover making me stupider? I've no clue what she's talking about.

'I just mean that Mr Graham's death means extra steps in the process. It'll also add extra time to the case.'

I hold the phone next to my ear, trying to comprehend what's happening.

'He… my dad's… dead?'

The silence on the other end is palpable.

'Oh... I'm… I'm so sorry. I had absolutely no idea. I thought you'd been informed. Your father passed away last week. I just assumed that someone – the police or the hospital – would have told you.'

'…. No. I, err… we didn't know.'

'Again, I profusely apologise that you had to find out this way. Please tell your mother to contact me whenever she's up to it, and we'll go through the next steps.'

She seems genuinely remorseful but can't hide her desire to end the call quickly.

'I will. Goodbye.'

The phone lands on the receiver with a clunk. I stand rooted to the spot staring at the device. It's ancient – still uses a cord, for God's sake. Why haven't we bought a modern wireless one yet? That would be so much easier. Why didn't I just go out and buy one earlier? I'm such an idiot.

I reach the sofa without touching the floor, floating over the carpet before collapsing face-first on the cushions. My heartbeat's deafening. Why do I feel like this? It's not like I've had any contact with him for years, nor did I ever intend to. It just all feels so… final. I know he would never have admitted to any past crimes, but maybe, just maybe, there was an ember of hope in me that he would change. That one day, he'd have a moment of clarity and express remorse, explaining that he knows he did wrong but doesn't understand what compelled him. That'll never happen now. The chance is gone forever. I'll never have one last opportunity to ask why. It's too late.

'Aria?'

No reply. If she were ever going to make another appearance, now would be the time. But her name hangs in the air, failing to conjure anything magical or imaginary.

It's another hour before Mum gets back. I'm still lying in the same position when she opens the door.

'I'm back, Dean,' she shouts, assuming I'm upstairs.

'In here.'

'Oh, what's wrong? Are you still tired from your festival?'

I drag myself into a sitting position.

'Susan rang.'

'Ahh, damn. I was hoping to catch her. What's the news? Don't tell me he's given in? Haha.'

'Errmm… you might want to sit down, Mum.'

She sits next to me. Her smile quickly turns to a look of concern.

'What's happened, Dean? Has he done something?'

'Dad's… dead. It happened last week. Susan thought someone must have told you… told us.'

The colour drains from her face.

'Oh… Oh God. Dean… I, I never wished him dead,' her voice cracking. 'I know what he did, but we… we had a lot of good years as well. And you were the best thing he could ever give me.'

Tears pour down her face.

'I know, Mum. But remember that he's been dead to us for six years. He was dead the moment we left that house. I'm sad, too. I'm sad that I'll never be able to find out if he was finally sorry for everything, for what he put us through, the damage he did. But it's over now. Maybe it will help us move on.'

'I know, son,' she says, the sobs slowing down. 'I just can't believe he's gone. I-I don't know. I feel silly for crying over him after everything that happened. But….'

'I know. He wasn't always that way.'

'Yes, exactly. You know, it's like something broke in him that night in Spain. His mother dying turned him into another person. I spent so much time hoping the old Bob would come back one day – probably why I tried to make excuses for him. I'm sorry, son.'

'You don't have anything to be sorry for, Mum.'

I hug her, and so ends the most defining chapter of my life – so far.

June 14, 2006

I dreamt of Dad last night. It was a memory of Spain long before that awful incident. I'd been playing outside our house when a cat ran under the neighbour's parked car, prompting young me to climb halfway beneath the vehicle to investigate. The old Spanish man next door seemed to hate two things: kids and foreigners. He often made his dislike of us evident and seeing me playing near his ancient Ford Escort sent him into a rage.

I never heard Paco storm out of his gate. He grabbed a handful of my hair, using it to lift me to my feet. The shock and pain made my six-year-old self scream, bringing Dad flying out of our house like a sprinter. He grabbed my attacker by the shirt, pulling back his fist before screaming, 'DON'T YOU EVER FUCKING TOUCH MY BOY. I'LL FUCKING KILL YOU!' If Mum hadn't dragged him away, I believe he would have.

Instead of returning to my awful job today, I phone up and ask to speak to my supervisor. Usually, I'd be nervous about asking for a day's absence following a holiday, but nobody's going to object to this.

'Hi, it's Dean,' I tell my line manager, Jamie, a young man who believes the best way to get ahead is to be unpleasant to everyone. 'I know I was supposed to be back today, but I just found out my dad passed away. I need to sort everything out as I'm his only next of kin.'

Silence on the other end.

'Riiiiight. So, will you be back in this afternoon?'

'Errmm… well, I assumed I'd have some compassionate leave. Isn't that the policy for the death of a parent?'

'Well, yes,' he says with a groan. 'Sorry, it's just that we're struggling right now for numbers. I didn't mean to come across insensitive. You have up to five days. There's no obligation to use them all, though I imagine you will.'

'Right. Yes. I'll be in next week, then.'

If I'm sure of anything, it's that Jamie thinks I'm lying about my dad's death to get more time off. A workmate confirmed the theory; as soon as the call ended, he asked my

243

team members if I'd ever talked about my dad and whether he was already dead – what a prick.

I've now got the unenviable task of tracking down my father's corpse, starting with a phone call to the police. I get put through to the correct department and speak to someone who's very adept at dealing with the recently bereaved. After a couple of minutes of searching, she gives me some unexpected news.

'Mr Graham. I've just checked my records and, well, I'm very happy to tell you that your father is alive.'

'He... he's not dead?'

I'm stunned. How could Susan be so completely wrong? I'd accepted his death, and now it turns out he's still alive!

'Oh... Mr Graham, I'm so, so sorry,' the lady sounds like she's about to throw up. 'I... I was looking at the wrong report. I'm afraid to inform you that your father *did* pass away last week. I can't apologise enough for my error.'

In the last 48 hours, one person told me my dad is dead when I thought he was alive, while another told me he is alive when he's dead. The officer is very upset about her mistake, whereas I feel nothing. Not angry, sad, happy, relieved – nothing.

'Oh, it's okay. We all make mistakes. So, could I ask where his body is?'

There's a short silence while she reacts to my apparent indifference at a faux pas that, had she been talking to someone else, might have got her fired.

'Errm... of course. He's actually in the hospital near you.'

'Really? Huh, okay. Thank you for your help.'

'You're welcome. And sorry, again.'

'That's okay. Goodbye.'

All I can think about is how Dad ended up in a local hospital when there are two others much closer to where he lived.

It's doubtful that anyone likes hospitals. Some view them as a place to get better, while others only associate death and despair, but everyone would prefer to not be in one. The thought runs through my head while passing through a cloud of cigarette smoke coming from patients crowded around the doorway, holding onto their IV stands while indulging in something that contributed to their admittance. The double doors slide shut, trapping me inside with an aroma of disinfectant that barely conceals the stink of bodily fluids. Hospitals – I, for one, hate them.

Having phoned ahead earlier, I'm directed to the mortuary after informing reception of my arrival. At least I've found Dad. Making my way down to the basement level, a middle-aged man wearing a white coat greets me.

'Mr. Graham. Yes, your father's been here a few days now. We were starting to think the council would have to take care of the burial.'

'Yeah, we were... estranged.'

'You'd be amazed by how often this kind of thing happens. A lot of family members never turn up at all. So, would you like to see him?'

'Who?' I ask, perplexed by the question.

'Your father.'

I must have watched a thousand movies in which people are shown dead bodies in morgues, but I didn't think it would ever happen to me. I've never seen an actual corpse. There's no way I want to see him. My throat tightens at the idea. No chance.

'Yes, please.'

The attendant leads me down a hall to a room with a large window, whatever lies behind hidden by a yellow curtain. He pulls back the material to reveal another area, sterile and white. A spotlight attached to a long metal arm hangs from the ceiling, its beam focused on a metal trolley below. I see the face of a skeletal-thin stranger, most of him covered in a white sheet, eyes closed, mouth slightly open, head tilted back. What little hair is left has been brushed. There's even a pillow under his head. Is this another mistake? It takes a few minutes before accepting the truth.

Seeing Dad like this makes me wonder what the end was like. Was it filled with regret or hatred, sorrow or fury? Did he call out for me, for my mum, his mum? I'll never know. My lack of any reaction is concerning – it's like looking at a fake Halloween corpse. I nod at the mortuary technician after about 10 seconds of silence, thanking him for his help and promising to make funeral arrangements.

June 15, 2006

I've discovered a few facts. It turns out that Dad ended up in a local hospital because he moved to the city, albeit briefly. Records have his current address down as a retirement home, not ten minutes' drive from where Mum and I live.

Grampian Gardens Retirement Living is as stereotypically depressing as one would expect. It reminds me of the asylum from One Flew Over the Cuckoo's nest, complete with a Nurse Ratchet-like administrator who's initially quite hostile to the son that abandoned sweet old Bobby to die alone.

It seems my father really had been peddling the story about his wife winning the lottery and running off with another woman, taking their son along – a story I can only assume is so unbelievable that people believed it. After about five minutes explaining to the hatched-faced woman why he really had no visitors, her icy exterior melts, suddenly swearing that she 'never really trusted what Bob said.'

I'm told that Dad's prediction of ending up on dialysis – a result of diabetes-related kidney damage – really did come to pass, though it was five years later than my birthday letter claimed. Struggling to look after himself and knowing he lived alone, the hospital suggested he move somewhere that could take care of his needs.

I'll never know if he did intend to sell the house, as per Mum's request, but was too ill near the end to go forward with it, or if he'd been determined not to give in to his ex, knowing his death would make everything more complicated. Either way, Dad was only in the old folks' home for around three weeks before being taken into hospital following another episode. Death came about a week later. Despite all the pain he caused us, I silently hope that the end was easy, that they had him pumped so full of drugs that he just slept continuously until his heart stopped.

June 21, 2006

It's the day of Dad's funeral. A lack of a will means what assets he had passed to me. That included around £2,000 in a bank account, the vast majority of which went on this ceremony. My friends said I was crazy. 'Why would you do that for the old bastard?' Andrew and Paul repeatedly asked. I've tried explaining it: how this will draw a line under the past, bring a form of closure to it all, a way to say goodbye, even. They think I should have spent it on two weeks in Florida and let the council take his body.

I saw Dad again in the funeral directors before the cremation. He looked so different from the skeleton in the hospital. The morticians had performed their magic, turning this empty husk into the man I remembered, the original Dad. He appeared almost peaceful.

About ten people have turned up at the crematorium, more than Aria and I joked about all those years ago. Andrew, Paul, and I make up three of the crowd. The rest consist of his drinking buddies who saw the obituary in the paper and some family. Mum is a notable absentee; she insists her appearance would have been hypocritical.

My uncle Norman grabs me on the way in. The resemblance to his brother is unnerving.

'Hi, Dean. Sorry we had to meet again under such sad circumstances.'

I haven't seen my dad's only surviving sibling in a long time. I wonder how much he knows about what happened, about everything.

'Errmm... yeah, thanks for coming,' is all I can think to say.

'Bobby, he... he had some problems, but there was goodness in him. He called me a few times, you know, after you and your mum... left.'

Norman doesn't know about Dad graphically accusing him of sleeping with my mother. I doubt he'd have praised his goodness if he did.

'Hmmm...,' I grunt.

'Listen, let's get together after this and have a chat about things.'

'Sure,' I say. I'd rather extract my teeth with rusty pliers.

I met the funeral celebrant yesterday to run through the service. Trying to give insight into my dad and his past without revealing his real character wasn't easy. It involved a lot of talk about his days as a theatrical agent, Spain, and how he 'wasn't perfect,' which is quite the understatement.

A section of the humanist's eulogy arrives that I didn't expect: 'But maybe if Bob got the help he needed, things could have been different.' There's an urge to jump up and explain that we *tried* to get him the help he needed, on numerous fucking occasions, each one resulting in a night-long beating for my mum for trying to 'have him put away.'

The glossed-over recounting of Dad's life ends just before the coffin starts trundling down the conveyor belt towards the incinerator. Madonna's 'Oh Father,' one of her less popular songs, blasts through tinny speakers that distort the words. I felt it was an appropriate choice.

'You can't hurt me now,

I got away from you. I never thought I would.

You can't make me cry. You once had the power,'
sings the queen of pop.

The oak casket disappears behind a massive curtain. I used to hope that Dad would burn in hell, but I find myself praying he finds the peace in death that he couldn't achieve in life. My eyes stay dry throughout, the emotionlessness evident to the few attendees.

'Bye, Dad,' I whisper before leaving with my friends, purposely avoiding Norman on the way out. We go straight to the town, where I drink so much that they carry me out of a bar before 11 pm.

June 22, 2006

Although I picked up Dad's house keys from the hospital when I first saw his body, I've left it until now before visiting my former home. I kept telling myself it would be better to get the funeral out of the way first – deal with one thing at a time. In reality, the thought of going back fills me with dread. Nevertheless, if we're going to sell it, the place needs to look habitable

I persuaded Mum to let me go alone, at least this first time. Pulling into my old spot, I climb out into the hot summer's day and recall the hours spent in this little parking lot. How many cigarettes did I get through waiting for that living room light to go off, I wonder?

The garden's not too bad. A bit overgrown, though far from the Amazon-like nightmare I expected. An empty bin stands in the corner. The sight of it still makes me feel sick.

The front door jams halfway open, forcing me to squeeze through the gap to discover a massive pile of letters blocking it. Some have 'URGENT' or 'FINAL WARNING' on the outside; I must have inherited my own terrible financial acumen from him. That's when the smell registers, a wet dog mixed with rotting food and excrement stench that seems to cling to the inside of my nostrils.

Despite the sunshine outside, the closed curtains ensure it's dark and dingy beyond where the light from the open-door ends. Hitting the hallway switch reveals the smell's origin. If I thought the home was in a state of disrepair last time, this is a whole other level.

The carpet is saturated, the earliest letters absorbing some of its liquid. Puddles identify the water's source as the downstairs bathroom. I gingerly poke my head around the corner, discovering an overflowing toilet bowl. It's been blocked with tissues, some bearing signs of bog roll replacement. Why did he keep flushing? Was this an attempt to destroy the house, a final fuck you to Mum, or had his mind deteriorated to the point where it seemed normal?

Entering the kitchen brings an involuntary gag. It looks like something from a TV documentary about slums. The sink must have every piece of cutlery he owned packed inside and stacked precariously high like a Tom and Jerry cartoon. They're almost black from where the stuck-on food has started to go bad. The tower sits in stagnant brown water that's pumping a smell across the room. I imagine it's akin to a decomposing carcass that's started to liquefy, the odour of fleshy decay and sour dampness. Bits of food are strewn across the workbenches and floor; insects scuttle everywhere; a slice of bread lying on the counter is so mouldy that it could be harbouring new life. It would have taken a lot longer than the four weeks Dad was gone to make a mess of this proportion.

A small electric fire and a duvet sit in the centre of the living room. I'd heard that failing kidneys result in feeling constantly cold, and no matter hard they try, people with the condition can't warm themselves. There's a large urine stain nearby. Whether it was made accidentally or on purpose, I'll never know.

The rest of the house is no different: food, dirty clothes, general rubbish, and dampness everywhere. I've left my old room until last. Grabbing the handle, I envision the inside as it was before, an oasis of cleanliness in a desert of filth. But no. If Dad had ever kept it clean in the hope of my return a second time, he'd given up a while ago. It wasn't as bad as the other rooms, but there were layers of dust everywhere, a carpet that hasn't been hoovered in what looks like years, and the same smell of wetness. Blankets are rolled into in a ball in the middle of the bed like he'd stop changing them halfway through the process. The sight brings an overwhelming sense of sadness, memories of all the times I spoke to Aria, my imaginary Angel. How I still miss her.

September 16, 2006

It's taken weeks of repairs, red tape, solicitors, and lawyers, but the house finally sold today. Mum never did visit.

The first couple who viewed it got a shock when they discovered the place flooded for a second time, the result of a burst water pipe. The explosion happened in the few days between me finishing renovations and their visit, so I had no idea the replacement carpets were sodden. Despite nobody knowing what had happened, the prospective buyers felt the need to make an official complaint about a house in such a condition. 'Twats,' I thought to myself when informed of the pair's decision.

Thankfully, after more repairs and yet another new section of carpet, the house was purchased by a letting company. The firm's ability to pay in one go, thereby pushing through a faster sale, was worth the lower selling price.

November 14, 2006

After the bank took its share and some of Dad's outstanding debts were settled, Mum and I walked away with around £12,000 each from the house sale. Not a life-changing amount, especially once I pay off my monstrous credit card bills, but enough to quit the data entry job I despise and live off the rest until something less awful comes along. In the exit interview, I mention my line manager's apathy toward Dad's death.

'I don't even think Jamie believed he'd died,' I tell the shocked HR manager. 'He even asked if I was coming into work on the same day I found out!'

I walk out of the building for the last time after four years of mind-numbing, soul-crushing work, swearing never to end up in a similar job ever again, no matter what. Determined that this will be another turning point in my life, I go home, throw the remaining fluoxetine in the bin and promise to join a new gym.

CHAPTER THIRTEEN

JEALOUSY

February 14, 2007

Three months of failing to find a new job have me questioning whether I've made yet another rash decision. One thing is for certain, though, it's been less stressful – no forcing myself to endure indistinguishable workdays. I also get to stay up late, hit the gym every day, and still have enough money left to get plastered on weekends and, sometimes, weekdays.

Quitting the antidepressants was hard. The numbness they brought during years of use started to subside, occasionally replaced by painful emotions. I fought back by focusing on the positives: I've never been fitter, spend more time happy than depressed, and my confidence is growing. What doesn't help is being jobless and single; Valentine's Day is always a painful reminder of the latter.

March 10, 2007

I've never had the confidence to ask out a girl since my disastrous attempt to speak to Michelle back at uni. Not counting a couple of short-term flings, Emma has been my only real relationship – a tragic statistic for a 28-year-old – and that evolved organically from a close, long-term friendship.

Paul, Andrew, and his girlfriend, Ren, have invited me to a night in town. Not one to say no to a drink, I give my head its now thrice-weekly shave before slapping on some new aftershave Mum gave me. I've never heard of the brand, and it smells like patchouli mixed with a hint of diesel.

The evening follows the usual routine, starting with drinks at Andrew and Ren's plush new home. Their place is gorgeous but serves as another reminder of my own tragic living situation. We then hit several pubs before arriving at the club. It's your typical loud and packed venue, one of the few still using those UV lights that make your teeth look blindingly white.

The several previous hours of pissing away what little money is left from the house sale has left me at the perfect point of drunkenness, not so pissed that I'm unaware of what I'm doing but drunk enough that my inhibitions have disappeared. I feel amazing. This apex of boozing is challenging to maintain. While I crave alcohol to enhance the sensation, a couple more drinks will move me into the lost zone where I fail to make any new memories, and the often horrible and embarrassing things I do are beyond my control. I never *want* to end up in this state, yet it's the inevitable conclusion of every drinking session.

For some strange reason, people in the club seem to be checking me out as I lead my friends through the doors and toward the bar. My temporary, alcohol-induced self-confidence is convincing me that the gym must be paying off. Even the barmaid smirks when I order a double vodka and red bull, while Paul, Andrew, and Ren struggle to get served at different sections of the counter.

'Excuse me,' I hear a female voice shout from behind, barely audible over the sound of Justin Timberlake's SexyBack.

I turn round to face the most stunning girl I've ever seen: a mass of curly hair sitting atop a tanned, perfectly symmetrical face; the low-slung bell-bottom jeans and crop top showing off a belly button piercing and tattoos on an athlete's body. Someone like this would typically cause me to freeze in terror. Thank God the various spirits in my system stop me from turning into a cartoon character.

'Hi,' I yell.

She puts both hands on my shoulders and leans in, placing her mouth next to my ear. My heart flutters when our cheeks touch.

'You're glowing,' she whispers.

I'm confused by a compliment usually reserved for pregnant women. Is this some form of flirting?

'Errmmm… thanks?' I emphasise the confusion in my voice.

'No, no. You're literally glowing. Like, something on your face is making it glow. I think it must be the lights in here.'

I slowly lean back, my drunken mind trying to fit the pieces together; all the people looking at me, the smirks, the lights, 'literally glowing.' Oh, Jesus.

The aftershave.

In a scenario that could have come straight from a 1980s sitcom, it turns out that my aftershave was of the budget variety due to its unique feature of glowing a luminous blue/green colour under UV lights. I'm now standing at the bar with what looks like children's glow-in-the-dark face paint covering my cheeks and neck. A sense of panic comes over me. Should I run out of the door? Try to get to the toilets and wipe it off without anyone noticing? Collapse into a shivering puddle on the floor and hope the earth swallows me? Worst of all, the gorgeous girl who informed me I look like one of the Village People is still here, waiting for a response. She's not stopped smiling, which I take as a good sign. Maybe I could pretend it's intentional, a bit of laugh. No, I don't want to come across even worse than I must already appear.

'Errmmm... I...,' I mumble, failing to hide my painful embarrassment.

'Haha, that's what you get for buying cheap aftershave,' she says before opening her bag and rummaging through it. 'Which, by the way, makes you smell like my grandad.'

I resist telling her it was a gift from my mother, with whom I live.

'Here, you never know when these will come in handy.'

She pulls a tiny pack of wet wipes from her bag. Before I can even say thanks, she removes one and rubs it around my face. I'm shocked by her forwardness and that she's doing this to a stranger. Maybe I should have worn comically defective toiletries on previous nights out. I say nothing as she moves her hand around. Her face, full of concentration, is almost touching mine as she removes my shame. She's so gorgeous that I wonder if her eyesight is okay, or could this all come from a place of pity? Does she think I'm out with my carer?

'God, thank you so much. I think I'd have run home if you hadn't been here.'

'You're welcome, though a thank-you drink would be appreciated.'

'Of course. It's the least I could do.'

'Hmm… we'll see,' she says with a smile that makes my knees go weak.

'I'm Dean,' I say, and without stuttering, surprisingly.

'Nice to meet you, Dean. I'm Justine.'

March 21, 2007

I met up with Justine after my night wearing clown makeup thanks to a combination of drunken gusto and an ability to make her laugh. We've been officially together just over a week now. She doesn't even care that I'm jobless and live with Mum.

April 23, 2007

I've seen Justine every single day in the three months since she wiped my face clean in that club. We've tried on more than one occasion to take at least a day-long break from each other's company but relent every time, agreeing to get together after just a few hours apart. She has quickly become an extension of me. I sometimes feel like a smitten teenager, unable to breathe when she's not around. It's the first time I've known the kind of love you hear described in songs and poems. It's as if nothing in the world other than her exists or matters. I've never, ever felt happier. Life would be perfect were it not for my self-destructiveness.

June 23, 2007

Being with a girl like Justine is a new experience for me. Not only is she breathtakingly beautiful, but she's also a party girl, flirtatious, and – something I never realised when we met –eight years my junior. The chasmic difference between our attractiveness levels and that near-decade age gap has caused more than one person to assume she's my sister. I'm sure people look at us and imagine I must "have money", which couldn't be further from the truth.

Justine's personality is one of the many reasons I love her so much, but it also worsens my insecurities. I hate myself for wondering what she's doing when I'm not there, who that late-night text was from, the way she talks about her 'wildcat' past and how I've 'calmed her down.' It plays into my long-held fear that the older I get, the more I'm turning into Dad. Maybe suppressed feelings of jealousy and low self-esteem were the seeds that sprouted into his violence and madness. No, I'm better than this; I'm better than him.

Tonight is Justine's best friend's birthday. We're all supposed to be going on a big night out in the nearby city to celebrate. Unfortunately, what little money I have left is almost gone, so an expensive drinking session is a luxury I can ill afford right now. I insist Justine goes and has a good time without me.

I spend the evening trying to drown out uncontrolled thoughts by jumping between the TV and computer. It's not helping. Paranoia keeps seeping through the cracks, whispering in my ear: why is she even with me? What if she meets someone her age who's also a ten? When will I get dumped?

A text arrives from Justine at about 8 o'clock. Judging by the spelling mistakes and missing words, she's already pretty drunk just two hours after getting on the bus – not that I'd be any different. Reading it makes my heart sink.

'Hya it me. Jst wantd u 2 know Jon is here. Never knew wud b. Didnt want u to hear from sum1 else n think I was trying 2 hide it. Luv u xx,' the message reads.

Another surprising fact about Justine is that she was engaged at 17, moving in with this Jon. Like me, he's a good deal older than her. She left after realising that being tied down so young wasn't a fun life. The split devastated him, and her constant mention of his name makes me wonder if she doesn't also regret the decision.

'Okay,' is all I write back. The coldness suggesting it's Justine's fault, as if she knew he'd be there.

Maybe she did know. Fuck. I need to stop imagining these things. I should text back, tell her to have a good night, or at least a 'love you' in return.

'U OK? :/,' comes the next message.

'I'm good,' I reply, not thinking about what I'm writing until it's on the screen. 'Just watch out for him lol Have a good night. Love you 2 xxx.'

I hit send and instantly regret it.

'OK Going 2 stay at Claires tonite & get bus back in morn. Save money on taxi.'

A wave of heat spreads across the back of my neck.

'Ok, gud idea,' I reply, crushing each key of my phone to the point of near destruction.

I sit motionless for two minutes.

'She didn't plan this. She didn't plan this,' I keep repeating.

Claire, her long-time friend and the birthday girl, had remained close to Jon after Justine ditched him, so it's natural he'd be there. And my girlfriend *asked* me to come. Yeah, I'm being stupid – a paranoid lunatic.

Unless…

What if she *knew* I'd say no. It's no secret I'm almost totally broke. What better alibi than to say, 'but I asked if you wanted to come'? My suspicion starts turning to sadness. I would rather she dumped me than cheated on me. How could she do this? I've never loved anyone the way I love her. I've never loved anyone. No… I'm… it's crazy.

June 24, 2007

No more texts arrived yesterday. I never slept at all, an entire eight hours lying wide awake as my mind raced through every single conceivable scenario.

It's 7 am. Justine will know something's wrong if I text this early on a Sunday. I just wish she were here with me right now. I know what I'm doing, exhibiting the same possessiveness, jealousy, and lack of trust that made me hate Dad so much. God, why didn't she text me? Too busy with Jon, no doubt. Jesus, stop it! Where are you, Aria? You always said I wouldn't be like him. How could you be so wrong?

Justine finally texts at 10 am.

'On bus back now. Was fab nite. U Ok? Xxx'

Just the mention of last night makes me shudder.

'Good thnx,' I lie.

Justine arrives at mine after she's 'caught up on her sleep.' The wait for her arrival felt as long as the hours I spent awake in bed.

'Hey. Good night?' I ask.

'Aye, it was mint. Claire got soooo pissed. Honestly, it was hilarious.'

She looks so happy. How could anyone act this way after cheating on their partner the night before? It's ridiculous to think such a thing.

'That's great, wish I could have been there.'

'Aww… me too. You would have loved it.'

'So, was it just you and Claire who went back to hers?' I try to make the question sound as innocent as possible, removing any hint of accusatory tones.

'Eh? Of course. Why do you ask?'

'I just wondered if any of your mates went back with you, that's all, thought she might have had an after-club party or something.'

She looks at me for a couple of seconds. I feel as transparent as a piece of glass.

'For fuck's sake. I knew I should have kept quiet,' she says, a mix of anger and disappointment in her voice.

'What? What are you talking about?'

'Do you think I'm stupid, Dean? Your texts last night, you said to watch out for him, remember? And now you want to know if we all went back for a party. So, what then? Do you think I fucked Jon?'

Hearing those words feels like a punch to the heart.

'Justine. I… I didn't mean….'

'Dean…,' she sighs while looking away.

'I'm… I'm sorry.'

'How often are we going to end up here? I honestly thought you'd appreciate me telling you. Can you imagine how you'd feel if I'd said nowt then you found out he was there? You'd be like, 'Why didn't you tell me? Did you fuck him?' So, I do tell you, and you still go on like… this.'

I can't argue with that logic. Jon being there was always going to be a no-win situation for her.

'Dean, you know how much I love you, but I hate this side. Always asking about my texts, where I was, what I've been doing. You know, I don't like telling you anything in case you get upset. It's not a nice way to live.'

'Justine, please… It's just that I've never been with someone like you. You make me feel happy. I don't think I know how to deal with it. I've never loved anyone the way I love you. I can change.'

'I love you, too, and that's the only reason I'm still here. But I need some time to think about things, okay?'

It's hard to understand the term heartbreak without experiencing it. The actual physical pain of losing someone you love so deeply is akin to your most vital organ ripping in two. A feeling made all the worse when it's your fault alone. She was the best thing to ever happen to me, and I've ruined it. Maybe it's for the best. She deserves better.

'…okay,' I say. If there's one thing I know from my time with Justine, it's that there's no changing her mind when she's made a decision.

'Look, Dean, this isn't goodbye, okay. I just need a while to decide what's best for both of us. And I think you need to do the same thing.'

We hug.

'I'll call you, okay,' she says.

My emotions pour out only after she's gone. Was I so awful to her? I knew there'd been times when I was suspicious, but it wasn't as if I'd ever raised my voice. Perhaps, in time, I would have screamed at her, directly accused her of sleeping around, done something worse. Are we destined to become our fathers, no matter how hard we try to avoid it?

I know what I must do.

June 25, 2007.

'Hello, Jameson and Son's funeral directors. How can I help?' the voice at the end of the phone sounds as sombre as one would expect from someone in the profession.

'Hi, I'm ringing to enquire about my dad. His ashes have been with you for a long time – picking them up was just too difficult,' I explain, not lying, though not being totally honest, either. I just didn't want anything more to do with him. 'But I just wondered if I could get them now, assuming they're still there.'

'I'll just have a look for you. What's the deceased's name?'

'It's Graham, Robert Graham.'

'I'll just check the computer… Ah yes. Well, I'm pleased to say that you're a very lucky man, Mr Graham. It's our policy to dispose of ashes that haven't been collected after 52 weeks. It's happened a few times – some families find it's too hard. Your father's remains were due to be taken away tomorrow, if you can believe that.'

'Wow, that… that does seem like fate, doesn't it?'

'It certainly does. Will you be collecting them today? I can hold onto them for the week if required.'

'I'll be down in the next hour, thanks.'

One day. One more day and he'd have been gone forever. It's hard to believe it wasn't destiny.

The reception area of the funeral home is tiny and has the same calming aesthetic favoured by dentists: landscapes adorn the white walls; a small fish tank sits in the corner. A man in his 50s stands behind the desk. He's obviously spent years practising how to smile without it looking like an expression of happiness.

'Hello, can I help?' he asks.

'Hi, I'm here to pick up my dad... errr... his ashes. His name is Robert Graham.'

I wonder if I should have used the past tense. That *was* his name. My knowledge of movies and TV tells me that people get referenced in these situations as if they're still alive.

'Ah, yes. From earlier. If you'd just like to take a seat, I'll retrieve him.'

I think my lack of experience around death is showing. My Dad's mother was the only one of my grandparents alive when I was born, and I don't even remember her. I wonder what Dad's father was like. It wouldn't surprise me if he had mental problems as well.

A family walks in while I'm waiting. It's two young kids – a boy and a girl – and their mum and dad. I imagine it's one of the mother's parents who's passed away, judging

274

by her crying. They're all dressed very smartly. It makes me feel self-conscious in my old hoody and baseball cap. The kids look positively bored.

'I'll be with you in just a second,' the funeral director tells them as he walks in carrying the off-bronze urn. The sight sends an icy shiver down my spine.

'Here you go, Mr Graham. Thank you for using our services.'

He holds the ashes at arm's length. All I can think is not to freak out and embarrass myself. Moving my hands up slowly, I clutch the cold, smooth container. It feels as if I'm holding a stick of plutonium. Its invisible radiation blasting through my cells, killing me.

'Thank you,' I reply, a feeling of shame stopping me from making eye contact.

The walk back to the car takes forever. I can't shake the feeling that I'm going to re-enact so many comedies by dropping Dad's ashes, watching as they blow into the road and cover passing cars' windscreens. But we, I, make it back safely. Placing the urn upright in the passenger seat, I wrap the seatbelt around it.

'Well, Dad, sorry you've spent the last year sitting on a dusty shelf in a funeral home. But hey, it could be worse; one more day, and they'd have poured you down the drain, haha. Might have been a fitting end for you, given everything.'

I take a deep breath in, letting the air slowly escape my mouth.

'Nah, sorry. I saw the state of the house – looks like you got your just desserts. Fucking hell, I don't know. I wish… I wish you could have just admitted to it. Said you were sorry, you know? Not blamed it all on Mum. I'm still not sure if I remember… everything.'

I look out the window and see the same family from the funeral home walking past, husband and wife holding hands, kids skipping.

'Hey, you might be pleased to know I've taken after you,' I continue. 'The most amazing girl in the world has left me because I'm a jealous, possessive, paranoid arsehole. Who does that sound like, eh? Maybe that's why Aria left as well.'

My efforts to stay off cigarettes have gone from bad to terrible. I was already struggling to stop lighting up, and I've gone through an entire pack in the near 24 hours since Justine left. Any relapsed smoker will tell you the same thing: you smoke even more when restarting the habit. It's like your body missed them so much that the pleasure and cravings are intensified once nicotine is reintroduced to the system. I light up a Regal King Size and take a long draw, letting the poison fill my lungs.

'I'm blaming you for this as well, you twat,' I tell the urn, waving the ciggy in front of it. 'Remember when you used to get through a hundred a day in the house? Or when you'd sit on the edge of my bed and smoke God knows how many? Bet I was addicted before I even started tabs.'

I take another long drag. 'Look, Dad, I don't know if you can hear me or if I'm just sitting here talking to some ash, but I just wanted to say… I wish things could have been different. Remember what you were like before that night in Spain? When you nearly knocked out that old bastard neighbour we had because he grabbed my hair? I wish you could have just stayed that way. Mum says something broke inside you when grandma died, that you couldn't be fixed. So, I'm going to do something for you, for both of us, really. I just hope it'll make a difference.'

Finding out where Dad's mother is buried wasn't easy. I didn't want Mum to know what I was doing, so it involved some subtle, innocent questioning about grandma Graham's resting place. She's local to the area, meaning the drive isn't too lengthy. It's pretty small as cemeteries go, so I won't spend hours walking around trying to find the grave.

My initial optimism that this wouldn't take ages has proved naïve – how tightly do they pack these plots? If this trip has taught me anything, it's that there are few things more depressing than looking at gravestones. The ones with photos of people who passed far too young are the worst. Some are kids – teenagers or younger. 'Loving son, beloved daughter,' they read. Then I see it: a small, faded stone, the text so weather-beaten that it's hard to read.

Mary Graham

Beloved mother to Robert, Norman, and Raymond. Wife of William Graham

Born: February 3, 1909

Died: August 5, 1988

Seeing the last date fills me with sadness. August 5, 1988, the same day I died. The person I was, the potential for me to become someone better, happier, a normal human being. All wiped away.

'Hi, nana. Sorry, I've not visited for, well, ever. It's funny; even though I don't remember you being alive, I'm the way I am now because of you. Your Robert, he... he didn't take your demise too well. Now, don't get me wrong, I love my mum, too. But I'd like to think her death won't turn me into a full-blown fucking schizophrenic.'

I light up another cigarette.

'Yeah, it's not like any of this was your fault. I'm sure you didn't *want* to die or for your son to be so…,' I trail off.

'Maybe your husband was an abusive prick as well? Anyway, Bob obviously loved you to bits. I'm pretty sure he loved me as well, despite actions to the contrary. Maybe this will draw a line under everything. I can't go on living this way, in the shadow of my past. Wishing things had been different. It's like the fear of becoming Dad is turning me into him. I need… I need to let go.'

Dropping to my knees, I'm grateful the muddy ground's softness makes it easy to scoop up clumps of earth. It doesn't take long to create a shallow, bowl-shaped hole in the plot.

'Your turn, Bob.'

The urn's lid feels stuck. I should have expected this after it sat undisturbed for so long. What an anti-climax – unless I dig even deeper and bury the entire thing. I let out a roar, giving the top a massive twist. It finally pops, and without the contents pouring all over me.

'I'll say goodbye again then, Dad, properly this time. I promise not to blame you anymore, to stop thinking about you, no more wondering about what really happened. I think it's what we both want.'

His ashes come pouring out like water, spilling into the makeshift grave. All I can think is how fine they are, like sand. I break down. It's the last time he'll ever be responsible for my tears. Sadness crushes me as all the memories, the bad and the few good, hit at once. The last few grains tumble out, leaving me with an empty, useless container.

CHAPTER FOURTEEN

THE DANGEROUS WORLD OF RETAIL

March 17, 2014

A lot has happened in the last six and half years. Justine and I got back together after she agreed to give me one more chance. We then did something crazy: moving in together and opening a dog grooming salon in the middle of the worst economic downturn the world had seen since the great depression. It was very successful, but living and working together, especially when there's just the two of you, puts a strain on even the strongest relationship.

While the parts of me I hated so much were buried with Dad, I still struggled with relationships, and there's no doubt being with me 24 hours every day couldn't have been easy. It led to us separating four years after opening the business. It couldn't have been more amicable. We even continued working together in the salon after splitting up. Things were fine for a while, though finding prospective new partners who were okay with our strange arrangement wasn't easy. I eventually left, Justine's new boyfriend taking my place.

I'm now 35, unemployed, and back living with my mum. It's like it's 2007 all over again. Anyone self-employed for a long time will know the difficulty that comes with finding a new job once working for yourself ends.

I used to bathe the dogs and handle the business side of the salon while Justine groomed the animals. Given the scarcity and minimum-wage salaries of dog-bathing positions, a change of career is in order. Out of desperation, I applied to a nationwide retail store/chemist for a van driver and merchandiser position. I'm sure my previous shelf-stacking experience will help, and while I've never been behind the wheel of anything bigger than a car, I assume a van won't be too different. An interview followed soon afterwards, and thanks to me being the candidate with the best customer service skills, today's my first day. Sure, I'm starting an entry-level job, but this could be a fresh start. By the time I'm forty, I might be running the store – or, more likely, still driving the van.

Meeting your future workmates is always a nerve-wracking experience. You want to come across friendly and eager without looking false or manically enthusiastic.

'Dean, this is Gina,' my supervisor tells me. 'She'll be showing you the ropes, so just do what she says. And don't let that tough exterior scare you. She's a softy, really.'

Gina is in her early 50s with a short blonde mop of hair. Skinny and only about 5-foot tall, there are a considerable number of wrinkle lines surrounding her mouth. I've only ever seen them on much older women who've smoked since they were old enough to hold a match. It reminds me what a good decision quitting was; they make her oral area look like a cat's bum. Fittingly, her breath smells like an untreated long-term mouth infection. I shouldn't judge on appearance – Christ, I'm far from an oil painting. She could be a lovely woman. I hold out my hand.

'Hi, Gina. Nice to meet you,' I say.

Gina's arms remain folded.

'Look, son, I've got two rules: I'm not your mother, and I don't suffer fools gladly,' comes the scowling response.

March 18, 2014

Following yesterday's arduous induction with some other new starters, I get to see the van I'll be driving today. My expectation of something resembling a long car turns out to be wishful thinking: it's enormous; a 3.5-ton 'Luton' van with a mechanical lift at the rear. It resembles a slightly smaller version of a lorry. Don't I need a special license for one of these? I suddenly regret my hubris in the interview when asked about my driving skills.

'Hope you can manage this. We had one new lad come in, looked at the van, quit on the spot,' Gina tells me, failing to hide her glee.

'I'll do my best.'

'Aye, we'll see if that's good enough.'

My first assignment is to drive a load of cages and pallets to the shop in town. Gina runs through how to operate the tail lift with such speed and lack of clarity that I wonder if she's doing it on purpose. Already scared of her, I'm too nervous to ask for a repeat of the instructions; this turned out to be another poor decision. Gina tells me I'll be doing this first task alone because she's busy.

The two-mile journey is terrifying, but I somehow make it to the loading bay intact. The rear entrance where staff bring in stock is a 5ft x 8ft rectangular hole in the store's back wall. It's positioned about four feet above the road, with a small lip jutting out the bottom for the tail lift to rest.

I manage to back up to the right spot without reversing through the building before jumping out to inspect the controls. It takes a few minutes to recall Gina's instructions on unlocking and raising the vehicle's sliding door, but I eventually figure it out. The sturdy tail lift moves from a vertical to a horizontal position, and I drag three 5-foot-high metal cages, all packed with stock, onto the van's metal platform, being extra careful not to let them fall off the edge. Now it just needs lowering to the point where it's flush with the entrance.

'Errrmm… so I hold this button down?' I speak the question aloud, hoping that doing so will somehow avert disaster. Gina said the red button lowers the platform, possibly. I press it down and the device springs into life, descending at a slow pace.

'Piece of piss.'

I release the button once level with the entrance, my newfound confidence disappearing as we continue to drop. Now caught on the large lip, the platform starts tilting diagonally, an orientation it wasn't designed for. The mechanism screams in protest as metal drags across brick. SHIT!

The downward force being applied to the van's rear is lifting its front wheels off the ground. I slam and poke and plead at the different buttons, but the heavy cages slowly roll toward me, leaving the choices of certain death or jumping out the way and dying of shame later.

'FOOOOOOK!' I howl while flying through the air, thankful to be in an enclosed parking lot.

The deafening noise is drawing gawkers from a nearby high street. Somehow, one side of the tail lift is still dropping while the other remains stuck on the lip. It's almost at a 45-degree angle. The cages have become trapped between the van and the platform. It's like watching a train hurtling towards another train; you know that the impending carnage is going to be horrific but can't look away.

The tail lift sounds like a high-speed car crash when it finally snaps, the heavy cages' smashing down into the tarmac below. Their metal gates fly open on impact, emptying the contents like spilt guts. Shampoos and other liquids come spilling out. Boxes tumble everywhere, sending deodorant bottles rolling toward the gathered crowd. It doesn't surprise me to see some opportunists pocket the items before casually walking off.

'OH MY GOD! WHAT HAPPENED?'

My interviewer, the same woman who decided a few days ago that I was the best candidate, stands at the back door, surveying the carnage while doubtlessly regretting her decision to offer me the job.

'I... I didn't know how to stop the tail lift,' I tell her, still lying on the ground.

'Are you okay?'

'Yeah, I'm okay, I think.'

That's slightly untrue as the shame and embarrassment are causing substantial physical pain. A few people in the crowd are doing a slow clap. As second days on the job go, this wasn't one of the best.

April 21, 2014

As hard as it is to believe, causing thousands of pounds worth of damage during my first week didn't get me fired. The bosses were far from happy, of course, and there was an inquiry, but I'm pretty sure the company feared any legal repercussions. The inadequate training and being left to operate the machinery solo didn't reflect well on the firm; I could have been injured or worse. But one serious consequence I'm experiencing is Gina. She made it clear from the offset that making friends with new co-workers wasn't a high priority, and any suggestion that her instructions were less than perfect hasn't gone down well.

'Next time I tell you how to do something, you're not going to fuck it up again, are you?' were the first words she snarled upon seeing me after the incident.

'No... I'll make sure to understand everything. I'm really sorry,' I replied.

'Make sure you do. I don't fancy getting blamed for your stupidity.'

I've since become used to this sort of passive-aggressiveness from her, though it's not so much passive as just aggressive. I've been called names, given demeaning work, laughed at, berated, and more. Gina once made me clean the warehouse toilets because there 'was nothing else to do.' Not wanting to piss her off even more or risk losing my job, I spent two hours wiping porcelain. Washing shit off a labradoodle's arse would be a blessing right now.

I've lost count of the number of times I've apologised to Gina during my five weeks here. I repeatedly emphasized during the investigation into my disaster that she wasn't to blame. Plenty of lies were told: there was nothing wrong with her training, the length of time she spent going over it was adequate, etc. But her absence from the van was a punishable offence.

There's just the two of us in the warehouse where we spend around seven hours of an eight-hour day. Gina talks to me only when barking orders or saying something degrading; her talent for making me feel bad is exceptional. The only time I hear her speak more than a few sentences is while using the work phone to talk to friends.

'Aye, he's here somewhere. Hope he's not smashing the place up again, the stupid twat. Honestly, I think they must have hired him on a bet, haha,' she once told someone at a volume loud enough for me to hear. I've mentioned her behaviour to other staff members, their responses varying from 'it's just the way she is' to 'then do something about it? She's just a little woman.'

Slumping onto my couch after another gruelling day, I decide there's no way I can keep enduring this crap. But what other choices are there? No degree, few skills, and little experience at my age isn't an attractive combination for potential employers. I lament my lack of good looks. Had I only been taller, better looking, less bald, and with better skin, perhaps prostitution or webcam work would have been an easier alternative?

Clicking through job websites is a depressing pastime comparable to choosing one's burial site. I jump between admin jobs, factory work, retail, and warehousing, knowing that whatever I pick will be a replica of what I currently have: a shit, menial job with piss-poor pay. At least Gina won't be there.

After a very miserable 45 minutes of browsing, I expand my horizons by selecting the 'show all' option. Interesting – could my future lie as a 'flood defence advisor?'

Maybe a dental nurse isn't that bad. Or how about a school crossing guard? Then I see it: video game reviewer. I always loved writing at school – English was my favourite subject – but my affinity for technology pushed me in another direction. Gaming remains an obsession even as I age. Once, during an icebreaker session at my old data entry job, we were asked to name the best moments of our life. Considering 'leaving my dad' too controversial, my highlight was 'completing a vampire role-playing game.' I still remember the look of pity from the guy who'd been moved to tears while describing his son's birth.

My heart sinks when I see the job is 'unpaid but offers great experience.' It's a shame that experience isn't accepted as currency when buying food and paying bills. I'm about to skip onto the next position when I have a rethink; thanks to being broke and single, my evenings are spent alone on either a PC or console, so at least I'd be doing something productive and bettering myself. Who knows, maybe it could lead to something else.

November 7, 2014

Considering how long I've been using the internet, the amount of abuse aimed at me since being published shouldn't have come as a surprise. I'm now in the position where I get called a twat at work and a cunt online. But I love writing and those occasions where random strangers say they liked my work or found it funny outweigh the misery of receiving death threats. It took only a few weeks before a larger gaming site invited me to produce content for their readers. It's still unpaid, but the audience is bigger and the setup more professional.

After about three months of writing for this new site, something happened that would set me down a path I could never have imagined. An article I wrote went viral, reaching a few hundred thousand people, one of whom happened to own a popular YouTube gaming channel. I was offered a job as a scriptwriter, and they were willing to pay! While it meant being at the keyboard ten hours per day earning less per hour than my current shitty occupation, I didn't care.

I wanted to tell Gina what I thought of her when my last day arrived, how her incessant barrage of abuse and bullying made my life a constant hell. But face-to-face confrontation isn't my style; instead, I pissed in her favourite cup while she was out of the warehouse, making sure to soak up the excess with a tissue before replacing it in the cupboard, ready for her next coffee.

The first time I heard a voice-over artist speaking my words on one of the UK's ten most popular YouTube channels was joyous. Previously, the extent of my ambition stretched no higher than having a job – any job – and a roof over my head. Dad's constant jibes about becoming a street sweeper leaving an indelible mark, convincing me I was useless and should be grateful for any employment.

I've already written about 25 video scripts and helped edit others. The work fills me with pleasure, bringing a desire to push further into this world, so I start checking industry websites for similar positions. It takes a few weeks before one sticks out: a home-based news reporter/feature writer for a big US technology site. Not only is the money more than I've ever earned in my life, but there's mention of travelling around the world to cover tech events; a prospect that would have once been terrifying now makes me salivate.

The application process is demanding, but I beat around 500 applicants to join nineteen others in the final round, which involves writing three news stories and a minor feature. Today's the day I discover if my dreams come true.

Covering part of my monitor's screen with a hand, I open the email that holds my destiny. It's a technique I've long used when reading anything that could contain good or bad news, slowly sliding my palm across the display to reveal one letter at a time.

Blah, blah, blah, 'Thank you for applying for this position,' blah, blah, blah, 'congratulations on reaching the final round of interviews....'

Everything hinges on the following letter. I want to avoid a 'U' as it would likely be the start of 'unfortunately.' My hand slows to the point where it's uncovering one individual pixel at a time.

Is it a 'U'? No, it's a 'W.' I yank my arm away.

'We're pleased to offer you the position.'

It's as if I've passed my driving test all over again. The sheer elation is overwhelming, another nail in the coffin of my past.

December 4, 2016

My thirty-eighth birthday. Finally, I'm at peace. I've twice been sent to Barcelona and Berlin to cover huge tech conferences over the last few years. I will never forget my first time in Germany's capital, watching the sunrise from the top floor of a hotel so posh that other guests likely assumed I was the cleaner. It's a moment I still call my happiest memory.

Thinking things couldn't get better, I was promoted to senior editor and met a wonderful, beautiful, kind girl called Marie. We now live together with a west highland terrier and two cats.

So, here I am, truly happy and content, no more mental anguish or talking to people who aren't there. I wish I could say this was the end of the story, that we lived happily ever after. But the worst was yet to come.

CHAPTER FIFTEEN

LIFE BEGINS AT 40

March 3, 2019

Everyone tells me the same thing: I look better at forty than I did at 18. I don't disagree with that statement; eating well, replacing alcohol with water, and returning to the gym have seen the weight fall off. The 46-inch waist once sported in my twenties now has a circumference under 30 inches. I feel great but sitting down all day and getting older means aches and pains, especially in my lower back and legs.

April 20, 2019

We've hired a cottage for a weekend in the Lake District, a place of almost unparalleled beauty. It's also perfect for dogs, which means lots of scenic walks with Buster. I notice that my feet are throbbing like hell after just an hour of hiking around hills and dales, which is a bit embarrassing, considering I'm on the treadmill so often. Buying a new pair of walking boots in the nearby village seems to help.

June 3, 2019

My age remains a surprise to most people, albeit only when a hat hides my Yul Brynner haircut. On the inside, however, I'm feeling the advancing years more and more. The age-related issue of getting up to pee in the middle of the night is becoming an increasingly common event. I'm also visiting the toilet more often during the day than ever before, doubtlessly resulting from the massive amount of water I consume, my protein shakes, and all the coffee and sugar-free energy drinks.

July 7, 2019

Being a gym addict is a funny thing – I'm constantly exercising to stay healthy but squeezing in high-intensity workouts around a job leaves me exhausted. I fall asleep within literal seconds of my head hitting the pillow at night, and I'm often still tired when waking the next day. A result of my bladder screaming at me to get up at 3 am, no doubt.

August 20, 2019

It's ironic that furniture labelled as a 'gaming chair,' designed to be sat in for hours, can be so uncomfortable.

The leather cushions on the one I reviewed for my website felt pretty good at first, but they must lose their shape after prolonged use. The only time my back, hip, and legs don't seem to hurt these days is while I'm working out, strangely, and I'm sure the chair has made things worse. It's time to splash out on an ergonomic office seat.

September 5, 2019

The worryingly expensive new chair I bought has brought little relief. I do believe that I've deduced the actual cause of my pain: the sofa. It's an electronic model that can recline almost flat with the press of a button. I remember reading that these aren't recommended for people with back pains; it certainly seems to aggravate mine. New sofas aren't cheap, and I've just spent a fortune on a new chair. But you can't put a price on your health, so they say, which is why I'm thankful for credit cards.

September 21, 2019

As much as I enjoy people commenting on my weight loss, the gym is beginning to do more harm than good, so I've decided to quit temporarily – just until I feel better. The sofa doesn't arrive until early November. In the meantime, I'm using my new office chair for watching TV. I'm also applying deep heat creams and painkillers before bed. There are few perks to ageing.

October 8, 2019

My discomfort has developed into something worse over the last few weeks. From the general kind of soreness you'd expect after physical exercise into incessant, grinding pain that can't be ignored. The burning in my lower back makes me rub my kidney areas whenever I'm moving. My left hip feels like it's been hit with a baseball bat, waves of agony radiating into my buttock. And both my thighs and quads have horrible, deep dull aches that never ease. I've decided that if things don't improve soon, I'll finally go to the doctor. I can't blame the gym anymore.

Marie and I have decided to go on a day trip to a beachside town. It's always a fun experience that involves playing arcade games, eating ice cream, and a lengthy stroll down a beachfront, activities we both enjoy. This will be our third visit and the most memorable, for all the wrong reasons.

The two-hour car journey certainly doesn't help my various ailments. I park in our usual spot once we arrive, a 40-minute walk from the main promenade.

They say there's always a moment when you realise something is very wrong with your body. When shrugging off mounting symptoms is no longer an option, and you finally accept their seriousness. For me, it's the second I get out of the car. It's not my legs, back, or hip, though they're causing the usual amount of misery; it's my feet. Standing up after the long drive sends bolts of electricity through both my soles. The pain makes me yell.

'What's the matter? Are you okay?' asks Marie.

'Fucking hell. Errmm… I don't know. I've no idea what that was. Something wrong with my feet.'

'Dean, you have to see a doctor. It might be connected to the other problems you've been getting.'

'I know, I know,' I say in a tone that doesn't disguise my regret at not taking this advice sooner. 'I'll make an appointment once we get back.'

Hopes that I might be able to walk it off prove fruitless as I hobble toward the beach, every step sending shockwaves through my feet and into my calves. The pain is exacerbated by a sensation akin to each foot being crushed in a vice.

The walk is the longest half-hour of my life. Marie suggests turning around and going home, but we've been looking forward to this trip for months, and I'm not going to ruin it. I try to convince myself that whatever's wrong will be addressed next week. I've been here before: develop weird symptoms, visit a doctor once they become unbearable, receive a simple treatment. It's called being male.

Once we arrive in town, the relief I feel is overshadowed by the onset of agony in my lower back area. It's as if my kidneys have been replaced with hot coals that are slowly melting all the surrounding tissue, the sort of pain that makes you feel like vomiting. I'm grateful whenever we play an arcade game with seating. Bowling is off the agenda as I genuinely believe it would kill me right now.

October 9, 2019

The long and painful ride back home was capped off by troubled sleep. Needing the toilet during the night started as a once-per-week inconvenience when the year began. As the months passed, it progressed to a nightly occurrence, then *occasionally* twice per night. Now, I can't remember the last time I didn't get up to pee at least twice. I broke my record with five nightly pisses yesterday. I would be concerned about my prostate if I didn't urinate like a racehorse.

Keeping my promise, I call doctors, happy to learn that an appointment is available tomorrow due to a cancellation.

Looking up potential illnesses online is never a good idea – convincing yourself you're dying is easy with Dr Google. I search for 'pains in legs and feet,' along with the latest thing I have to worry about: a bizarre tingling in my right thigh that only began this morning. A few conditions sound similar to what I have, including restless leg syndrome, vitamin deficiency, hip bursitis, a trapped nerve in the spine, spinal injury, but none seem to cover every symptom.

I read about thyroid issues and cancers, bringing a nervous sweat to my brow. I've also noticed that diabetes came up when Googling 'frequent urination,' but I find nothing about it causing extreme pain. Other signs such as urinary tract infections, blurry vision, and slow healing cuts aren't something I experience. Plus, I'm super fit. Jesus, the idea of it; I remember Dad's insulin needles. No way I could ram something like that in my stomach. I hate needles. No, it's not worth considering.

October 10, 2019

My hatred of hospitals remains as strong as my fear of seeing doctors. I view the latter as places where we're informed that a seemingly innocuous issue needs investigating further, or that 'something has shown up in a routine test.' Much sadness begins here.

'So, Mr Graham. How can I help?' asks the physician.

'Well, I've been getting these awful pains in my hips, legs, and feet for months now, and they're getting worse. I thought it was just muscular, but I stopped the gym a while ago, and they're still there. Painkillers don't seem to work at all. I've bought a new chair, new sofa, tried all sorts.'

'Hmm... my first instinct would be to blame overexertion, yes. Have you had any other symptoms?'

'A sort of tingle in my leg's just appeared.'

'It could be several things, perhaps even something as simple as vitamin deficiency. We'll need to do some blood tests.'

Vitamin deficiency. That would be great – easily curable and not serious.

'I'll ask them to check your thyroid as well.'

'Errmm… could I ask something? You don't think it could be diabetes, do you?'

'Oh, I can't imagine it would be. Diabetics only get pains like the ones you're describing after years of high glucose levels. Why do you ask?'

'Well, my dad and uncles all had type 2, so I was just worried.'

'Do you drink and urinate a lot? Get infections often? Blurry vision?.'

'I suppose I do a drink a lot of water and wee more than most, but I can't remember a time when I didn't. I don't get many infections, and my eyesight's fine.'

'Hmm… it doesn't sound like diabetes, to be honest, but I'll add it to the list for your peace of mind.'

'Thanks.'

'You can pop over to the nurse and get the bloods done now. If you like.'

Sitting outside the nurse's office is more nerve-wracking than waiting to see the doctor. My enormous coat might be suitable for this freezing day, but the heating in here is intense. Sweat dribbles down my back, making me even more aware of how thirsty I am. Nerves, probably.

My heart skips a beat when they call my name.

'I'm not good with needles,' I tell the nurse, trying to justify my saturated shirt.

'You're not the only one, love. Don't worry about it.'

I hate this process: the strap tightening around the arm, my vein fattening with each tap, mentally preparing myself for the flesh-violating needle. No wonder people have phobias of this shit.

'You'll feel a sharp scratch.'

I look away before it enters. There's minimal discomfort; it's the idea that makes me queasy. The whole thing is over in a couple of seconds.

'Right. I'm afraid that arm doesn't want to give up any blood, so we'll have to try the other one.'

Fuck.

We go through the whole rigmarole again: strap, tap, pierce vein. This time it does hurt. I wince as the needle travels even deeper.

'Ahh… you've got stubborn veins. I'm afraid nothing's coming out of that one either,' she says while removing the syringe. 'Could be that you're dehydrated. Or just too nervous.'

'I'm definitely both.'

'Right. I could try again using the back of your hand, or we can give your arms another go at a later date.'

There's no way in hell I'm having a needle put in the back of my hand. The only thing I want at this exact moment is to be out of here.

'I'll just try again later if that's okay.'

'If you're sure.'

She checks the computer.

'We need to give your arms about a week to heal. And that takes us right to when the nurses are on holiday. I'm afraid the earliest we have is October 22.

'That's fine, thanks.'

Truthfully, I don't mind suffering in pain for almost two more weeks if it gets me out of this fucking place right now. I've never needed a drink, a shower, and a piss more in my life.

October 11, 2019

Could I be diabetic? Dad smoked like a trooper for decades, loved pork, drank heavily, and never exercised a day in his life before being diagnosed in his fifties, whereas I've been using gyms on and off most of my life, eat well, and stopped binge drinking and smoking years ago. And I'm only for forty! Several symptoms do fit, including difficulty in extracting blood, but I lack many common signs. Nah, in all likelihood, it'll be something easily fixable, leaving me to wonder why I never visited a doctor sooner.

October 22, 2019

The big day. I'm grateful that my appointment isn't until 2:30 as it gives me plenty of time to prepare. I've read that being well-hydrated can help the blood flow freely, so I up my regular consumption of two litres of water per day to around four; I actually worry that I might drown. I peed about ten times before setting off to the clinic.

During the walk from the car, I notice that my legs and feet aren't feeling too bad today. I bought one of those electronic massage guns; it works remarkably well, despite looking like a vibrator. Maybe I've been a bit of a hypochondriac about all this. My biggest concern right now is whether they'll be able to extract any blood.

There's no sweat when I remove my massive coat in the nurses' room this time.

'Fingers crossed we'll get a better result,' chirps the lady.

'I hope so. I don't fancy you going through my hand.'

I look away as she puts in the needle, feeling nothing.

'There you go. All's good. We'll let you know the results next week.'

I breathe a massive sigh of relief. All the months of pain will soon be over. Now it's just a case of waiting for the results. With my mood buoyed, I decide to stop off at a café on the way home for a well-deserved coffee and piece of cake.

I'm standing in the kitchen waiting for dinner to cook when my mobile ringtone goes off at 5:55. The handset's in the living room with Marie.

'Dean, your phone's ringing. It's the doctor,' she shouts, the display revealing the caller's name.

'Ugh! I bet something's happened. They'll have lost my blood, or there's been a mix-up,' the only conceivable reasons I can think of for them ringing so quickly. I run to the upstairs bedroom for a better signal – one of the drawbacks of living in rural areas.

'Hello?.'

'Hello, is that Mr Graham?.'

'It is, yes.'

'Hello, Mr Graham. This is Doctor Pritchard. It's about your blood tests.'

Here we go. I can't believe I'm going to have to get jabbed again.

'I'm afraid your blood glucose levels are high, extremely high. A normal reading would be anywhere between around 4 and 7; yours is 48. I'm sorry to say that you have diabetes. You need to come back to the surgery right now.'

The small amount of strength it takes to hold the phone disappears. I stare at my reflection in the wall-sized mirror attached to the wardrobe, recalling the day Marie and I bought it. Sunday shopping in Ikea is a ritual many dread, but I remember the simple contentment of picking a piece of furniture for our home. There I was, finally doing everyday things like an average person. All my life, even during my time with Justine, there was a fear of what the future held, a fear that disappeared soon after meeting Marie. The first person I envisioned growing old with.

The mirror reflects the dull glow behind me. Its luminance grows, moving across the room just like that first time. I see the wings spread out as if they're attached to my own back.

'Never expected to see you again,' I say without turning around.

'Ditto. You managed pretty well on your own for a while there.'

'Yeah... I... I think that's about to change.'

'Yes, me too.'

I turn around to look at Aria. How long has it been? Fifteen years? More? Her eternal youth still surprises me.

The same angelic beauty, unchanged after three decades. Features created by my mind, frozen forever.

'Hello? Mr Graham? Hello?'

The doctor sounds quite frantic. He probably thinks I've fainted. I put the phone back to my ear.

'Hi, sorry. Will I have to inject myself?.'

The memory of Dad ramming that giant needle into his stomach is all I can think of right now.

'Well, we don't know what type it is just yet, but it's likely, I'm afraid.'

That hot sickness I haven't experienced in so long crawls from my gut into my chest.

'I'll, errmmm... I'll be straight down.'

I hang up. Aria wears that same expression I saw so many times as a kid.

'Jesus. I don't believe it. How... how can this have happened? I tried so hard to put things right. I haven't been hammered or smoked in years. I'm only forty, for fuck's sake. What did even bother going to the gym for?'

'Life isn't always fair. Think you know that better than anyone.'

'Is this some kind of ironic punishment, Aria? I left him to die, and now I've got the same disease that killed him. Do I deserve this?'

'No. Don't blame yourself. Listen to me, Dean. This is not your fault, and never, ever, think that it is.'

People rarely heed good advice. I can't help but believe that one way or another, I caused this illness. I wonder what Dad's thinking, wherever he is.

'Yeah, thanks. I missed you.'

'And I missed you, too.'

I really did miss her, despite understanding how the angel's absence reflects my level of sanity. I'm glad she's back, but the cost is too high.

Marie looks like someone about to hear bad news. The length of time I was upstairs and the look on my face don't help.

'I have diabetes,' I tell her. We hug, crying into each other's shoulders.

The drive back to the clinic was completed mostly in silence, shock keeping us from discussing what this all means. Dr Pritchard explains my results but taking anything in right now is difficult. He repeatedly mentions one term.

'Diabetic ketoacidosis. When blood glucose levels have been extremely high for a while, which appears to be the case with you, a body stops using sugar for energy and starts using fat. That causes a build-up of ketones that turns blood acidic, leading to severe complications,' he says, emphasising the word 'severe.'

I'm given a vial.

'If you can get me a urine sample, I'll check your ketone levels. We'll just take things from there.'

Filling the vial in the surgery's bathroom isn't difficult. I piss so often these days that I can do it on demand, another one of the many diabetic warning signs I refused to acknowledge. That's the thing about being in denial: you never wonder to yourself, 'am I in denial?.'

Back in the consultation room, Dr Pritchard takes the container and places it on the table. There's a tube full of what looks like little strips of paper on the desk. He takes one out and unscrews the lid on my piss pot.

'Right then. For a non-diabetic, we'd be looking at below 0.6 for normal ketone levels, but yours will be higher. We just have to hope it's not too high.'

'Okay,' I reply, not wanting to ask what constitutes too high or what it would mean.

He dips the testing stick into my bodily fluid. The end of it starts changing colour, quickly going from beige to pink to very dark purple, almost black.

'Wheeeeeeeee!,' the doctor squeals.

'Have you come down here with anyone?' he asks.

'Err... yes. My girlfriend.'

'Do you want to ask her to come in.'

I collect Marie from the waiting room, still unsure why. She fails to hold back the tears when I ask her to join us.

'Hello, Marie. Nice to meet you,' the doctor says. 'Okay, I'm afraid Dean here is in what we call diabetic ketoacidosis, or DKA for short. Ketone levels would normally be under 0.6; his is over 11. He needs to go to the hospital this instant.'

The shock nearly knocks me off my chair. I was expecting to be slowly introduced to insulin injections or something. Hospital? Ketoaci-what? What's going on?

'I won't have to be in overnight, will I?'

The doctor looks me straight in the eyes.

'Dean. I'll be honest. I have no idea how you are walking around right now. Most people in DKA are extremely sick. Do you not feel ill?'

'Well, I mean. A little ropey, but I wouldn't say I felt sick.'

'I'm not trying to scare you, but if this had gone unchecked, you would have passed out in a few weeks or sooner. At that point, the risk of diabetic coma, and possibly worse, would be high. It's lucky you asked for the diabetes test.'

My head starts to spin.

'Is this type 2, doctor? My dad and uncles all had it.'

'We can't say for certain without more tests. But to be honest, given your body shape, I'd say it's highly likely to be type 1.'

Not what I wanted to hear. Dad always said he had 'type 2 diabetes' when explaining his condition to people. I'd never even heard of the other kinds. Unlike type 2, which is usually related to lifestyle or age, it's unclear why people develop type 1, which results from the body's auto-immune system destroying insulin-producing beta cells in the pancreas. Insulin regulates blood glucose, aka blood sugar. When we don't have enough of this hormone, glucose levels rise dangerously high and can eventually cause devasting effects, including blindness, amputations, and death. There is no cure.

'We really need to get you into hospital without delay,' I'm told in a stern voice. 'I expect they'll have you in there for at least three days.'

THREE DAYS! AT LEAST! What that fuck! Coma? Death? I know I've not been well lately, but...

'Doctor, is Dean going to be okay?,' asks a tearful Marie.

'It's good that we've caught it now. Things would have been a lot worse if this had gone undiagnosed.'

He avoids answering a 'yes or no' question with the skill of a politician.

'I'd normally call an ambulance in cases like these, but seeing as you feel okay, somehow, I think it would be okay if you make your own way to hospital. I'll phone ahead and let them know you're coming.'

Marie spends the journey googling diabetic ketoacidosis on her phone. I'm not sure I should be driving in my current state, a mixture of trauma and fear. And to think, my biggest concern about being diabetic was the needles.

'Listen to all these symptoms of DKA, Dean – peeing loads, thirsty, losing weight, falling asleep all the time, short temper. You've got all of those.'

'I… I never....'

'How many ties did I tell you to go the doctors? It's not normal to go to the toilet fifteen times a day and drink four massive bottles of water. You fall asleep the second you sit down and eat like a horse but keep getting skinnier. You've been dead snappy recently, too.'

How could I have been so blind? I had an excuse for everything: drinking loads of water is something I've done for years, explaining the frequent peeing; I'm an early riser and work out regularly, so tiredness is natural; the gym and a high metabolism stopped my 4,000 calories per day turning to fat; I'm stressed and tired a lot, making me sleepy and snappy; and loads of men my age go to the toilet multiple times during the night, don't they?

'I'm sorry. I love you,' I tell her.

'I love you, too.'

The story of how I met Marie is one we often tell at parties. A mutual filmmaker friend of ours was shooting a local band's music video and looking for extras. We didn't know each other beforehand but hit it off on the set. I was required to be shirtless at one point while wearing a white cowboy hat and dragging her along the floor as she sat in a sink.

All the other extras and even some band members were flirting outrageously with Marie, whereas I just tried to make her laugh. It worked. Five-foot tall, blonde, beautiful, and the sweetest, nicest person I've ever met. More than one of my friends has accurately commented that I'm punching above my weight. I feel terrible that she has to go through this. What kind of future does she have in store with me now?

I tell Marie to take the car back home once we reach the hospital. There's no point in coming in this late as I imagine they'll just stick me in a ward for the night on a drip. I promise to keep her up to date with what's happening via text.

There's no receptionist after 6 pm. Excellent, what am I supposed to do now? All I can think is to ask at the accident & emergency ward located on the other side of the building. The hospital is massive. It takes about ten minutes of going up and down stairs, through long halls, and getting lost twice before reaching A&E, at which point I'm gasping for breath, and my chest is killing me. Maybe I'm having a heart attack. That would cap off the perfect day.

The place is packed. I wait in line to see the nurse behind the smash-proof screen, trying to control my breathing.

'Hi, I'm Dean Graham. My doctor phoned ahead earlier on. I'm... I'm diabetic,' I tell her. Words I never thought would leave my mouth. 'And I'm in DKA; I believe it's called. Sorry, I've literally just been diagnosed.'

'One second,' she says, picking up a phone and leaning back in her chair, ensuring the short conversation is out of earshot.

'Just take a seat, Mr Graham. We'll call your name.'

There must be over fifty people in here. Checking the LED screen on the wall confirms that I'm in for a long wait: approximately two hours. Despite feeling pretty rough, hunger pains stab at my stomach. I buy a packet of Nik Naks spicy crisps from the waiting room vending machine. If I knew they would be the last 'naughty' food I'd ever eat without manually injecting insulin first, I would have chosen something tastier.

'Mr Graham to room 3, please.'

What? Did I mishear? I only checked in five minutes ago. I knock on the door before entering, just in case.

'Come in,' shouts the voice from inside.

'Hi, was it for Dean Graham?' I ask the nurse.

'Hi, Dean. It was for you, yes. Please, sit down. How are you feeling?'

'Errmm... pretty overwhelmed, to be honest. I'm starting to feel a bit sickly. I was only diagnosed about an hour ago.'

'Oh, you poor thing. That must have been such a shock. I can tell you're in DKA; I can smell it on you.'

'Sorry?'

'Diabetics give off a distinctive smell when they're in DKA. It reminds me of nail polish remover. It's coming off you.'

I'm speechless. How long have I reeked of polish? Did people think I was sniffing it?

'I'm just going to take some blood samples and do a ketones check.'

Great, more needles. As per the usual routine, I look at the wall as it's plunged into my arm. The lack of pain suggests the nurse has had plenty of practice. It's now time for my first ever finger prick. A pen-like device is placed on the tip of my finger that fires out a tiny, retractable needle to draw the blood. The unexpected sting makes me jump a little. A paper strip is dabbed into the forming pool of red before being placed into a handheld machine.

'Oooo… that's not good,' she mutters.

The nurse presses a button on the comms radio pinned to her chest, speaking a load of codewords and numbers that I don't understand.

'I've got a young man here who's newly diagnosed diabetic. His ketones are at 12.5. Please advise.'

'Aww… bless him,' the voice on the other end replies.

After everything I've gone through, all I've been told, the severity of my situation only hits home upon hearing that comment. Nurses see the worst illness afflicting humanity. For a medical professional to react in that way illustrates how sick I am. I'm shaking, though whether it's the DKA or my nerves is unclear. The nurse, presumably noticing my deterioration, leans forward and holds one of my trembling hands.

'Dean, I know you must be terrified, but I want to know that this will be the only time you'll have to go through all this. I work with diabetics all the time. Nothing is stopping you from living a long, happy, and healthy life.'

322

Nurses don't get the credit they deserve. During my darkest moment, feeling so scared and confused, those words were like a beacon of light. Reassurance that I wasn't going to die soon, something I'd started to believe was a real possibility.

I'm taken from the triage section to a small room deeper in the hospital and told to wait on a trolley. A doctor arrives after about fifteen minutes to ask the same questions. Have I been sick recently? Urinating frequently? Drinking lots of water? I give the same excuses as to why I ignored the symptoms, prompting feelings of guilt.

'I'll be honest, Mr Graham. Your glucose and ketone levels are what we'd classify as horrendous. I'm baffled by how you're not vomiting and close to passing out. We need to get you onto the HDU.'

'HDU?'

'High-dependency unit. It's essentially a level down from intensive care. You can be monitored more extensively and quickly moved to ICU if required.'

I suspect the vomiting and passing out everyone's expecting is about to arrive.

The HDU is awful. Most of the twelve beds' occupants look like they're at death's door, and none appear under 60 years old. I feel almost embarrassed to be here. One family sits around an older man. His closed eyes and drool-covered chin indicate their hysterical cries are warranted.

Another nurse comes over and introduces herself, informing me that I'm going to be given fluids and insulin. A needle attached to two tubes is placed in my left arm.

'We're going to have to place this other cannula in your right forearm, okay, love?'

'Errmm…'

The colossal needle burns as it pierces my limb, several inches below the wrist. The thought of it burying into the muscle makes the pain ten times worse. It's then time for another finger prick, which feels relatively insignificant given what just happened.

'We're going to keep checking your blood sugar levels every hour until they're stable,' the nurse explains.

'How long do you think that will take?' I ask. It's almost late evening, and I'm shattered.

'At least 24 hours. Then we'll start checking it every two hours.'

I gasp. How can they prick my finger while I'm asleep? The last time I stayed awake for 24 hours was after taking a massive wrap of speed at university. I struggle to make it past 11 pm these days.

Thoughts run through my head as I sit watching the other HDU patients. Will I be okay? What's life going to be like now? And how will Mum react to this? It could kill her.

No matter how often I'm told that type 1 diabetes is an autoimmune disorder with no known reason behind its cause, I can't stop feeling like this is my fault. Aria's assurance that I'm not being punished is unconvincing, and even if this isn't some karmic retribution, it's hard to believe years of abusing my body didn't play a part.

October 23, 2019

Last night never ended. It wasn't as if sleep came easy, but on those occasions where I became too tired to keep my eyes open, it wasn't long before a nurse shook me awake to request a 'quick finger jab.' My blood was checked every hour on the hour, as promised.

Being attached to numerous machines meant going to the bathroom involved asking staff to unplug me. Sick of bothering them, I decided to use one of the cardboard urinal bottles, which is a first for me. Trying to piss into this tube while lying down proved impossible due to my bursting bladder refusing to cooperate, so I left the bed, closed my cubicle's curtains, and tried to perform while standing next to the trolley. The surrealness of the situation caused more shyness, but it eventually started to flow at a mighty pace. Sadly, it was too powerful to stop instantly when a nurse walked through the curtains, causing me to pull out and splash everywhere like a dog marking its territory.

Things got worse at around 5 am when, for some reason, I started sweating profusely. My head buzzed, eyes lost focus, a sickness washed over me, and there was a bizarre feeling as if my tongue had gone completely numb. I would later learn that this was my first ever hypo.

There are no windows in the HDU, intensifying the misery of the room. I check my mobile – 7 AM – time to make the call I've been dreading.

'Hi, Mum. It's Dean.'

'Dean, what's the matter? Why are you calling this early?'

'Mum… listen. I'm okay, alright. I'm honestly okay. But… I'm in hospital right now. Remember I had those blood tests yesterday? Well, they discovered I was… I'm diabetic.'

'Oh, Dean,' she cries, in a way that I haven't heard in a very long time.

'Mum, please. I swear I'm okay. They were lucky to find it when they did, could have been really bad.'

'I knew it. I knew something wasn't right. This is my fault.'

'Mum. It's not what Dad had. They think it's type 1. It's an autoimmune disease that just happens for no reason, I think.'

'So, do you have to inject yourself like him?'

'Yeah, it looks like it. They're going to tell me more today.'

'Oh… Dean. I love you, son,' she wails.

'Mum, I'm not dying.'

'If this… if this is because of that bastard….'

'I don't know if it's hereditary or anything. Suppose Dad and his brothers all having diabetes might have played a part.'

Or it could be entirely my fault.

'He's making us miserable even when he's dead,' the sadness in Mum's voice changing to anger.

'Don't think like that, Mum. Look, my phone's running low on power. Visiting hours start at 2, so come over to the hospital then. I'm on the HDU ward.'

'Okay. I love you.'

'I love you, too.'

I've noticed that the food they serve here is incredibly bland. Whether it's just hospital meals in general or the diabetic-friendly option, I don't know. More finger pricks follow throughout the day – half of my tips are bruised already, leaving nasty yellow stains that remind me of once smoking 20 cigarettes in one night. A new orderly approach at around 10 am.

'Dean Graham?'

'Yes.'

'I'm here to take you for your X-ray.'

'X-ray? Are you sure it's for me?'

He checks his papers.

'Dean Graham. Aged 40. Diabetic. HDU. Yup.'

'But why do I need an X-ray? I've not broken anything.'

'Afraid they don't tell me that stuff, mate.'

I'm wheeled through to the X-ray unit and left outside the door, dazed and confused. A radiologist steps out.

'Hi, Mr Graham. We're just going to take a quick look at your heart.'

'My heart? Why?'

'The doctor wants to make sure everything's okay. I assume it's just a precaution, what with your ketones levels being so high.'

This comes as a particularly sickening revelation, especially as I'd just assured Mum that I'm fine. The procedure itself is over in seconds. I'm wheeled back to the HDU feeling like I've been hit by a car. There have been occasions, quite a few, if I'm honest, over the last few months when I felt a strange sensation in my chest as if my heart is itchy. It was often accompanied by slight breathlessness. All related to indigestion, I assumed, or perhaps from working out too hard. Now I discover it was one of the many symptoms of DKA, one that could have permanently damaged my most vital organ. This whole experience has been terrifying, though the X-ray's been the worst – so far

Lunch arrives at 12. I'm starving, but I look at the meal and am scared to eat anything, worried it could kill me. Is this life from now on, never being able to consume anything without stressing over the consequences?

The nurse, noticing me staring at the food like it's from another planet, says that everything I need to know about my new lifestyle will be explained later. She assures me it's okay to eat the veggie pie as they can adjust the insulin I'm currently receiving.

A doctor arrives at my bedside at around two. I hope the fluttering sensation is nerves and not my heart shutting down.

'Mr Graham?'

'Hi, yes.'

'I'm just here to tell you about your X-ray. It's good news – your heart is fine. And your ketones and glucose levels have come down, so we're moving you to the diabetes and endocrine unit.'

The diabetic ward is an improvement over the HUD, mainly because there are no grieving families or screaming patients. What instantly strikes me is that out of the eight men here, all but one is an overweight, older gentleman. A few say hello as I'm wheeled in, making me feel like the newest member of a club I never wanted to join.

Some people on the ward are talking about their routines. One mentions that he injects morning and night, which doesn't sound too bad. Another says he only needs one injection per week. Maybe this new life won't be as awful as I imagined. A doctor arrives about half an hour later to smash my optimism into tiny pieces.

'Hi, Dean. I'm Dr Stephenson,' he says. His blonde hair and glasses remind me of the actor Ed Begley Junior during his St. Elsewhere days.

'So, this is probably all a big shock to you, yeah?'

'Yeah,' I say, wondering if some medical handbook recommends that line to newly diagnosed diabetics.

'We're pretty sure you've got type 1, I'm afraid, but we won't be able to confirm it until we get the results of your GAD antibody test. It takes a while for the blood sample to be sent off and checked. You might need a scan of your pancreas if it comes back negative, just to make sure there's nothing nasty going on.'

Nastier than type 1 diabetes?

He flips through some of the pages in the file.

'I see your dad had diabetes. You're familiar with injecting insulin?'

'Well, yeah. I suppose,' I reply, praying for no more than a couple of daily injections.

'Right. You'll be injecting yourself at least four times per day, maybe more, depending on what you eat.'

I'm not sure I can take any more shocks.

'Four times! I hate injections!.'

'Yes, I'm afraid so. Type 1 is quite different from type 2. You need to inject every time you eat, and you also need to take background insulin each day. These will help.'

He hands me what looks like two small magazines and a thick leaflet: Type 1 diabetes for the newly diagnosed; Eating well with type 1 diabetes; and How to identify DKA.

'We'll be back later to show you how to inject and test your blood.'

I've lost count of how many times my finger's been pricked. Some of them were surprisingly painful.

'How often will I have to prick my fingers, doctor?'

'Errmm… usually around seven or eight times per day, though some people do it more often.'

Fuck.

Dr Stephenson, who now appears more like the grim spectre of death than an actor, gets up and leaves.

I'm going to be stabbing myself at least four times per day and putting a needle into my fingertips eight times daily for the rest of my life. Even thinking about the upcoming first-ever injection fills me with dread. I guess it's something I'll have to get used to when the alternative is dying. Maybe the reading material will offer some comfort.

The 'newly diagnosed' booklet starts with a classic shit sandwich, explaining that while type 1 diabetes 'is in no way a death sentence,' there can be 'extreme complications.' However, the chances of experiencing them can be lessened with good blood sugar management. Its reassurance that not *everyone* has their feet amputated or goes blind is, in fact, not hugely reassuring.

The diet book explains the need to count carbs in every food, using this information to work out exact insulin doses based on specific ratios. Maths was my worst subject at school. Now I'm going to kill myself unintentionally because I'm crap at sums.

'Hey, mate.'

I look up to see the voice coming from the only other skinny person in the room. He's likely in his thirties, though he could be younger; the hard-lived life etched onto his face and basin haircut are very ageing. There are black bags under his eyes, tattoos on his neck and knuckles, and some of his teeth are noticeably absent.

'Anyone ever tell you that you look like Moby?'

I really have lost a lot of weight.

'Ha, my mate points it out all the time, aye.'

'Haha! Fucking hell! You sound like him as well.'

'Shame I can't sing like him.'

'I bet. I'm Barry.'

'Dean.'

'Alright, Dean. I heard the doctor say you're a type 1 like me, eh?'

'So they think, yeah.'

'He didn't tell you that type 1's much worse, did he, though?'

'No, but I had heard that.'

Barry grabs the bedsheet covering his lower half and yanks it off, exposing a left leg amputated just below the knee.

'Believe it, son. And I'm blind in one eye, too.'

My jaw falls open. I remember Dad telling people about how diabetes could lead to his feet being cut off and blindness. 'I'd rather be dead than blind' was the quote he used to love throwing around. Guess he got his wish in the end. I wonder if I'll feel the same way.

'You know why I'm in here, Dean?'

'I'd assume it was diabetes-related.'

'Aye, in a way. I tried to kill myself. Fuckin' sick of life and this disease. Third time I've tried an' all.'

'Three times! Wow… you mustn't be very good at it'

I know I'm taking a risk with that line. After a tense second of silence, Barry howls with laughter.

'Haha! I guess I'm not, nah!.'

Barry spends the next few hours telling me about his past, most of which invovles tales about multiple stints behind bars for petty crimes. He passed out while walking down the street seven years ago. 'Thought it was from a fucking weekend bender,' he said. The reality was undiagnosed type 1 diabetes and DKA.

'Tell you the truth, mate, I've never looked after it, kept on drinking and taking drugs, though I knocked both of them on the head recently. I still smoke, mind you – hardest bastard of them all to quit. Aye, I'd forget to take me insulin. Eat the wrong stuff. I remember, me bloods were getting higher and higher every day, couldn't figure out why. Turns out the pop I was drinking wasn't sugar-free. Got an ulcer on me foot a couple of years down the line that turned bad. Said it spread into me bone and up me leg, so they had to take the thing. Lost the sight in this eye not long after. It's a fucking cunt of a disease, don't let anyone tell you otherwise. Got sick of life a few times. Tried a paracetamol overdose the last time, but me ma found us before it were too late.'

'Fucking hell. So, I've got a lot to look forward to, then?'

'Well, they say you don't get too bad if you control it, but I've never been able to. Maybe you'll do better.'

'I hate needles.'

'Hahah! A diabetic scared of needles! You best get over that, mate. Don't want to end up like me.'

That was a sobering conversation.

A nurse arrives not long afterwards with my first injection. I'm relieved to find that things have come a long way since Dad's day. The insulin is now stored in a pen device, and the enormous needles have been replaced with tiny, disposable ones.

After being instructed on how to set the correct dosage, I steel myself, trying to remember that I'll be doing this at least four times per day, every single day, forever. A deep breath in and a slow exhale while pushing the sharp point into my stomach near the belly button. There's no pain at all – a bit of good news at last.

Marie and Mum arrive later in the day. They got a shock earlier when, due to the poor mobile reception in the hospital, I couldn't tell them about my transfer from HDU. They walked in to find an empty bed where I was supposed to be, causing them to assume I'd died. The story made me laugh; they didn't think it was funny.

While seeing me sitting up in bed and looking well came as a relief to both, there were many tears during the visit. I feel a lot better physically since being pumped full of insulin and fluids, though the tingle in my leg has become more noticeable in the last 24 hours. Itchy, almost. How I feel mentally is a different matter.

October 24, 2019

The big guy in the bed next to me spent most of last night groaning in pain. He's been in here ten days already and is supposed to be getting discharged later, though that seems a bit premature. I see him struggling with a pair of compression socks, every pull of the tight material bringing a yell and more profanity.

'FUCK!' He shouts to himself, 'I don't care what anybody thinks; diabetes is worse than cancer.' Words no newly diagnosed diabetic want to hear, especially after discovering they have the 'worst' type.

Somewhat surprisingly, I'm also being discharged today, providing my glucose and ketone levels remain stable. Barry considers this an outrage.

'When they first diagnosed me, Dean, I was in hospital for a week, showed me how to do everything loads of times. It's fucking scandalous they're letting you out after two days, mate. State of the bloody NHS.'

I couldn't be more relieved. The thought of being in my own home, in my own bed, and without constantly being told I'm very sick has kept me sane. My wish is granted when the doctor returns to say everything looks good. He also has some less welcome news: a list of dates next week for various tests, checks, classes, and more.

It's time to call Marie and let her know what's happening. I swing my legs over the side of my bed and stand up.

'Owww!.'

The now-familiar crushing sensation in my feet remains, joined by something else. The tendons in my heel and ankle areas are on fire, burning, shooting pains blasting through them. It's especially bad when walking, causing me to hobble. What's also weird is that the tingling in my right thigh has also appeared in my left one.

'You should stop trying to kill yourself and find something you're better at, mate,' I tell Barry on the way out.

'Maybe I will, Moby. Hope you manage alright.'

'Same to you, mate. Don't give up.'

October 25, 2019

Being back home helps mitigate the awful reality of my new life. I spent most of yesterday playing with Buster – looking up type 1 diabetes online was almost as horrible as being in the hospital.

My tendons have got worse; every step feels like they're going to snap. Additionally, my feet have developed a strange tingling, much like that in my legs. They've also become so sensitive that any physical contact hurts. Even my soles touching the floor is teeth-grindingly awful.

I've been told to inject the same dose for every meal until they can work out my insulin-to-carb ratio next week. It's important to rotate injection sites between the stomach, arms, thighs, and bum cheeks to avoid lipodystrophy, a condition where fat breaks down or builds up under the skin. Wanting to avoid a stomach covered in unsightly lumps, I've tried injecting in my arm (usually painless but awkward), my leg (sometimes painful and prone to bleeding), and my bum. If you've ever tried to jab something sharp into your buttock, for whatever reason, you'll know that doing it incorrectly hurts. I made the mistake of hesitating and repeatedly stabbing myself in the ass cheek like it was a pin cushion. I've never used that location since. The regular finger pricks can be worse than the injections, especially when the results show my glucose levels are through the roof, inducing stress like little else and pushing me higher.

I told my boss that I need a week off work for the numerous clinic appointments coming up. I'm not sure what I'll do with my time outside of these visits. I've already tried watching TV, playing games, reading, but I can't concentrate on anything, like the information isn't reaching my brain.

My 'introduction to type 1 diabetes' book explains that the newly diagnosed need to go through a grieving period, similar to when someone close dies. I suppose someone has: me. The person I was, who could eat and drink whatever they wanted, whenever they wanted, without thinking twice, is gone. The man who never had to worry about forgetting his insulin and glucose tablets when leaving the house, who could exercise without the threat of a hypo, who never contemplated going blind, kidney disease, or losing a limb, is dead.

October 27, 2019

The tingling in both my thighs is becoming more pronounced. Not exactly painful, but noticeable no matter what I'm doing. Driving to the shops saw me almost crash into another car when my increasingly useless foot failed to summon enough force to depress the brake pedal. I expected the other vehicle's driver to get out and punch me, so I decided it would be best to allow this attack rather than shout, 'It wasn't my fault; I'm diabetic.' He just hurled verbal abuse while I gave him a nod that wordlessly acknowledged my error.

Walking is the worst part of all this, thanks to a horrible foot numbness combined with intense pain from every tendon. I have to rest on the supermarket trolley's handle while pushing it, my limping inducing looks of curiosity mixed with pity from some customers. Is this what it's going to be like from now on? I've also noticed a weird lump that's appeared high in my stomach. Google says it's one of the symptoms of pancreatic cysts.

October 28, 2019

My new daily routine.

6:30 - Get up, finger prick to check blood

6:35 - Inject insulin

7:00 - Breakfast

9:00 - Finger prick

11:30 - Finger prick

11:45 - Inject insulin

12:15 - Lunch

14:15 - Finger prick

17:00 - Finger prick

17:15 - Inject insulin

17:45 - Dinner

19:00 – Inject long-lasting insulin

19:45 - Finger prick

22:45 - Finger prick

23:00 - Bed

And that's not including any correction doses or the extra required for snacks. It makes me wish I didn't take my old life for granted.

It's a strange feeling, knowing that my entire existence now depends on a medicine manufactured somewhere in the world, that if I don't take it several times each day, every single day, for the rest of my life, I will die. Should something cause me to lose access to insulin, I will die, and it will be a painful death that arrives within a few days. I am sick, and I will never get better.

October 29, 2019

Today's my first appointment of the week. It's a lengthy introduction to type 1, involving even more blood testing, carb counting, and a very long chat with a dietitian.

The clinic's scales show I've dropped down to a weight not seen since my schooldays. It doesn't come as too much of a surprise – while lying on the living room floor last night, what I presumed was an object sticking into my back turned out to be my spine. I mention the worsening tingling in my legs and the issues with my feet to the doctor.

'Hmm… could be neuropathy. Or it could be from your glucose levels being high for so long then dropping overnight. The tendon thing is a bit unusual. We'll know more when they screen your feet later this week. They'll be checking your eyes, too,' the endocrinologist explains.

'Right. That's… good to know. I guess. Have you got the results of my other blood test back yet? The one that indicates whether I'll need a pancreas scan?'

'I'll just have a look,' he says, moving over to the keyboard and hammering away at some keys.

'Nothing yet, I'm afraid. The antibody test can take quite a while to carry out.'

As much as I want to tell him about the lump in my stomach, I don't. It's as if talking about it will make a cancer diagnosis more likely. Just the fact that I've lost an astonishing amount of weight is worrying enough.

I'm lost in my thoughts as the evening passes. Am I going to die? From what I've read about neuropathy, an irreversible condition, death might be the better option. And God only knows what they'll find wrong with my eyes. Never think things can't get any worse. I learned that the hard way.

October 30, 2019

My foot and eye exams take place at a new medical facility larger than a clinic but smaller than a hospital. I tell the receptionist I'm here for my 'diabetic screening,' the words causing physical discomfort as I try to form them in my mouth.

A nurse calls me after a few minutes of sitting in the grim waiting room. I struggle to keep up with her as she walks ahead. At this point, the skin on my soles feels like wet tissue paper, as if every step could rip it wide open. Just moving my toes has become almost impossible without an enormous amount of pain.

A patient about ten years older than me exits the room as we approach. She's on crutches, barely managing to drag her feet along the floor.

The foot test is painless, thankfully. It involves poking a nylon stylus into the soles while my eyes are closed to determine sensation levels.

'Just let me know if you feel it,' the examiner says.

I almost go through the roof the second the material makes contact. Everything seems to be going pretty well until there's a long pause between jabs.

'Can you feel anything there, Mr Graham?'

Is she even doing anything?

'Err… no. Nothing.'

'Right, how about here?'

'Oww… yes.'

'Okay then. You are experiencing oversensitivity in your feet, but that could ease in time. There's one small area at the back of your heel that seems to have lost sensation. Again, though, it could be nothing to worry about and may not spread elsewhere. The best course of action would be to bring you back in six months instead of the usual year so we can check them again.'

'Right. Errmm... could I just ask: what can the lack of feeling lead to?' I say, hoping the answer isn't as bad as I suspect.

'In a worst-case scenario, you could get a cut or dry skin on your foot that you can't feel and never heals. That leads to infection and, well... complications. That's why we tell diabetics to check their feet and apply moisturiser every day.'

I move into a different room for the eye test, the image of Barry's stump stuck in my head. I've not noticed any changes in my vision; it's one of the reasons I never imagined my pre-diagnosis symptoms could be caused by diabetes.

The procedure is very similar to the kind you'd get at an optician. Following the standard distance-reading test, which I breeze through, the nurse uses a periscope viewer-style device to photograph the back of my eyeballs. She pours over the resulting images with a furrowed brow that makes me nervous.

'Okay,' she begins. 'I'm afraid you do have what appears to be small burst blood vessels at the back of your eyes. What I'll do is send these off to a specialist and see what they think. You might have to go to the local eye infirmary for a different type of test in a few weeks.'

This has not gone as well as I'd hoped.

November 1, 2019

It's time for my last appointment: a consultation with yet another doctor involving more blood samples and setting up repeat prescriptions. That nurse's words about diabetics living normal and healthy lives are ringing hollow right now. I feel anything but ordinary, which isn't helped by all these fucking visits to different medical centres.

The tingling in my thighs has quickly evolved into a horrible burning sensation that's spread to the skin on my stomach, upper back, and upper arms. It's as if someone is pressing a hot iron onto my body. My feet are getting worse. I can walk up stairs normally but descending them involves taking one step at a time while gripping the banister. That lump in my abdomen appears to be getting bigger and adding to my worries is a crippling pain in my gut whenever I eat, bringing back unwanted memories of the ulcer.

The doctor examines my torso like a mechanic looking over an old banger, letting out sighs and shaking his head as he pokes around at a piece of machinery that's seen better days.

'Yeah, this is from injecting in your stomach,' he says, jabbing a finger into the protruding mound. 'Use other sites.'

Weird, I thought diabetics didn't experience injection site lumps until they'd been using the same spots for years. I've been injecting for a week. I tell the doc about the pain after eating, for which I'm given acid reflux tablets.

I mention my feet and the spreading burning sensation, prompting a look of concern on his face.

'It sounds like peripheral neuropathy in your legs and feet, but I've never heard it affecting a stomach or back area.'

'Yeah, the endocrinologist mentioned neuropathy,' I reply. 'It's horrible. Like, I can't even bear clothes touching my skin.'

'We'll do some extra tests on your bloods. If nothing shows up, we can start ruling out neurological conditions.'

'Neurological conditions?'

'Yes. Don't worry, though, checking for conditions such as motor neurone disease is standard.'

'Errmmm… wow…. okay.'

'I wouldn't worry about that. I'm prescribing a drug called Pregabalin used to treat nerve pain like yours. Most patients say it works really well.'

'So, does it ever go away?'

'Well, neuropathy itself is considered irreversible. But it can usually be managed to the point where you live without discomfort.'

'What if it never gets better, or it gets worse? I mean, just moving is a nightmare right now.'

'Well, the hard truth is that's a possibility. We can send you to the pain management clinic and look at options to aid your mobility: crutches, wheelchairs, scooters. But hopefully, it won't come to that.'

November 3, 2019

I was convinced the pain couldn't get any worse, another reminder never to assume anything. Now accompanying the burning is a sensation akin to knitting needles violently piercing various locations across my body at random intervals. I had to sleep without a blanket last night as its touch has become like scalding sandpaper. Hot showers offer very temporary relief, but my feet have become so sensitive that even the tiny, anti-slip dimples on the bottom of the tub are agonising to stand on, forcing me to sit down as I bathe. Baths are even worse; submerging my feet entirely in water causes all feeling in them to disappear.

I've spent virtually every waking moment this weekend lying on the couch, half-watching TV. Nothing distracts me from imagining the worst possible outcomes: blindness, being confined to a wheelchair, amputations, constant pain, drugs, and I might still die.

No matter what happens now, best- or worst-case scenario, I will always be a diabetic, spending the rest of my life in a constant state of worry and stress, different from everyone else. How did this happen? I'd turned things around. I was so fit and healthy, and even my once broken mind was improving. Of all the things I've been through, I'd never faced such a glaring inevitability: this will never improve. I battled through every hardship by holding onto the belief that, in time, life would get better. But not now. The hopelessness of the situation has brought absolute despair.

November 4, 2019

My first bad hypo hits while watching TV. It seems I misjudged the number of carbs in my vegetables and dosed way too high. The first sign is dizziness, reminding me of the initial stages of drunkenness only with none of the pleasure. My eyes go next – everything becomes blurry and out of focus. Voices sound far away or underwater, then comes the sweating and numb tongue and lips. Hands shake uncontrollably. You were right, Dad, this is awful. There are weirdly overwhelming feelings of sadness and confusion. My mind is a fog. Vocabulary and rational thought disappear.

I try to stand, but weakness combined with the pain in my feet sends me to the ground. I'm suddenly grateful for the numbness that prevents me from feeling the floor's impact. My brain is shutting down. Drool slides out of my mouth. I want to close my eyes.

Marie, having heard the clattering thud, comes running downstairs. She says something I can't decipher before flying into the kitchen, returning with some sweets. It makes me thankful I told her of my previous experiences with Dad's hypos. As I struggle to hold on to consciousness, her pushing glucose tabs into my mouth to keep me alive, the sense of déjà vu makes me wonder if this is all just life's ironic joke. Had it not been for the encroaching coma, I'd probably laugh.

November 7, 2019

Many people look at famous diabetic athletes, musicians or movie stars and think it doesn't seem that bad. Eat well, take your insulin, exercise – easy! The harsh reality is that it's not like that for most of us. Diabetes is like having a full-time job that requires your attention 24/7 with no breaks. Instead of being paid for the constant work and stress, you get to stay alive.

The condition affects every little thing in your life, the kind of stuff everyone else doesn't even think about: eating, drinking, holidays, alcohol, exercising, driving, partners, sex, work, and even sleep. People rarely get to see the pain, frustration, misery and fear it can cause. The way diabetes makes you feel so different from everyone else and wish to be normal again. Even those with no physical symptoms struggle when first diagnosed. Dealing with neuropathy and a host of other problems exacerbates an already challenging situation.

November 10, 2019

The last week has been hell. My pains get worse every day. Pregabalin does nothing other than cause facial twitches, extreme tiredness, and constipation; the inside of my stomach often hurts as much as the outside. Walking has become so painful that I avoid it whenever possible. The lump remains, and I *still* don't have confirmation of whether I've got pancreatic tumours. Not to mention that the diabetes lifestyle of carb counting, multiple injections, fingerpicks, and hypos is causing mental burnout less than a month after diagnosis. I am falling.

Does anyone enjoy washing dishes? I find it particularly awful as the mundaneness of the task makes my mind drift. The monotony of scraping some crud off a plate sends me back to a friend's birthday last year. Being his fortieth, I made a rare exception to my 'no drinking to excess' rule. We had pizza at his place in preparation for the night out, which involved boozing, laughing, and dancing like maniacs. It was the most fun I'd had in years.

The realisation is like a sledgehammer: I will never be able to experience something like that again for the rest of my life. Pizza is a nightmare food for diabetics, causing glucose spikes no matter how we dose for it. Alcohol makes sugar levels drop dangerously low, as does vigorous exercise like dancing – not that I can even walk across the kitchen right now without wincing in agony. My incurable disease has taken so much, including the ability to experience fun like everyone else. No matter what, this fact will never change. Never. It is the straw that breaks the camel's back.

I step away from the sink, pulling out my phone to search for the local taxi firm's number. Aria appears next to me.

'Don't do this, Dean.'

'Tell me another way, then.'

'Think of Marie. Think of your mum; this will kill them.'

'They'd want this if they knew what I'm going through.'

'You're not the only one to experience shit like this, you know.'

'Yeah, I know. But I am broken, Aria. I am too fucking tired to keep on fighting. There's nothing left in my tank. What do I have to look forward to? Going blind, unending pain, losing a leg? I've already become a burden to them. I just… I just can't anymore. It's the logical solution. I'm sorry.'

The taxi ride to the seafront goes in the blink of an eye. I've never been so grateful for a driver who isn't chatty. He seems amazed when I give him a £20 note for the £11 fare and tell him to keep the change.

I like this place. The high pier curves out into the sea for about a quarter of a mile, a lonely lighthouse standing guard at the end. There are benches placed along its entire length. Despite being sunny, the temperature's close to freezing right now. The only people dotted about are the few fishermen sitting in their deckchairs, wrapped in blankets on the distant beach.

A walk that would typically take a couple of minutes lasts ages as I limp and hobble at a snail's pace, a bracing wind slowing me further. The red and white striped lighthouse gleams in the late afternoon sun, waves crashing around the rocks below. A waist-high metal barrier sits on both sides of the pier, which, while preventing people from falling into the sea, does little to keep sightseers dry on days like this.

Reaching the end of the walkway, I rest on the top railing and look out at the horizon. Did I make the most of my life? Was I a good person? The recurring thought that I deserve all this, that I'm destined to end up here, remains hard to shake. I swing one leg over the rail, followed by the other, leaving me standing on the edge, peering into the rough, inky-black water about ten feet below while gripping the bar behind my back.

My fingers unfurl, letting go of a life I can no longer endure.

The seconds-long fall takes forever. Freezing wind belts against my face as I instinctively pull my knees up just before impact. It's like hitting a thick pane of glass. Icy water rips into skin, so cold it burns. Muscles lock, refusing to move. I taste the salty liquid entering my throat and nose.

I'm sinking fast. The massive walking boots I bought in the hope of easing my foot pains are like a pair of anvils. Every inch deeper feels another degree colder. It's getting harder to hold my breath as the cold constricts my chest, paralysing my diaphragm.

The light dancing on the surface looks incredible from beneath the surface. Darkness envelops me. I open my mouth so water can fill my lungs, bringing this to an end. There's a moment of utter terror before I drift away. It's over. And I'm glad.

'Bloody cold today, eh?' says the voice, easily distinguishable as belonging to an old man.

I'm still standing on the pier, gripping the bar from the safe side of the barrier. Was that a trance? Another psychotic episode?

'I say, it's a bloody cold one today, eh?'

An elderly gentleman sits on the bench a few feet away. He wasn't there before. In his late 60s, portly and wearing a crumpled grey suit with a massive puffy green jacket over the top, the stereotypical look completed by a flat cap that's somehow staying on his head despite the wind. A ruddy complexion and thread veins in his large nose suggest a love of alcohol.

'Errmm… aye, biting,' I say, still in a near-stupor.

'Used to go hiking with the wife in weather like this. That were years ago, of course. Getting to the end of this bloody pier's hard enough these days, heh.'

'I… I can imagine, yeah.'

'Mind, don't be fooled by this old bugger. I was fit as a lop up until a few years ago, liked nothing better than walking holidays with my Susie. That stopped after she was gone, of course – not mad on the idea of holidaying alone.'

'Gone?'

'Dead, lad.'

'Oh, God. Sorry. Sorry for your loss.'

'Cheers, been a lot of years now. Not that it doesn't hurt any less. You okay, son? You were standing still for so long there; I was going to check your pulse, ha.'

Son. I remember the last person to call me that.

'Yeah. I'm… I was just thinking. I guess.'

'Aye, got to be careful with thinking too much. Can drive you mad.'

The statement's accuracy makes me snort, though he either doesn't hear or chooses to ignore it.

'I try not to think too much, myself. Truth be told, had some hard times, suppose most people have. We had a son, Susie and me, loved him in a way I never thought was possible. He started getting ill when he was 12. Took him to the doctors – leukaemia. Treatments back then weren't what they are today. Said it was an aggressive form. I remember… I remember asking God to take me instead, but Michael died before his fourteenth birthday. Felt like part of me went with him. Susie never really got over it, but we carried on, 'cos that's what you do, isn't it? Never had any more children, kept saying we were too old, but I think we were scared of going through that kind of pain again. Bastard cancer took Susie away from me as well a few years back. In her lungs – and she never smoked a bloody cigarette her entire life.'

He looks out to the sea, the tears in his eyes unlikely a result of the cold.

'Aye, had some hard times, but I never lost hope, still haven't, despite everything. You'll probably think I'm a mad old sod who talks too much. But what do we have without hope, eh? I hope Michael and Susie are somewhere better and that I live the rest of my days in a way that makes them proud. Never lose hope, son. Never. It's what gets us out of bed in the morning. Even in our darkest moments, hope, well, it keeps us alive, doesn't it?'

It was the absolute absence of hope that brought me here. I believe my life will never get better. It's just a fight to slow down the degenerative process.

But what about this old man? How could he have buried his son and wife yet still hang on to hope? Maybe he's a God botherer. Perhaps he's not even real, and this is a trick by Aria. No, there are signs that he's no figment of the imagination: the smell of Old Spice aftershave, an unfamiliar look that I doubt my mind could have manifested. He really is sitting there, opening his heart to me, a stranger. Could he tell what I was planning?

'How do you keep going after... everything?' I ask. He looks right at me, a hint of a smile flickering across his face.

'Because we have to, you daft bugger. Life, any life, is a gift. Most folks don't realise that until it's being threatened. A lot of people get a bad roll of the dice – maybe you did as well – but that's not a reason to give up. No matter how many bad rolls we get.'

He turns to look at the sky. The sun blasts through gaps in the metallic winter clouds, sending pillars of light falling into the dark sea below.

'I was never really a religious man, given everything, but when you look at something like that,' he points upwards, 'you've got wonder whether there's… something… out there, eh? A reason for it all?'

I look up. It really is something.

'Well, here's hoping. I'll see you later, son. Take care now.'

I watch him slowly walk down the pier toward the beach, occasionally glancing skyward. Once faded from my life, I follow in his footsteps.

CHAPTER SIXTEEN

HOPE SPRINGS ETERNAL

November 11, 2019

I wake to a different world. My pain is still intense; moving is an agonizing process; the diabetes and threat of related complications remain; but I'm different. The despair has gone, replaced by the same hope present in a man who lost everything. I put on a pair of running shoes I haven't worn for months and set off for a walk around the streets. The internet says exercise is the best way to alleviate neuropathy, so let's give it a try.

Forcing myself down the road brings back childhood memories of wearing Dad's oversized shoes. My feet are foreign bodies attached to the end of my legs, flopping around as I swing the withered appendages back and forth like a Sesame Street puppet – a comparison made all the more accurate by my yelps every time a shoe connects with the hard surface. The drop from the curb is going to be a problem. Not being able to control my feet properly means keeping my head down and eyes on them at all times. Seeing the end of the pavement approach, I stop, mentally determining the best way to get myself onto the road four inches below.

Taking a deep breath and ensuring no cars are nearby, I lift my right leg, pulling it back slightly before swinging in the opposite direction, letting inertia propel me forward. My foot lands squarely on the tarmac. Success! But I didn't give enough consideration to my left side, which is now collapsing in slow motion as the opposite leg drags behind my body. I flop face down in the middle of the road like a sack of potatoes.

'You should get up before a car finishes the job,' Aria says from somewhere above.

'Is it always going to be this hard?'

'Things are always difficult in the beginning. It will get easier. Come on, son. We've been through worse than this.'

I climb from the floor and bound off into the distance, legs flailing wildly.

November 15, 2019

One of those good news/bad news letters lands on the carpet. The good part is that my C-peptide blood test confirms I have Type 1 diabetes, thereby ruling out pancreatic cancer or other damage to the organ. Talk about the lesser of two evils.

The not-so-good news is that I now have an appointment at the local eye infirmary to assess the damage diabetes has done to my eyes.

November 18, 2019

I've been walking every day for a week now. Locals, presumably thinking I'm just another eccentric drunk, often nod or say hello as I swing myself down the street. The act of moving forward remains incredibly difficult, and my various foot and leg pains are just as intense, but the routine's increasing familiarity makes each subsequent 20-minute trek slightly less arduous.

November 20, 2019

The eye infirmary's waiting room is full of diabetics, all looking petrified. Few things scare people as much as the thought of losing their sight. Dad's quote of death being preferable to blindness have rung in my head since they discovered the burst blood vessels. If anything is going to test my newfound optimism, it's this.

The process is pretty much the same as my previous eye exam, albeit using a larger machine. Images of what looks like a vein-covered pool ball appear on the computer display before being examined in agonisingly slow detail by the consult.

'It does appear you have diabetic macular oedema. That's damage to the part of the eye that provides your central vision. It's very minor right now, no leaking or anything, so the best course of action is to continue checking them every six months instead of the usual year.'

'And if it gets any worse?'

'Oh, there are plenty of treatments for this sort of thing. We would start off with laser surgery to seal any leaks. There's also the option of anti-VEGF injections.'

'Injections?'

'Yes. Into your eyeballs.'

Just when I thought diabetes couldn't get any worse, I'm now faced with a Hellraiser-style torture method.

'I thought this kind of thing only happened after you'd had diabetes for years?'

'That is usually the case. But you'll find undiagnosed diabetics whose blood sugar is very high often get complications like these when it drops rapidly.'

So, the process of saving my life has caused potentially irreparable damage to my body. Not going to the doctor sooner was the worst mistake I ever made.

November 25, 2019

I must have grabbed about three hours of sleep last night due to my neuropathy flaring up recently; I did read that the Pregabalin can take weeks to work. Yet again, the pain was so bad that even my blanket's weight became unbearable. There were times when I thought a vial of acid had been thrown over my thighs. I kept imagining the skin on my stomach and back was being slowly removed with a vegetable peeler, and my feet somehow felt like they were burning and freezing at the same time. This is in addition to the unending pins and needles that force me to keep my socks in bed. The constant thought of a life without sight didn't help me nod off, either. I kept repeating a 'don't lose hope' mantra, hoping I heed my own advice.

November 30, 2019

My number of daily walks has increased from one to two. Whether each step is becoming easier or I'm just getting used to the pain is unclear. I haven't gone arse-over-tit since that first fall.

December 1, 2019

The variation in the types of pain my feet experience is astounding: numbness, oversensitivity, burning, freezing, tingling, pins and needles, random stabbings, a weird feeling like I'm walking barefoot on rocks, and splitting-skin sensations. It's made worse by tendons that refuse to work properly, like they're too tight for my body.

The diabetic life remains tough. I've noticed people staring at me when I inject in public, their looks varying from pity to disgust and even anger. Do they think I've figured out how to store heroin in an easy-to-use pen dispenser? And my previous bad hypoglycaemic attack has made me paranoid about suffering something similar while asleep, resulting in never waking up.

December 4, 2019

Forty-one years old. It wasn't long ago when I never expected to see this milestone. Marie and Mum have chipped in on the best birthday present I could ask for: a constant glucose monitor. This tiny device sticks to a body with a plaster and features a small, wire-like needle that inserts just under the skin. It sends blood glucose readings to my phone every five minutes, which not only means finger pricks are mostly unnecessary, but it also sounds alerts when I'm going too high or low, vastly lessening the risk of hypos – no more going to bed wondering if I'll see the following morning.

December 20, 2019

I notice something today: I can move my toes slightly while walking. This allows me to land each step heel first, rather than slapping the entire foot down flat like a child having a tantrum. Thinking about the mechanics of how we move was something I never did before diagnosis.

December 22, 2019

An early Christmas present arrived today. Lying on the sofa in my socks – the only time I'm allowed to have my slippers off in the house due to the risk of foot injury – I wiggle my toes freely and without pain, something I haven't been able to do for well over a month. Moreover, that weird lump in my stomach is shrinking.

December 31, 2019

Diabetics are advised to go easy on alcohol. In addition to being more at risk of damaging organs such as kidneys, it can worsen nerve pains. But the biggest problem is that booze reduces a body's ability to recover when blood sugar levels drop, leaving us at massive risk of hypos. I wasn't going to drink at all this New Year's Eve, but my new blood monitor gives me more confidence, and I could certainly use a tipple. Other type 1s recommend vodka and diet coke as a no-carb option, so I give it a try. My glucose levels remain steady after one glass.

So, I have another.

And another.

And a double.

And another double to celebrate the clock hitting 12.

A deafening alarm screams in my ear as I'm shaken violently. The realisation that I'm in bed and the noise is my low blood sugar alert slowly dawns. Marie is trying to rouse

371

me from a drunken slumber, demanding I eat some glucose sweets. I reach over and check my phone. It reads 1.9. Anything below around 3.4 is considered hypo territory. How ironic it would be that after having decided against suicide, I kill myself accidentally soon after. The alarm goes off three more times during the night. I vow never to get this drunk again.

January 7, 2020

Every day, every walk, it gets a tiny bit better – less painful, faster. When I first started these strolls, a man with a walking stick who must have been in his 70s overtook me, grinning as his hobbling outpaced mine. I'm now close to the speed of a young child. Suck it, grandad.

January 10, 2020

While I'm making progress, my neuropathy is still a constant source of misery. The Pregabalin has finally taken the edge off, but only after I upped the dose on the doctor's advice. There remain days when it's difficult to concentrate on anything other than the horrific burning coming from my nerve endings.

An article in a diabetic forum mentions that neuropathic pain can be alleviated through weightlifting in addition to aerobic exercise. It's been so long since I've been to a gym, and I'm certainly in no condition to go back to one just yet, so I buy a couple of dumbbells for home use.

January 12, 2020

My weights arrive. After putting them together in the spare room, I stick a few plates onto the little bars. About ten kilos in each hand should do – that used to be my warm-up weight. Struggling to curl the dumbbell toward my shoulder, there comes an acceptance that I'm not the person I was. This is going to take a while.

January 26, 2020

My walking speed has now increased to a sort of gentle trot. Slow but steady. It means people tend not to stare as much. I did have a slightly embarrassing incident today when, just as a young girl approached, I stepped off the curb with a little too much confidence, causing shooting pain in my foot when it touched the ground. The scream I let out in her face for seemingly no apparent reason ensures she'll be taking a different route from now on.

January 31, 2020

A virus originating in China that's been spreading around the world is confirmed in England. I remember Swine flu and other similar, less-concerning diseases, and how they all came with the caveat of 'tends to only cause problems in older people and those with underlying health conditions.' I never thought I'd end up in the latter category. It scares the life out of me.

February 11, 2020

The World Health Organization has called this virus 'COVID-19.' A word almost every person on earth will come to know.

February 18, 2020

I contact the doctor about my neuropathy to see if anything else can be done. Some days it's not too bad, but there are plenty of times when it verges on crippling – just walking from one side of the kitchen to another is a night-mare as my clothes rub against my legs and stomach. The suggested solution? Another dosage increase. I'm now at the highest recommended level for Pregabalin, a controlled drug that's popular among prisoners, apparently.

March 5, 2020

The first death in the UK as a result of COVID-19 has been confirmed.

March 26, 2020

With cases spiralling out of control and more deaths, England enters a national lockdown. Never have I appreciated my work-from-home job more. The rules state we're only allowed out to exercise once each day. As my two daily walks are dropping to one, I'm increasing the length.

April 2, 2020

Marie is still travelling to an office job. Her place now allows anyone who falls into the 'at risk' category, such as those with diabetes, to work from home. Sadly, employees living with a person who has a severe health condition must still come in, meaning I'm in constant fear of her unintentionally killing me.

April 10, 2020

The streets are deathly quiet during my walks. Whenever a person appears, we lock eyes in a silent duel to decide who will cross the road first, scared that one of us might be carrying a virus. It's surreal. While my diagnosis was a horrible experience, I can only imagine how hard it must be for others going through the same thing right now, a time when hospitals have become a place of terror for many.

April 20, 2020

Marie's business is making every one of its employees work remotely. The relief we both feel is immeasurable.

April 24, 2020

With everything going on in the world, I've barely registered my improvements over the last four weeks. Today, I managed to descend the steps of my house without holding onto both sides of the wall for the first time. My feet do still hurt, but it's a different kind of pain, a bearable one. Even my tendons are getting better. What also comes as a surprise is that I no longer keep my head down 90 per cent of the time while walking, continually watching where my feet land.

May 2, 2020

I can move normally again, having gained complete control over my legs, feet, and toes. The next stage in my quest towards the old me is running.

I look for a street without people or cars – easy to find in lockdown times – and mentally prepare. I start by walking at pace before moving to a very slight shuffle-jog, the kind you see older adults enjoy. There's a mild numbness in my feet, though it's expected. With Nine Inch Nails blasting in my earbuds, I take my first leaping stride into a sprint, crumpling into a ball almost instantly. It seems I need to add some muscle to my now sparrow-like legs.

May 15, 2020

Right, this time. This time I'll do it. After three-quarters of a year, I swear I will run again. The location of my previous attempt seems like a good place for another try. It's been almost two weeks since I last ended up on my arse, two weeks of leg exercises and speed walking. Instead of listening to a classic industrial rock band for inspiration, I choose the cheesiest option available: Chariots of Fire by Vangelis. For all it's been parodied, the tune remains a favourite of mine. I hit play on my phone and slowly jog as the synthesizer kicks in.

The start of the piano section is my cue. After launching into the air with possibly too much enthusiasm, my heart skips as I descend. Foot meets pavement solidly, my pace unaffected by the slight leg wobble. I'm running. Wind whistles past my ears, air tearing through lungs that haven't worked this hard in a long time.

Vangelis' theme reaches its central crescendo. Unconcerned by potential witnesses, I laugh maniacally, throwing my arms in the air. It has taken months of pain and suffering and work, but here I am, finally, running again. I remember the doctor who suggested a wheelchair; I remember hopelessness; I remember the pier. I've never been happier to be alive.

I didn't hear the middle-aged woman open her front door, nor did I see her walk onto the pavement until it was too late. She also failed to see or hear the strange man hurtling down the road like he was crossing the finishing line at the Olympics. I crash into the unfortunate lady just as Chariots of Fire nears its end. We both go flying. Soaring through the air, I instinctively spin us 180 degrees mid-flight, breaking her fall on top of me. The wind is knocked from my body as she crashes down on my sternum.

After helping her up and repeatedly asking if she's okay, I burst into a lengthy explanation as to why I was running down the street while looking at the sky, hoping to justify an oafishness that could have been fatal. Luckily for me, she's incredibly understanding.

'Awww… it's fine, son. My nephew's got the diabetes as well. It's a bastard. I'm glad you're feeling better.'

May 20, 2020

A story in The Guardian reads: 'Type 1 diabetics more likely than Type 2 to die of coronavirus.' Seeing my condition singled out like this is crushing. The article highlights an NHS study that discovered people with type 1 are 3.5 times more to die in a hospital with COVID-19 than those with no underlying health conditions. Anyone with type 2 is twice as likely to die compared to non-diabetics.

You can be determined, motivated, full of righteous anger to battle against life's injustices, but there'll always be times when something comes along and punches you in the gut, a blow that knocks the will out of you. Looking at that headline, I wonder if I'm wasting my time. Is all the effort going to be for nothing? It sounds as if my compromised immune system could be responsible for my death after all.

'Is there any point in trying?' I ask Aria.

'This is your tipping point, really? I mean, I'd have thought the prospect of going blind or hopping around on one leg would have been more disheartening.'

'Ha, yeah. I suppose. Fuck life's shitty rolls of the dice, eh?'

'Exactly. Do not go gentle into that good night, and all that.'

I was never one for poetry at school, but Dylan Thomas's most famous work always struck a chord. To fight against the inevitability of death, to rage against it with every ounce of strength. It's a stark contrast to my previous outlook. But now, understanding the preciousness of existence and the importance of making the most of life, these words take on new meaning.

'Ha, yeah, rage against the dying of the light,' I finish.

'It's not the end, Dean, just the beginning of a new chapter. No matter what else this world throws at us, we'll never stop fighting. Remember, hope for a better tomorrow; it's what gets us out of bed in the morning.'

Today.

Things are constantly changing. The big news is that the Pregabalin finally started working. My neuropathy, once unbearable, has regressed to the point of occasional irritation. A doctor suggested I come off the medication to see what happened. Stopping the tablets was a lengthy, cautious process that involved a dosage reduction every two weeks. Each time I decreased by 25mg, the pain returned with a vengeance, ripping through my body but lasting only for a couple of days. Going drug-free was the worst, leading to pain so bad that I wanted to restart the course. Again, though, this dissipated in time. It's incredible how much I appreciate being able to do simple tasks without suffering. Flare-ups do occur, but their rarity and brevity make them little more than a nuisance.

I also joined a new gym; the fact that the owner is a former professional bodybuilder who is also a type 1 made my decision a lot easier. Like so many things – laughing, being happy, living a full life – it's something I never expected to do again but was ultimately proved wrong. Ironically, diabetes has made me fitter and healthier than ever, and I can still have fun.

My eyes are currently stable, my blood glucose levels are usually in the same range as a non-diabetic, and my feet, while not always perfect, are good enough to hit a treadmill and stairmaster three times per week. I have bad days, of course, when my sugars skyrocket for no reason and I feel sick, or the frustration of another hypo at an inopportune moment pushes me close to the edge, days when I wish to be like everyone else. But the feelings always pass, and I get back to work.

Diabetes is a fight, and while there's no cure, we never give up. It's frustrating, exhausting, and utterly unfair, but this disease brings out a strength in people they never knew was present, turning them into the absolute best version of themselves.

Marie, Buster, and our cats keep me smiling, and I still have the occasional night out with Paul, Andrew, and Ren, though I usually stick to a two-drink limit.

On December 5, days after my 42nd birthday, Mum was taken to hospital after suffering a fall. Tests confirmed she had both COVID and double pneumonia. Her condition worsened over the following days; our communications limited to phone calls. On December 18, a doctor told me to prepare for the worst and that I'd soon be allowed in to say my final goodbyes.

On December 26, three weeks after her admission, my mother walked out of hospital unassisted. Despite being 82 and suffering from hypertension, PTSD, a leaky heart valve, thrombocythemia, goitres, and a host of other conditions, she called on the same strength that got her through decades of marriage to an abusive man. It was a miracle. She's now 83, a milestone that would have been inconceivable had she never left my father.

Speaking of Dad, I don't think about him anymore. It's not a conscious choice; he's just gone from my mind, part of a past I no longer need or want to revisit. I've never been to grandma's grave where I poured his ashes, either. Whether I do recall everything that happened, or if my brain blocked out some of it, I'll never know for sure. But it finally feels like ancient history, the kind that doesn't affect me anymore.

Finally, there's Aria. Her visits are few and far between these days. Not that I mind; it's a sign that life is going well. But she's always there during the occasional moments when I falter. The angel's message remains unchanged from that first moment I laid eyes on her so many years ago: never lose hope.

THE END